W9-BLA-172

Books by J. A. Jance

J. P. Beaumont Mysteries
UNTIL PROVEN GUILTY • INJUSTICE FOR ALL
TRIAL BY FURY • TAKING THE FIFTH
IMPROBABLE CAUSE • A MORE PERFECT UNION
DISMISSED WITH PREJUDICE • MINOR IN POSSESSION
PAYMENT IN KIND • WITHOUT DUE PROCESS
FAILURE TO APPEAR • LYING IN WAIT
NAME WITHHELD • BREACH OF DUTY
BIRDS OF PREY • PARTNER IN CRIME
LONG TIME GONE • JUSTICE DENIED
FIRE AND ICE • BETRAYAL OF TRUST

Joanna Brady Mysteries
DESERT HEAT • TOMBSTONE COURAGE
SHOOT/DON'T SHOOT • DEAD TO RIGHTS
SKELETON CANYON • RATTLESNAKE CROSSING
OUTLAW MOUNTAIN • DEVIL'S CLAW
PARADISE LOST • PARTNER IN CRIME
EXIT WOUNDS • DEAD WRONG • DAMAGE CONTROL
FIRE AND ICE • JUDGMENT CALL

Walker Family Thrillers
HOUR OF THE HUNTER • KISS OF THE BEES
DAY OF THE DEAD • QUEEN OF THE NIGHT

Ali Reynolds Mysteries
EDGE OF EVIL • WEB OF EVIL
HAND OF EVIL • CRUEL INTENT
TRIAL BY FIRE • FATAL ERROR

J.A. JANCE

INJUSTICE FOR ALL

HARPER

An Imprint of HarperCollinsPublishers

This is a work of fiction. Names, characters, places, and incidents are products of the author's imagination or are used fictitiously and are not to be construed as real. Any resemblance to actual events, locales, organizations, or persons, living or dead, is entirely coincidental.

HARPER

An Imprint of HarperCollins*Publishers*
195 Broadway
New York, NY 10007

Copyright © 1986 by J.A. Jance
Excerpt from *Queen of the Night* copyright © 2010 by J.A. Jance
ISBN 978-0-06-195852-6

First Harper Premium paperback printing: January 2010
First Avon Books paperback printing: May 1986

HarperCollins® and Harper® are registered trademarks of Harper-Collins Publishers.

Printed in the United States of America

Visit Harper paperbacks on the World Wide Web at
www.harpercollins.com

10 9 8 7 6 5

To Norman and Evie,
from their "only" child

INJUSTICE FOR ALL

CHAPTER 1

THERE'S NOTHING LIKE A WOMAN'S SCREAM TO BRING a man bolt upright in bed. I had been taking a late-afternoon nap in my room when the sound cut through the stormy autumn twilight like a knife.

I threw open the door of my cabin. The woman screamed again, the sound keening up from the narrow patch of beach below the terrace at Rosario Resort. A steep path dropped from my cabin to the beach. I scrambled down it to the water's edge. There I spotted a woman struggling to drag a man's inert form out of the lapping sea.

She wasn't screaming now. Her face was grimly set as she wrestled the dead weight of the man's body. I hurried to help her, grasping him under the arms and pulling him ashore. Dropping to his side, I felt for a pulse. There was none.

He was a man in his mid to late fifties wearing expensive cowboy boots and a checkered cowboy shirt. His belt buckle bore the initials LSL. A deep gash split his forehead.

The woman knelt beside me anxiously, hopefully. When I looked at her and shook my head, her face contorted with grief. She sank to the wet sand beside me. "Can't you do something?" she sobbed.

Again I shook my head. I've worked homicide too many years not to know when it's too late. Footsteps pounded down the steps behind us as people in the bar and dining room hurried to see what had happened. Barney, the bartender, was the first person to reach us.

"Dead?" he asked.

I nodded. "Get those people out of here, every last one of them. And call the sheriff."

With unquestioning obedience Barney bounded up the steps and herded the onlookers back to the terrace some twenty-five feet above us. Beside me the woman's sobs continued unabated. It was a chilly autumn evening to begin with, and we were both soaked to the skin. Gently I took her arm, lifting her away from the lifeless body.

"Come on," I said. "You've got to get out of those wet clothes." She allowed me to pull her to her feet. "Is this your husband?"

She shook her head. "No, a friend."

"Are you staying here at the hotel?" She nodded. "Where's your room?"

"Up by the tennis courts."

She was shaking violently. The tennis courts and her room were a good quarter of a mile away. My cabin was just at the top of the path. "You can dry off and warm up in my room. The sheriff will need to talk to you when he gets here."

Like a dazed but pliant child, she followed me

as I half led, half carried her up the path. By the time we reached my room, her teeth chattered convulsively. It could have been cold or shock or a little of both. I pulled her into the bathroom and turned on the water in the shower. "Get out of those wet things," I ordered. "I'll send someone to get you some clothes."

Kneeling in front of her, I fumbled with the sodden laces of her tennis shoes with my own numbed fingers. "What's your name?" I asked.

"Gi . . . Ginger," she stammered through chattering teeth.

"Ginger what?"

"Wa . . . Watkins."

I stood up. Her arms hung limply at her sides. "Can you undress, or do you need help?"

Clumsily she battled a button on her blouse, finally unfastening it. Leaving her on her own, I let myself out of the bathroom. "I'll be outside if you need anything."

Alone in the room, I stripped off my own soaked clothing and tossed the soggy bundle on a chair near the bed. I pulled on a shirt, a sweater, and two pair of socks before I picked up the phone and dialed the desk clerk. "This is Beaumont in Room Thirteen," I said. "Did someone call the sheriff?"

"Yes we did, Mr. Beaumont. The deputy's on his way."

"Have someone stay down on the beach with the body until he gets here. Make sure nothing is moved or disturbed. The woman who found him is here in my room. She was freezing. She's taking a hot shower. Her name is Watkins. Can you send someone to her room for dry clothes? Does she have a husband?"

"There's no Mr. Watkins registered, Mr. Beaumont, but I'll send someone after the clothes right away."

"She'll need the works, underwear and all."

"I'll take care of it as soon as I can."

"Good," I replied. "And when the deputy comes, be sure he knows she's here with me. Since she's the one who found the body, he'll want to talk to her."

The desk clerk himself brought the clothes, handing them to me apologetically. His name-tag labeled him Fred. "I hope I have everything," he said.

I opened the bathroom door wide enough to slip them inside onto the floor before turning back to Fred. "The deputy isn't here yet?"

"There's an accident down by the ferry dock. He can't come until he finishes with that."

"Did the dispatcher call for a detective from Friday Harbor?" I asked.

He shrugged. "I guess, but I don't know for sure. You seem to know about this kind of thing, Mr. Beaumont."

I ought to. I've worked homicide in Seattle for the better part of twenty years.

Fred moved uncertainly toward the door. "I'd better be getting back."

"Who was he?" I asked. Fred looked blank. "The dead man," I persisted.

"Oh," he replied. "His name was Sig Larson. He was here with the parole board."

"The parole board!" Cops don't like parole boards. Cops and parole boards work opposite sides of the street. Parole boards let creeps go faster than cops can lock them up. "What's the parole board doing here?"

Fred shrugged. "They came for a three-day workshop. They'll probably cancel now."

I glanced toward the bathroom door where the rush of the shower had ceased. "And her?" I asked.

"She's a member too, as far as I know. Her reservation was made along with all the rest."

"But her husband isn't here?"

"No, she's by herself."

"What about Larson?" Asking questions is a conditioned response in a detective. I asked the question, ignoring that I was more than a hundred miles outside my Seattle jurisdiction. Someone was dead. Who, How, and Why were questions someone needed to ask. It might as well be me.

"His wife is due in on one of tonight's ferries. I don't know which one. She isn't here yet."

I went to the bathroom door and tapped lightly. "I'm going to order a couple of drinks from Room Service. Would you like something?"

"Coffee," was the reply. "Black."

I turned back to Fred. "Did you hear that?"

He nodded.

"Send up a pot of coffee for her and two McNaughton's and water for me. Barney knows how I like them."

"Will do," the clerk replied, slipping from the room into the deepening darkness.

The door reopened. "I almost forgot. She's

supposed to call Homer in Seattle. It's urgent. He said she knew the number."

Fred shut the door again, disappearing for good this time. Still cold, I turned up the thermostat in the room, mulling the turn of events. The lady showering in my bathroom was a married member of the Washington State Parole Board. The dead man on the beach was married too, but not to her, although it was evident there was some connection.

Room Service was on the ball. Coffee and drinks arrived before the bathroom door opened. Ginger Watkins, wearing a pale green dress, stepped barefoot into my room, a huge bath-towel turban wound around her head. She was fairly tall, five-eight or five-nine, with a slender figure, fine bones, and a flawlessly fair complexion. Her eyes were vivid uncut emeralds.

Coming up from the beach, I hadn't noticed she was beautiful. Standing across the room from me, swathed in the gentle light of the dressing room behind her, she took my breath away.

She returned my unabashed stare, and I looked away, embarrassed. "Better?" I managed.

"Yes, but I'm still cold."

I rummaged through the closet and brought out a tweed jacket which I put over her shoulders. I handed her a cup and saucer. "Here's your coffee."

She slipped into one of the two chairs at the table. "I left my wet clothes on the floor," she said.

I pointed to the chair. "There mine are." I poured more coffee. Her hands trembled as she raised the cup to her lips.

"What did you say your name was?"

"Beaumont," I answered. "J. P. Beaumont. My friends call me Beau."

"And I'm Ginger Watkins."

"You told me. The desk clerk said the man's name was Larson. You knew him?"

She nodded somberly, her eyes filling with tears. "Sig," she murmured, her throat working to stifle a sob.

"A friend of yours?"

She nodded again.

"How did you happen to find him? It wasn't much of a day for a walk on the beach."

"We planned to meet down there to talk, after the meeting. I was late. Darrell called. I didn't get there until forty-five minutes after I was supposed to."

"Who's Darrell?" I asked.

She gave me a funny look, as though I had asked a stupid question. "My husband," she answered.

The name sounded familiar, but I didn't put it together right then. I let it go. "Why meet him there? Why not in the lobby or the bar?"

"I told you, we needed to talk."

She set her coffee cup down, got up, and walked away from the table, her arms crossed, her body language closed.

"What about?"

"It was personal," she replied.

That's not a good answer at the beginning of an inquiry into death under unusual circumstances. Accidental drownings in October are unusual. My gut said murder, and murder is very personal. The ties between killer and victim are often of the most intimate kind. "How personal?"

She turned on me suddenly. "You don't have any right to ask me a question like that."

"Someone's going to ask it, sooner or later."

She met my gaze for a long moment before she wavered. "Sig had some business dealings with my family. That's why I needed to talk to him."

"Privately?" I asked. She nodded. "Do you know his wife?"

Her mouth tightened. Her fingers closed tightly on her upper arms. "Yes. I know her."

"What's she like?"

"Mona's a calculating bitch." It was a simple statement spoken with a singular amount of venom.

"I take it you're not friends."

"Hardly." She walked back over to the table and sat down opposite me. "Mona thought Sig and I were having an affair."

"Were you?"

She looked at me, her eyes clear and steady in the glow of the light. "No," she said.

Irate husbands and wives don't always verify their spouses' indiscretions before they rub out a presumed lover. "Is Mona the jealous type? Or Darrell?"

She laughed. "Darrell? Are you kidding? He could care less. Mona called him with the story, and he was afraid it would hit the papers and screw up his campaign."

Suddenly the names shifted into focus. Darrell Watkins, candidate for lieutenant governor. Boy

Wonder tackling the longtime incumbent. I whistled. "You mean *the* Darrell Watkins?"

Ginger Watkins peered at me across a cup of coffee. "One and the same," she said softly. "The sonofabitch."

It was no wonder I forgot to give her the message that someone had called.

CHAPTER 2

DEPUTY JAKE POMEROY ARRIVED ABOUT SEVEN. HE made a very poor first impression. He was a fat-faced, pimpled kid who looked like he had stepped out of his high school graduation picture into a rumpled deputy sheriff's uniform. Until the detective arrived from Friday Harbor, Deputy Pomeroy was in charge. The deputy considered Sig Larson's death to be the crime of the century on Orcas Island.

He was trolling for suspects. He tossed his first hook in my direction. "Your name's Beaumont, is that correct?" I nodded. "What do you do?"

"Homicide detective. Seattle P.D." I handed him my ID.

He gave me a shrewd, appraising look. "I understand you moved the body. Is that also correct?"

"Yes."

His look became a contemptuous sneer. "Surely you know better than that."

I wanted to slug the officious bastard, but I answered evenly. "We thought he might still be alive."

"When you say 'we,' you mean you and Mrs. Watkins?"

"She found him. I heard her scream."

"And what time was that?" he asked, addressing Ginger.

"A quarter to six," she replied, "I was late."

"Late for what?"

"I was supposed to meet Sig there. At five."

The deputy tapped his front teeth with the eraser of his pencil and eyed her speculatively. "Why?"

"To talk."

His look narrowed. "Wasn't it cold down by the water?"

"We wanted to talk privately."

Pomeroy said nothing as he made a note. "How would you describe your relationship with Mr. Larson?"

"Friends."

"That's all?"

"That's all."

"How long have you known Mr. Beaumont here?"

"We just met. Down on the beach."

She was in my room, wearing my robe, her hair wet from my shower, with my bath towel wrapped around her head. She was also barefoot, because the desk clerk had forgotten to bring her shoes. Jake Pomeroy didn't believe for one minute we were recent acquaintances.

I attempted what must have sounded like a lame explanation. "We were freezing. I was afraid she'd go into shock. Her own room is way up the hill."

Jake gave Ginger an overt leer. "You're sure the two of you never met before this afternoon?"

"I'm sure!" Ginger snapped, a tiny flush marking her delicate cheekbone.

"You did say 'Mrs. Watkins,' isn't that right?" She nodded. "But your husband isn't here with you?" He recast his hook.

"I'm here on parole board business. So was Sig." She was rapidly losing patience.

"Was your husband also a friend of Mr. Larson's?"

The emerald in her eyes gleamed hard and brittle. "They had some business dealings, that's all."

"We'll check this out, of course," he said.

His questions had gone far enough. I resented the insinuations in his clumsy quest for an infidelity motive. "Look, Pomeroy," I told him, "if you want to ask questions about the position of the body, or what time it was, or whether we saw anyone else on the beach, that's fine. But if you're making accusations, you'd better read us our rights and let us call an attorney. If not, I'll shove that gold star where the sun don't shine."

A stunned expression spread over his flabby countenance. He lumbered to his feet. "I'll go back and wait for Detective Huggins."

"You do that."

I banged the door shut behind him and returned to the table. Ginger had unwrapped her turban and was toweling her hair dry. She looked relieved.

I picked up the phone and dialed the desk. "You didn't bring shoes," I growled when Fred answered.

"I didn't? Sorry. I can't do anything about it right now. A whole bunch of people just got here. I have to get them settled."

"Never mind," I told Fred. "I'll get them myself."

Ginger gave me her key. I walked to her room through a lightly falling evening mist. Opening her door, I expected to find the room well ordered and neat. Instead, it was a shambles. The place had been ransacked. I picked up the telephone receiver. Holding it at the top in an effort to disturb as few prints as possible, I called the desk. "Was Mrs. Watkins' room torn apart when you came after her clothes?" I asked.

"Why no, Mr. Beaumont. It was fine."

"It isn't now," I said grimly. "When that detective gets here, send him up."

"He's right here. Want to speak to him?"

"Put him on."

"Hello," a voice mumbled. "This is Detective Huggins."

"I'm Beaumont."

"J. P. Beaumont? Are you shitting me? This is Hal, Hal Huggins. Haven't seen you since I left the force ten years ago. How the hell are you?"

It took me a minute to place the name and the face and the mumbling speech. Hal Huggins had opted for being a big fish in a very small pond when he left Seattle's homicide squad to go to work for the San Juan County Sheriff's Department in Friday Harbor, hiring on as their chief detective. Probably their only detective.

"I'm fine," I replied.

"What are you up to?"

"I was with the woman who discovered the body this afternoon."

"No shit. Pomeroy is lining me up to go talk to her."

"You'd better come to her room first. Have the desk clerk bring you up."

"Okay, we'll be right there. Hey, by the way. There's someone else here you know. I just ran into him in the lobby. Remember Maxwell Cole?"

Does Captain Ahab remember Moby Dick? Cole is a crime columnist for the *Post-Intelligencer.* He's been on my case ever since I beat him out of a college girl friend, packed her off, and married her. As a reporter, he has dogged my career for as long as I've been on the force. Karen and I have been divorced for years, but I'm still stuck with Max. It's like I threw out the baby and ended up having to keep the dirty bathwater.

"Don't tell him I'm here," I cautioned. "What's he doing here anyway? The Sig Larson story?"

"Probably, although he didn't say."

"Don't ask. And don't bring him along."

Fred led Huggins and Pomeroy into Ginger's room. The clerk's mouth gaped. "What happened here? It wasn't like this when I picked up her clothes."

"What time was that?" Huggins asked.

Fred walked around the room as if at a loss for words, examining the debris. "What time?" Huggins repeated.

"Forty-five minutes ago," Fred replied. "No more than that."

Huggins looked at me. "So what's this got to do with the stiff on the beach."

"I took Ginger Watkins to my room to warm up after we left the beach. Fred here," I said, indicating the desk clerk, "came up to get her some dry clothes. Not quite an hour later, I discovered this when I came to pick up a pair of shoes."

"Maybe she trashed it herself."

"No. She's still in my room. It's too cold to be wandering around barefoot."

Huggins glared sorrowfully around the room before turning to Pomeroy. "Call the crime-lab folks, Jake. Have them come take a look. Coroner's got the body, and the beach is covered with water, but they'd better see this all the same." He turned stiffly to me. "Take me to the lady. She can answer questions barefoot. Nobody's taking any shoes out of this room until the lab's done with it."

Pomeroy lingered near the door. "I told you to get, Jake, and I mean it," Huggins growled. Jake got, with the desk clerk right behind him.

Hal and I strolled back toward my room. "You're a little out of your territory, aren't you, Beau?" It was a comment rather than a question, asked without rancor.

"I'm here on vacation, an innocent bystander."

"Pomeroy seems to think otherwise."

"Pomeroy's got a dirty mind."

He chuckled. "How'd you get dragged into this, anyway?"

"I heard a lady scream and went to check it out. I never saw her before six o'clock this evening."

"Pomeroy says if you only met her tonight, how come she's sitting in your room barefoot with a towel around her head, wearing your bathrobe? He told me she had just stepped out of your shower. He thinks you're a hell of a fast worker."

"She was cold, goddammit. I tried to tell him that."

"He's not buying. Envious, I think. Claims she's pretty good looking."

"She is that," I acknowledged.

"What did you say her name is?"

"Ginger Watkins. Her husband's Darrell Watkins."

He stopped short and whistled. "The guy who's running for lieutenant governor against old man Chambers?"

"That's right."

Huggins shook his head. "What did I ever do to deserve this?" he asked plaintively.

"I don't know," I said, "but whatever it was, it must have been pretty bad."

Ginger rose to let us in, a worried frown on her face. "What took so long?" she asked. "I was afraid something had happened to you."

"This is Detective Hal Huggins," I said as he stepped forward, hand extended. "He's from the sheriff's department in Friday Harbor. Hal needs to ask you some questions. Hal, Ginger Watkins."

She offered him a firm handshake, while Hal examined her with care.

"Glad to meet you, Mrs. Watkins, but I'm afraid I have some disturbing news."

Her face darkened. "What?"

"We've just come from your room. The place has been ransacked."

She paled. "Ransacked! When?"

"Between the time the desk clerk picked up your clothes and when I went to get your shoes," I told her.

"But who would do something like that?" she demanded.

"We were hoping you could tell us, Mrs. Watkins." Hal settled himself on the edge of the bed. "Any ideas?"

Ginger shook her head. "None," she said.

"No one else had a key to your room?"

"Sig did. We always kept keys to each other's rooms on trips, as a precaution in case one of us was sick or hurt. I was sick once and he had to break in. It was just a safety precaution."

Huggins looked at her closely. "We'd better go over the whole thing," he said, leaning stiffly against the headboard. "Tell me everything. From the beginning."

CHAPTER 3

HUGGINS HAD BARELY ASKED HIS FIRST QUESTION WHEN the phone rang. I answered it—the phone, not the question. The voice on the other end of the line was one degree under rude. "I'm told Ginger Watkins is there. Let me speak to her."

"May I say who's calling?"

"No you may not! If she's there, put her on."

I don't like imperious *schmucks*. I fought fire with fire. "Mrs. Watkins is busy at the moment. Can I take a message?"

He fired off a verbal volley. I held the phone away from my ear long enough for the shouting to stop. "Give me your name and number," I told him. "She'll call back."

"I already left one message, damn it. Put her on. Tell her it's Homer."

When I heard his name, I remembered the forgotten message. I hung up the phone, cutting short his tirade. "It was Homer," I told Ginger. "He wants you to call."

Something flickered across her face, but I

couldn't tell what. Anger? Fear? She turned her attention back to Huggins. "What were you saying?"

He regarded her with a sad-eyed glower. "I understand you discovered Mr. Larson's body. Now someone has ransacked your room. These incidents may or may not be related. We can't afford to assume they're not." He shifted on the bed, trying to find a more comfortable position. "Isn't it unusual for coworkers to have keys to each other's rooms?

"Sig and I were close." Huggins waited as though expecting her to say something further. She didn't.

He sighed. "Did you have any valuables in your room? Items of jewelry, something like that?"

She shook her head. "No."

"Anything else of value—cameras, prescription medications?" Again she shook her head. He continued doggedly. "Any paperwork concerning parole board business that might be considered damaging or in some way usable? Maybe something you and Mr. Larson were working on together?"

There was a slight hesitation. "I brought some papers from home. They have nothing to do with work."

"May I ask what they are?"

"I'm filing for divorce on Monday," she said levelly. "I brought the paperwork with me. Sig and I planned to discuss it this evening." Her answer was calm, but her eyes betrayed a turmoil of warring emotions. I noticed it. So did Huggins. "That's why I was late to see Sig," she went on. "Darrell called. Someone told him."

Hal sat up. "You didn't tell him before you left?"

"No." Ginger gave him a wan smile. "It was a surprise."

"Someone told him. Who?"

Ginger shrugged. "I don't know, not for sure."

"Did he mention what time?"

"Sometime today, I know that much."

"Can you guess who it was?"

"Probably Mona."

"Mona?"

"Sig's wife, Mona Larson." The antagonism in Ginger's voice set little alarm bells ringing. Had Sig Larson died in a matrimonial crossfire between his wife and Ginger's husband?

"But how did Mrs. Larson know?"

"I wrote Sig a letter last week, the day I made up my mind. He suggested I not file until after we had a chance to discuss it."

"Why talk it over with him? What did he have to do with it?"

"I told you before, he was my friend. . . . My best friend," she added defiantly. "Why wouldn't I discuss it with him? We weren't having an affair, if that's what you mean." Her denial of an unspoken accusation gave credence to Huggins' line of questioning. Sig's having her room key made it even more plausible.

Hal's disbelief must have showed. She continued. "Our families were involved in a joint venture, a condominium project in Seattle. I didn't want to jeopardize Sig's position."

"Would you have?"

Her smile was caustic. "Evidently not. Homer

and Darrell seem to have covered all possible contingencies."

I had sat quietly as long as I could. "Who the hell is Homer?" I demanded.

"Homer Watkins," she replied, her answer permeated with sarcasm. "My illustrious father-in-law."

"I don't know him."

"You haven't missed a thing."

Huggins pulled himself to a sitting position and studied his notes. "How will a divorce go over with the voters?" he asked, approaching from another direction.

Ginger bit her lip. "It won't make much difference. No one will pay any attention. It certainly won't cost him the election." She looked at Huggins closely. "Does Mona know about Sig?" she asked.

"Not yet. We still haven't located her." Huggins sighed. "Let's talk about today, from the beginning."

"I came over on the ferry early this morning," Ginger said.

"Alone?"

She nodded.

"Did you bring your car?"

"No. It's in Anacortes. I didn't think I'd need it."

"What time did you check in?"

"Our meeting started at one. I checked in sometime before that."

"What time did Mr. Larson get here?"

"I don't know. I didn't see him before the meeting. During our afternoon break we arranged to meet on the beach. That's when I gave him my key."

"Do you have a key to his room?"

"No. Mona was coming." Her answer spoke volumes.

"Oh, I see," Huggins said. "Was anyone else aware you planned to meet on the beach?"

Ginger shook her head. "Not as far as I know."

Hal Huggins was meticulous. "You got out of the meeting at four. What did you do then?"

"I went back to my room. I took a nap. Then Darrell called."

"What time?"

"I was almost ready to go meet Sig. It must have been right at five."

"What did he say?"

"He asked me to reconsider."

"And you said?"

"No."

Huggins reminded me of a doctor, probing and poking to find out where it hurts. "Was he upset?"

"He seemed to be. That surprised me. If I didn't know him better, I would have said he was jealous." Her tone was resigned. Ginger Watkins had long since come to terms with her losses, whatever those might be.

"Why wouldn't he be jealous?"

"He's not the type." She gave a half-assed grin, the kind people use to cover their real feelings, to hide something that hurts more than they're willing to admit. Huggins skirted the issue, leaving me wondering what kind of husband wouldn't be jealous of Ginger Watkins.

I had never met the man, but I decided I didn't

like Darrell Watkins, candidate for lieutenant governor. As a matter of fact, I was sure I wouldn't vote for him.

"Where did he call from?"

"He didn't say. It could have been anywhere in the state. He's out campaigning."

"You don't keep a copy of his schedule?"

"No."

"Supposing he were jealous. Would he have done something to Sig Larson or maybe hired someone to do it?"

"You mean put out a contract? No, for two reasons. Number one, he wouldn't have the money. Number two, I don't believe he's that much of a hypocrite."

"I see," Huggins said sagely. "You mean he fools around himself?" Ginger's lips trembled. She dropped her gaze and nodded.

Hal's questions had led circuitously to the heart of the matter. I had to give him credit. He made another note. "Watkins is an old, respected name in Seattle. Long on reputation and money both. Supposing Darrell did want to get rid of Sig Larson, why wouldn't he have the money? It only costs a few grand to put out a contract."

"Appearances can be deceiving," she said. "I'm not working gratis, you know."

"Which means?" Hal prompted.

"It means we need the money. Some of Homer's investments haven't turned out so well. The parole board job was designed to help out. Connections are nice. How else do you think someone without a degree could walk into a forty-thousand-dollar-a-year job?" Her voice carried a defensive edge.

The phone rang, and I answered, recognizing Deputy Pomeroy's officious voice. "Detective Huggins," he demanded.

I handed the phone to Hal. He listened for a few seconds before he said, "Keep her at the desk until I get there. And, Jake, if one of those goddamned reporters gets near her before I do, I'll have your badge, understand?"

Hal bolted for the door, then stopped, turning slowly back into the room. "It would be best if you stayed here," he told Ginger. "I'll let you know when you can return to your room."

She nodded. "All right."

"The lab guys'll call when they finish." He strode into the darkness to the sound of steady rain. I closed the door behind him, feeling uncomfortable, not knowing what to say. Ginger Watkins was a stranger I knew far too much about. "Warm enough?" I asked awkwardly.

"I am now." She paused. "I might as well call Homer and get it over with."

"Why call him at all? You can afford to ignore your soon-to-be ex-father-in-law."

She picked up the phone. "Ignoring him is the worst thing you can do to Homer." She dialed the desk to charge the call to her room number, but the desk didn't answer.

"Dial it direct," I told her, and she did.

"You called?" she asked. From across the room I could hear a renewal of his verbal barrage. "What do you want?" She interrupted him bluntly, dealing with rudeness in kind.

There was a long pause while she listened. I watched her. Her hair had dried. Honey-blond waves framed her face. She paced back and forth, tugging on a phone cord that didn't give her quite enough leash.

"I'm not going to change my mind, Homer," she said at last. "I've finally seen through the fog well enough to know what's going on."

Again there was a pause. "When I wanted to do something about it, he couldn't be bothered. Now it's too late. I don't care if he's upset. I'm getting out."

She waited. "That's not true, and you know it. What I do won't make a bit of difference, one way or the other. Besides, why should I care who wins?"

His answer to that question was brief, and she stiffened. "I've found jobs before. I'll find one again." She slammed the phone down, eyes blazing. "That bastard," she muttered.

The phone rang again, and she angrily snatched it off the hook. "Hello!" Sheepishly, she handed me the receiver. "It's for you," she said.

The desk had a message for me from Maxwell Cole. He would be in Room 143. He wanted to talk to me. I put the phone down and turned to Ginger. "Are you all right?" The phone call had genuinely disturbed her.

"I'm fine," she answered without conviction. She walked across the room and stared blindly out the darkened window like a lost, lonely child in need of comforting.

"He threatened to pull your job?"

"It's no idle threat," she returned. "He can do it."

I stood near her, wanting to put an arm around her shoulder and tell her everything would be all right, to give her some of my world-famous

Beaumont Bromides. Determinedly she wiped away a tear.

"I'm sorry," she apologized. "I didn't mean to cry."

"You have plenty of reason," I offered.

She looked up at me with a faint smile. "I guess I do. I was thinking about Sig."

"What about him?"

"He gave me back my self-respect," she answered. "Nothing's going to change that. I'll resign if I have to, work as a waitress or a salesclerk, but nobody can take away what Sig Larson gave me." She paused tremulously. "I can't believe he's dead."

Abandoning her attempt to stave off tears, she fell helplessly into my arms, sobbing uncontrollably against my chest. I held her and let her cry, hoping no one was outside my window. Ginger Watkins was, after all, still very much a married lady with a husband who was a well-known statewide political candidate. This would provoke a terrific scandal if it ever hit the press.

I wondered briefly how I had fallen into such a mess. As her sobs subsided, I decided what the hell. Lie back and enjoy it.

CHAPTER 4

ONCE GINGER REGAINED HER COMPOSURE, I suggested we order dinner from Room Service. It was close to nine. My three-meal-a-day system was going into withdrawal. I ordered two steaks medium-rare. "Some wine?"

She shook her head. "I don't drink."

I ordered two bottles of Perrier. When in Rome, and all that. With her emotional outburst quelled, we waded toward dinner through a mire of meaningless chitchat. "Where are you from?" I asked.

"Centralia. My dad runs the Union 76 station down there."

It was a long way from small-town girl to big-time politics. She readily followed my thoughts. "Good looks help," she said with a smile. "Add some stupidity, and this is what you get."

"What do you mean?"

"I was pregnant when we got married. Homer offered to buy me off, send me to Sweden for an abortion. Darrell only married me because his father was dead set against it. I was a first and last

gesture of independence." Her directness was unsettling. I was relieved when Room Service
knocked on the door.

Our waiter was a young, local kid with a mouth-
ful of braces and a winning smile. He wore a cut-
away coat with a white towel draped casually over
one arm. He spread the small round table with a
linen cloth and served us with the arch panache
of a British butler.

"That kid will go places," I said to Ginger after
he bowed his way out of the room.

"At least he seems to enjoy what he's doing,"
she responded.

I poured two glasses of Perrier and handed her
one. "You don't?" I asked.

"I was ready to," she began, "but then after
Sig—" She broke off, unable to continue.

"What about Sig?"

"He saved my life," she said. "It's that simple."

"What did he do? Pull you out of a burning
car?"

Ginger studied me in silence for a long time.
"Something like that," she said quietly. "He got
me to quit drinking."

"Drinking?" I'm sure I sounded incredulous.

She picked up the empty Perrier bottle and examined it. "I used to drink vodka, Wolfschmidts,
on the rocks."

I grimaced. "We're not talking one drink before dinner."

"I almost died, Mr. Beaumont."

"Beau," I corrected. "My friends call me Beau."

"Beau," she added. "As long as I drank myself
into oblivion every night, it didn't matter if Darrell

had a steady girl friend down in Olympia when the legislature was in session, or that he was screwing around with some secretary after work. If I drank hard enough and long enough, I could almost forget. Not forgive, just forget.

"Sig was like a father to me. Never laid a glove on me, as far as sex is concerned. He just kept telling me I deserved better."

"He was right," I interjected.

She smiled at me then, green eyes flashing momentarily. "Are you going to take up where Sig left off?"

"At your service." I waved my Perrier glass in a gallant flourish.

Her smile disappeared. "I can't understand why both Homer and Darrell are trying to talk me out of the divorce. Homer never liked me, and Darrell hasn't shown any interest in me for longer than I care to remember."

"Come on, you have to be kidding!"

"Do I?" Her face was devoid of humor.

I groped for a thread of non-threatening conversation. She had said she was pregnant when they married. "You have a child?"

"Had," she corrected. "A girl. Her name was Katy, after my mother. She was almost six months old when I found her dead in her crib. They call it Sudden Infant Death Syndrome, now. Back then it didn't have a name. I blamed myself. The kooks came out of the woodwork, told me God was punishing me for my sins. It was awful!" She closed her eyes, reliving the pain.

I wanted to say something, but it was a little late to offer condolences.

"That's when I started to drink," she continued as naturally as if she were discussing the weather. "I never got pregnant again. I couldn't sleep. I started having a drink or two in the evening to put me under, to blot out the pain. Eventually I had to drink to live. It's only been since I dried out that I've come to terms with Katy's death, accepted it, allowed myself to grieve. Booze is like that, you know. It buries feelings, keeps you from dealing with them."

The last sentence hit close to home. It was what Peters had told me I was doing, and Ralph Ames, and the chaplain. They told me to stop hiding out in McNaughton's and come to grips with grief. They said I should cry for Anne Corley and let her go. I wasn't ready.

I veered the conversation away from me and back to Ginger. "Sig helped you do that?"

She nodded. "We were in Shelton doing a series of hearings. Board members travel in pairs, like nuns. One morning I couldn't get out of bed. I had the shakes too bad. That was when Sig broke into my room. He dragged me to my first Alcoholics Anonymous meeting that night. We were scheduled to go home the next morning, but we stayed over. Sig got us rooms in a different motel. It took three days for him to walk me through the DTs. That's when Mona started thinking Sig and I were having an affair."

I looked at Ginger's trim figure and flawless grace. She didn't fit any of the standard stereotypes of a recovering alcoholic. Had she not told me, I never would have suspected.

"I won't go through that again, ever," she continued. "Nothing can be worse than DTs. Sig kept me in the program, talked to me when I got discouraged, kept telling me I was a worthwhile person long before I could see it for myself. I'd be dead by now if it weren't for him."

"He sounds like a hell of a nice guy," I commented.

"He was." She lapsed into silence.

"Do you love Darrell?" It was none of my business, yet I asked anyway. I already knew a great deal about Ginger Watkins, far more than our few hours together warranted, but I wanted to know more. It had nothing to do with Detective J. P. Beaumont. It was Beau, the man, who needed to know.

"I used to," she said softly. "Not anymore."

She met my gaze, then looked down at her plate. "I didn't mean to bore you."

"I'm not bored. What will you do?"

"Live one day at a time. I'll file on Monday, resign from the board if I have to, and go looking for a job."

"What kind of job?"

"Maybe I'll go back to school and get a degree in alcoholism counseling. I'd like to repay Sig Larson."

"Somehow I don't think Sig expected to be repaid."

"No," she agreed, "he didn't. That's why I want to do it." Suddenly she put the brakes on my questioning. "What about you? Who is J. P. Beaumont?"

I gave her an evasive grin. "A homicide cop in the middle of a mid-life crisis, trying to decide what I want to be when I grow up."

"Married?"

"Not anymore."

"Involved?"

I sighed. It was six months later, but the hurt was still there. Not bleeding, but raw nonetheless. "No, I'm footloose and fancy-free."

"You don't sound very footloose," she observed.

"That's very perceptive of you," I said. "You're right." I couldn't match her candor. The kind of open self-revelation that came easily to her eluded me. The telephone jangled a welcome interruption.

"Detective Beaumont?"

"Yes."

"This is Smitty with the crime lab. Could you bring Mrs. Watkins up to take a look around the room?"

"Sure. Find anything?"

"Can't tell." It was a standard answer. "Maybe she can tell us if anything's missing."

"Okay, we'll be right there."

I put down the phone and turned to Ginger. "Traveling time."

She peered in dismay at her stockinged feet. "What about shoes?"

Scrounging the bottom of the closet, I turned up my ancient bedroom slippers. "Put these on. They'll fit like a pair of snowshoes, but it's better than going barefoot."

Ginger stumbled across the room in a trial run. "Not much better," she commented.

The walk to Ginger's room was cold and windy. The rain had stopped. Wispy clouds scudded before a half-moon. Ginger scuffed along, gripping my arm in case she tripped over the outsized slippers.

"Have you ever been the victim of a break-in before?"

She shook her head. I wanted to warn her, to ease the shock of seeing her things strewn and disheveled by unknown hands. She knew of the break-in from Huggins, but hearing it and seeing it are two different things.

We made it to her room without incident. If Rosario was crawling with reporters, they weren't in evidence. Thank God Huggins had managed to keep Ginger's room out of the limelight. By now members of the Fourth Estate would have filed their stories. They'd be settled in the Vista Lounge, drowning their sorrows or entertaining one another. The Seattle Press Corps Traveling Dog and Pony Show.

Pomeroy opened the door, grunting with displeasure when he saw me.

I ignored him, pushing my way past without any kind of acknowledgment. His face flushed angrily, but he said nothing.

Ginger followed me into the room. She stopped short inside the door, her face blanching, her hands involuntarily covering her mouth.

A man came forward and introduced himself. "I'm Dayton Smith," he said. "Smitty for short. This your room?"

Ginger nodded.

"We've dusted for prints. We'll want your prints and those of any other people known to have been in the room—the desk clerk, maids, Room Service. That's the only way to discover unidentified prints. We'll go down to the lobby after we finish here."

Again Ginger nodded, incapable of speech.

"Look around. Can you see if anything is missing?"

Walking trancelike through the room, Ginger fingered the heap of clothing piled on the floor, sifted through the contents of her makeup case strewn on the counter while those of us in the room watched in silence.

All the officers, with the possible exception of Pomeroy, understood the deep sense of violation a break-in victim feels. Fear, anger, and outrage passed over her face in rapid succession. She knelt beside a scatter of papers dumped near an overturned Gucci briefcase, awkwardly attempting to straighten them. When she finished, I pulled her to her feet.

"Is anything gone?"

She shook her head. "I don't think so."

I looked at Smitty. "No sign of forced entry?"

"No. Whoever came in evidently had a key."

I looked down at Ginger. She was pale and shaking. "Gather what you need," I said. "You can't stay here. We'll have the desk send someone to clean up this mess."

She approached the task purposefully, moving through the room, scooping up nightgown, robe, and shoes from the tangled heap on the floor. She sorted through the things on the counter, placing makeup, hairbrush, and toothbrush in a small case along with her clothing. Pomeroy watched her leeringly from the door. I wanted to kick him.

At last, still wearing my slippers, she turned to me. "I'm ready. Can we go?"

I led her from the room. She sank against me. I supported her willingly, J. P. Beaumont, Good Samaritan in an hour of need.

"Thank you," she whispered.

"You're welcome," I replied, guiltily conscious of savoring the slight pressure of her slender body against mine.

CHAPTER 5

SMITTY'S PARTNER FROM THE WASHINGTON STATE Crime Lab took Ginger into the hotel kitchen for fingerprinting. I went to the desk where I tackled Fred, demanding another room. "I'm sorry Mr. Beaumont. We're full. We were almost booked before the reporters showed up, and now—"

"Look," I said. "The crime lab's still not done with her room. Besides, she can't go back there. The lock wasn't broken. Whoever got in had a key."

"As I said, we don't have any other rooms."

I turned away from the desk in disgust, only to run headlong into the mustached human walrus who calls himself Maxwell Cole. "Hello, J. P. Why didn't you return my call?"

"Didn't want to, Max. Get out of my way."

"You're being rude," he chided. "I only need to talk to you for a minute."

"What about?" I was pretty sure I knew what Max was after. For once in his life, he surprised me.

"Don Wilson."

"Who the hell is Don Wilson?"

"You remember, Denise Wilson's husband. DeAnn's father. The Lathrop case."

There isn't a cop in Washington State who isn't sickened by the very name. Philip Lathrop sits over on Death Row in Walla Walla, a slime thumbing his nose at the system. Seven years ago, he followed Denise Wilson home from the laundromat and raped her in front of her two-year-old daughter. Denise testified against him, and Lathrop got sent up. He went to prison vowing revenge.

Six years later he was placed in a work/release program. Nobody remembered that the Wilsons lived less than three miles away. He came back to their house one hot July day and finished the job, killing both Denise and DeAnn in a bloody carnage that left hardened detectives puking at the scene. It'll be years before he exhausts the appeals process. It's called a miscarriage of justice.

"What about Don Wilson?" I asked.

"I was to meet him here at four. He never showed."

"So? What does that have to do with me?"

"I wondered if you had seen him. He turns up at parole board hearings, demonstrating, protesting—that kind of thing. He's lobbying for a statewide victim/witness protection program."

"Look, Max, I wouldn't recognize him if I saw him. There hasn't been a protester in sight."

Max blinked at me nearsightedly through thick glasses. "You're sure?"

"Yes, I'm sure, goddammit," I snapped. "Now leave me alone." I was still worrying about Ginger, wondering if there might be a room available somewhere in Eastsound.

Max backed away from me warily. The last time he and I had a confrontation, I loosened a couple of teeth for him.

Just then Ginger returned from the kitchen. She walked past Cole. "I'm done, Beau," she said. "Did you get a room?" It was an innocent question, but I wondered how it would read in the morning edition. As recognition and wonder washed across Max's fat face, I wanted to crawl into a hole.

"Why, Mrs. Watkins, how nice to see you again."

Ginger turned on him coolly. "I don't believe I know you."

"Cole," he said with an affable grin. "Maxwell Cole of the *Post-Intelligencer*. Would you care to comment on Sig Larson's death?"

Her manner changed from cool to frigid. "I would not."

He shrugged and looked at me. "Doesn't hurt to ask."

"Get out of here, Max." I was in no mood to put up with any of his crap.

"Just one more question, Mrs. Watkins. Have you seen Don Wilson today?"

Ginger's reaction was totally out of proportion to the question. "Is . . . he . . . here?" she stammered. Color drained from her face. She groped blindly for my arm.

The change wasn't lost on Max. He stepped toward her, and she shrank against me. "He was supposed to be," Max continued lightly. "We had an interview scheduled at four. He called late this morning. Said something was about to break. I barely had time to get here."

I stepped between Max and Ginger. "Why did he call you? Why not someone else?"

"I've been working on a special piece—"

I took Ginger's arm, cutting him off. "Come on. Let's get out of here."

"But—" Max protested.

"Stay away from her and stay away from me, Max. If you don't, I'll give your dentist and your eye doctor a little more business."

His walrus mouth opened and closed convulsively. They weren't empty words, and he knew it. When Ginger and I left the building, he made no effort to follow.

I led Ginger back to my room and helped her into the chair before I went back to shut and lock the door. "What is it, Ginger?" I asked gently. "Tell me."

"He did it," she said decisively. "It has to be him."

"Who did what?"

"Don Wilson. He killed Sig, I'm sure of it. I had no idea he was here. I never thought—"

"What are you talking about?"

"Don Wilson. He threatened us, both Sig and me. Sig just laughed it off. So did Darrell. No one took it seriously."

"Why did he threaten you? I don't understand."

"We—" She swallowed hard. "Sig and I conducted the hearing that sent Lathrop to that work/ release program."

My gut gave a wrench. I remembered the public outcry. There had been talk that the parole board should resign *en masse*. I had been standing next to her. Turning, I moved away, distancing myself. I couldn't help it.

"Please, Beau, it wasn't our fault. We were given incomplete records. We made the decision as best we could with the information at hand." Her voice pleaded for understanding, for me not to abandon her.

"What did Wilson say?" My tone was flat and empty.

"That we'd pay for his wife and daughter. We didn't know, Beau. Can you understand that? There was an administrative foul-up. The rest of Lathrop's records weren't found until much later. We didn't know he had sworn to get even with Denise Wilson. We had no idea where she lived. Washington doesn't keep track of witnesses or victims, not even to protect them."

"When did Wilson threaten you?" I could tell from her voice it was important that I believe her.

"I don't know. Several times. He's always hanging around. In fact, Sig and I were surprised Wilson wasn't here today. He stands outside every meeting, carrying signs, passing out petitions, but I never thought he'd really do it."

"Petitions for what?"

"For a victim/witness protection program."

"But he wasn't here today?"

"No. Sig even mentioned it." I got up and went to the phone. "What are you doing?" she asked.

"I'm calling Huggins. He needs this information." Fred answered. "Is Detective Huggins still around?"

"No," came the reply. "He left in the police boat

right after the crime-lab guys took off. He's probably in Friday Harbor by now."

"Call him and tell him to come back," I ordered.
"It's urgent."

Fred's response wasn't hopeful. "I doubt he'll
want to come back tonight."

"Tell him we've got a suspect. That'll bring him
back." I hung up.

Ginger followed me to the door. "Where are you
going?" she asked.

"I've got to find Maxwell Cole. You stay here,
understand?" She nodded. "Lock the door behind
me. Don't let anyone in." I dashed outside and
headed up the path to Room 143. No one answered my knock. I glanced at my watch. It was
after eleven. The Vista Lounge was still open. I
hurried back toward the main building, a converted mansion that serves as lobby, dining room,
and bar. The lounge is a long, narrow room facing Rosario Strait. In its previous life it had been
a sun porch. Now it was a posh watering hole.

Maxwell Cole's ample figure slouched on a
stool at the end of the bar. He was downing hand-
fuls of salted cracker goldfish and regaling the
poor guy next to him with one-sided conversation. I tapped his shoulder.

"Hey, Max. I need to talk to you."

He heaved himself around on the bar stool to
face me. "What's this? A change of heart? Decided
you can afford to spend some time with your old
fraternity buddy after all? Fuck off, J. P. Who
needs it?"

He turned away and picked up his beer. I
tapped his shoulder again. "I want to talk to you."

Barney is a good bartender. He has a sixth sense for trouble and can spot it before it starts. He ambled down the bar to where Cole was sitting.

"What seems to be the problem?"

"This guy's bothering me," Max whined. "I was sitting here minding my own business."

Barney glanced up at me. "I need to talk to him," I said tersely over Max's head. "About what happened this afternoon."

Max set down his half-empty glass. Barney swept it away and poured the contents into the sink. "After you talk to this gentleman," he said, "I'll buy you another beer."

"Why you—" Max objected.

"You'd better go, fella, before I get upset."

Barney is a beefy former Green Beret who looks as though he could inflict a considerable amount of bodily harm with his bare hands. Max finally scrambled down from the bar stool and reluctantly followed me into the next room, muttering under his breath. Once we were out of earshot of the bar, I turned on him. "You have any pictures of Wilson on you?"

"Hell no. Why should I?"

"Because you just might."

"Maybe one, but it'll cost you."

"How much?"

"An exclusive interview with Ginger Watkins."

"Ginger Watkins is not for sale."

"You say that in a rather proprietary manner, J. P. You got something going with her? I heard what she said about getting a room. She's a married lady, you know. Her husband is big. Very big."

"I want the picture, Max."

"No way."

He was wearing an ugly striped tie, still knotted, but hanging loose around his neck. I grasped it in my fist and lifted him to the tops of his toes. "I'm not on duty, Maxey, so don't tempt me."

"Okay, okay," he sputtered. "It's in my room."

"Go get it and bring it to me. I'll wait in the lobby."

He shambled off. I hurried to the pay phone near the front desk and dialed Peters, my partner, at home, long-distance, collect. I figured that would get his attention. He sounded half-asleep when he answered the phone. "What's up?" he asked when he recognized my voice. "Where are you? And why the hell are you calling me collect?"

"Rosario," I growled. "Send me the bill. Now listen. Remember the Lathrop case? Get down to the department and gather everything you can find on it. A detective from Friday Harbor will be calling for it. I want it ready when he does."

"Just a fucking minute, Beau. Do you know what time it is? It's a long way from Kirkland to the department."

"So move to town. It's not rush hour. It won't take more than twenty minutes to get to Seattle."

"Beau, you're supposed to be on vacation, for chrissake. What's gotten into you?"

"I'm asking a favor, Peters. Please."

"Oh, all right, but I'm gonna remember this. The Lathrop case, you said?"

"Yes, and everything you can find out about the victims' family, particularly Don Wilson, the father."

"Anything else? I'm already awake. Don't you want me to pick up some groceries or a newspaper while I'm at it?"

Maxwell Cole was lumbering toward the building. "Cut the comedy, Peters. This is serious."

"Okay, Beau, okay. I'm on my way."

"Thanks. I owe you one."

"This better count for more than one."

"It does."

CHAPTER 6

I KNOCKED. "WHO IS IT?" GINGER CALLED.

"Me, Beau." I opened the door with my key. Ginger stood near the bed, her face drawn and wary. She glanced at the manila envelope in my hand. "What's that?"

I came inside, shutting and locking the door behind me. I opened the envelope and handed her the picture Maxwell Cole had given me. She looked at Don Wilson's likeness.

"Where'd you get that?"

"Good ol' Max saves the day for a change."

Ginger retreated to a chair in the corner of the room, where she curled up with her legs folded under her and began brushing her hair with a vengeance.

"Huggins is on his way," I told her. "He'll want to go to work on this picture tonight. He'll show it to everyone he can find on or near the ferries, passengers and workers alike. He'll try to get to them while someone still remembers seeing Wilson, either coming over or going back."

Ginger put the brush in her lap. Her voice when she spoke was very small. "Do you think he's still here?"

"I don't know. My gut instinct says yes."

"What can we do?"

"First we talk to Huggins. After that, I don't know."

"Can I stay here, Beau? With you?" Anxious green eyes held mine.

I felt a catch in my throat, remembering the feel of her body against mine as she wept for Sig Larson. "I don't know why not. I'd as soon have you here where I can keep an eye on you. I was going to see if there were any rooms available in Eastsound, but this makes more sense."

She picked up her brush and silently resumed brushing her hair. I called the desk. Fred and I had gone round and round over the room problem one more time after Max gave me the picture. I had pulled rank on him, hoping Detective Beaumont would elicit more action than Mr. Beaumont. No such luck. His tone was somewhat guarded. "Yes, Detective Beaumont. What can I do for you?"

"You have a roll-away bed down there?"

"Yes."

"I want one up here, on the double. Mrs. Watkins will stay here with me. We have reason to believe Larson's killer is still in the area. He may try to reach her next. Don't leak a word of this, is that clear?"

"Yes, sir. I'll deliver it myself. Not even the maids will know. I can pick it up in the morning before I leave."

"And if she has any calls," I continued, "put them on hold and check with me before you put them through."

"I understand."

"When's your shift over?"

"I'm pulling an extra one tonight. I won't get off until eight tomorrow morning."

"All right. Have the roll-away back out of here before you go. I guess that's all."

"Detective Beaumont?"

"Yes."

"Someone said Detective Huggins is just pulling up at the dock."

"Good. See if you can locate any coffee, would you?"

"Sure thing."

When Huggins knocked on the door, he was carrying a tray with a pot of coffee and three cups and saucers. "Somebody handed me this tray. Whatever you've got, Beaumont, it better be good."

"It is, Hal," I assured him. "Believe me."

Ginger poured coffee while I brought Hal up to date and showed him the photograph of Wilson. When I finished, he shook his head sadly. "It's a pisser. The wrong goddamned people get killed. Wilson'll end up on Death Row with Lathrop, and probably beat him to the gallows."

I interrupted Huggins' grim soliloquy. "Look, Hal, I called my partner in Seattle. He's gathering everything Seattle P.D. has on Lathrop and Wilson. It'll be ready when you call. He'll bring it out himself if you ask for him."

"Is he one of the old-timers?" Hal asked. "Somebody I'd remember?"

"No. He's brand-new, but a hell of a nice guy."

"What's his name?"

"Peters. Ron Peters."

He made a note of the name before turning to Ginger. "Can you remember exactly what Wilson said when he threatened you and Mr. Larson?"

Ginger shook her head. "Not the exact words. Just that he'd make us pay, that it wasn't fair for his wife and child to be dead while we were still alive."

"But you didn't think of him this afternoon when you discovered Mr. Larson's body. Why not?"

"I didn't think Wilson was here. If he's around, he's usually out front picketing with all his signs and paraphernalia. I forgot about him completely until that reporter said Wilson didn't show for a meeting."

"Which reporter?"

I answered him. "Max, Maxwell Cole. Wilson called him this morning and set up an interview here at Rosario at four o'clock. Max waited. Wilson never came."

Huggins focused once more on Ginger. "You said you mentioned the threats to your husband. He advised you to disregard them?"

Ginger nodded. "He said the world is full of harmless crazies."

"This one is far from harmless." Huggins sighed, glancing in my direction. "Any ideas, Beaumont?"

There was a quiet tap on the door. When I answered it, Fred stood outside with a roll-away bed. "This is the first I could get away," he said. "It's all right if Detective Huggins knows, isn't it?"

Since the bed was already there, it was too late to debate secrecy. I stepped aside and helped pull the bed over the threshold. He pushed the bed just inside the door, then ducked back into the night. Fearless Fred.

"This is my brainstorm," I said, turning to Huggins. "She stays with me tonight. Without knowing whether Wilson is still on the island, I'm not willing to risk leaving her alone."

He nodded in agreement. "Good thinking. I was going to suggest flying her to Seattle, but I'd prefer having her here in case there are more questions in the morning. The county budget doesn't handle a whole lot of commuting back and forth to the big city."

Huggins stood up. "I'm going, then." He held Wilson's picture up to the light, examining it minutely. "I'll copy this sucker tonight and plaster the island with it tomorrow—the island and every single ferry that stops here. I'll send someone by Wilson's house. It's late. I'd better hit the trail."

I followed him to the door. He turned to me and said in an undertone, "You got a piece on you?"

"It's locked up in a suitcase, but—"

"I'm deputizing you as of right now, Beaumont. I don't want there to be any jurisdictional fuss. Besides, I need you. Get it out, and keep it handy." He poked his head back inside the door. "You're in good hands, Mrs. Watkins. J. P. Beaumont is the best there is."

"You'll give me a swelled head, Hal," I said.

I came back into the room, once more carefully locking the door behind me. I went around the room, double-checking the locks on the windows.

Ginger watched me, her eyes gravely following my every move. I took my suitcase from its place in the closet and removed my .38. I put the gun on the bed beside me. Women usually retreat from firearms. Ginger held her ground.

"Are you?" she asked.

"Am I what?"

"The best there is?"

"I don't know about that." I sat looking at my revolver. A gun is a tool, an instrument, until it kills something you love. Then it takes on a life of its own, alien, evil.

"What are you thinking?"

"Nothing," I answered quickly. "Just wool-gathering."

"What happened to your wife?"

"Karen?" I shrugged. "She ran off with a chicken magnate from Cucamonga, California."

"Chicken?"

"Yeah. He was an accountant scouting for a new plant site for an egg conglomerate. Karen was supposed to be selling him real estate."

"He married her?"

"Eventually."

"Kids?"

"Two. A boy and a girl, Scotty and Kelly. They're mostly grown, thriving in California. I see them during the summers." I didn't mention Anne Corley. It was a deliberate oversight.

"Girl friend?"

"None at the moment. Why all the questions?"

"Everyone's been asking me questions all evening. Turnabout is fair play. You said earlier you were having a mid-life crisis. How come?"

"Mid-life crises are very trendy these days." I responded with a congenial grin I hoped would derail the question. I didn't want to go into that, to examine motives and lost illusions.

"Will you still be a cop?"

I shrugged. I couldn't imagine being anything else. "Unless you have some other bright idea."

She looked at me seriously, squarely. "You've been hurt too."

"Does it show that much?"

"It shows."

I winced at her direct hit and changed the subject. "You said something earlier that's been bothering me: that you were working because you and Darrell needed the money. How come?"

"We're part of a syndicate that put together a downtown luxury high-rise project, just before the bottom dropped out of the real estate market. Most of our capital—ours, Homer's, and Sig's—has been tied up keeping the project afloat, waiting for the market to turn. Meantime, ready cash is in short supply."

"That's why you and Sig ended up on the parole board?"

She nodded. "Sig was actually well qualified. He knew it from the inside out without ever being either a prisoner or a guard. He did volunteer work at Walla Walla for years. He used to live near there, even started an A.A. group inside. He had every right to be on the board. I was the hanger-on."

Ginger looked at me earnestly. "I tried, though, Beau. Especially after Sig got me dried out. I read everything I could lay my hands on. I did a good job. The Lathrop case was an administrative night-mare." She willed me to believe her. It was important to her that I not lay blame.

"Those things happen," I conceded.

She accepted my remark as a form of absolution. "Thank you," she murmured.

"What will you do if you resign from the board?"

She shrugged. "Something," she replied. "Homer told me tonight he'll see to it that I don't get a penny."

"That's just a threat. He can't get away with it. You have an attorney. He'll see that you get a fair shake."

She laughed. "You don't understand. Homer Watkins' name isn't up in lights. He doesn't make headlines, but he's a mover and shaker in this state. Stone-cold broke, he can still pull enough strings to get anything he wants, including elect-ing his son lieutenant governor. I'll be lucky to get out of the house with the clothes on my back."

"I have an attorney," I offered. "Maybe he could help." I was thinking about Ralph Ames, who even then was preparing for a custody hearing to wrest my partner's two kids out of a religious cult in Broken Springs, Oregon.

Ginger smiled, condescendingly. "How far do you think I'd get paying for an attorney on my own? It takes money to fight the system. I won't have any."

"Ames would do it if I asked him. He's from Ari-zona. Phoenix. He handles all my personal affairs. Let him take a look at your situation. It wouldn't cost you anything."

A smile flickered around the corners of her

mouth. "Beau, listen to me. These are big-time lawyers with big-time staffs. They'd chew up your little guy and spit him out. But thanks. It's kind of you to offer."

"Promise me you'll let Ames look it over first. Talk about the best there is, Ames is it."

Ginger laughed aloud. "All right, all right. If you insist, but he'd better not show up wearing cowboy boots and riding a horse."

CHAPTER 7

I SPENT SOME TIME LOOKING FOR A DELICATE WAY TO suggest we get ready for bed. There was no easy way. I finally said it straight out. Ginger retreated into the bathroom to change while I grappled with the Chinese-puzzle roll-away bed. Partial assembly required.

The bed was unfolded and sitting in front of the outside door when Ginger emerged from the bathroom. She wore a jade-colored silk robe with a hint of filmy nightgown underneath. Seeing her, I realized I didn't have a pair of pajamas to my name. I'd been a bachelor so long, my last pair of Christmas pajamas had bitten the dust.

"What are you staring at?" she demanded, one hand on her hip. "Haven't you ever seen a woman in a robe before?"

"Sorry. I was thinking about something else."

I retired to the bathroom to contemplate my dilemma, finally opting for skivvies and no lights. That, of course, presented another problem. No light in a familiar room is one thing, and no light in a city apartment is another. But no light in a strange room where they've never heard of street-lights can be murder on shins, toes, and other unprotected parts of the anatomy. I blundered my way into bed after a bruising game of blindman's buff.

Settling into the roll-away, I discovered the bed frame formed a rigid hump directly under the small of my back. It was a long way from the king-sized comfort I had grown accustomed to. At last I concluded the bed wasn't any worse than some of the rocks I had slept on just for the hell of it during my hunting and camping phase. This at least had a somewhat higher purpose.

I tossed around a few minutes before dozing off. I had just entered that deep, initial alpha sleep when I heard her say, "Beau?"

Adrenaline pumping, I made a dive for the .38 on the floor beside me. The roll-away tipped up on one corner, pitching me headlong onto the floor in a tangle of sheets, pillow, and blankets. Ginger switched on the bedside lamp.

"What happened?"

"I fell out of bed, goddammit! What's wrong? Did you hear something?"

"No, I was wondering if you were awake."

"I am now," I grumbled. I didn't want to get up. The light still blazed while I sat on the floor clad in a discreet loincloth of sheet. I glared at her, and she started to giggle.

"It's not funny," I muttered.

She nodded, covering her mouth with her hand to contain increasing ripples of laughter. "Yes it is," she gasped at last. "You ought to see yourself."

I looked down. I had to admit that what I could see was pretty funny. The gun had skidded under the bed. No way was I going to crawl around on hands and knees searching for it. With as much dignity as I could muster, I unraveled my legs. At last, wearing the sheet as a toga, I stood on my feet, surveying the debris that had once been a tidy roll-away bed.

"This is a very large bed," Ginger said seriously, stifling her mirth. "It's probably more comfortable than that thing, too." That much was inarguable. I said nothing. "Care to join me?"

"Come on, Ginger. Get serious."

"I am serious." All laughter was gone from her mouth and eyes. "There's plenty of room," she added. "We're consenting adults. We haven't crossed any state lines."

"But you're the wife of the soon-to-be-elected lieutenant governor."

"The soon-to-be-former wife of the soon-to-be-elected lieutenant governor," she corrected with a hint of a smile.

I moved to the far side of the bed and alighted cautiously on the edge of it. I waited for lightning to strike. It didn't.

"Would you like me to call the desk and see if they have any bundling boards?"

I turned on her. "You're making fun of me."

"I can't help it."

Tentatively I slid first one leg, then the other under the covers, clutching the sheet firmly in one hand as a security blanket. I settled warily on my pillow before I turned to look at her. She sat propped up in bed observing me with undisguised interest.

The deep neckline of her gown fell away revealing a firm swell of breast.

"Do you think I'm beautiful?" she asked gravely.

I looked up guiltily, convinced she had caught me peeking. "Of course you're beautiful. Very beautiful."

"Sig used to tell me that. I never knew if I should believe him."

"My God, Ginger! How could you not believe him?"

"I still see a drunk when I look in the mirror." It was a comment made without guile. She wasn't fishing for a compliment: she was attempting to understand, to sort out what was real and what wasn't.

Obviously we weren't going right to sleep. I propped my pillow next to hers, examining her carefully, critically in the golden glow of the bedside lamp behind her. I studied the curve of her forehead, the clear green eyes under delicately arched brows, the fine, straight nose, the gentle pout of her lower lip. "You're not the same person now. I think that's what Sig wanted you to realize."

She drew her knees up and rested her chin on them, musing aloud. "I thought that once I quit drinking, that I'd be good enough, that Darrell would finally pay some attention to me. There are a lot of stories like that in A.A., you know, marriages that bounce back from the brink of disaster. But this is a thirty-six-year-old body. I can't compete with tender blossoms from the secretarial pool."

Silence lengthened between us. Never glib, I could think of nothing to say. But then, I had never before found myself in quite this situation.

"What's the scar on your chest?"

"Huh?" Her question startled me. I looked down as though I had forgotten it was my chest and my scar, the stark white of an incision highlighted against the rest of my skin. "It's from a bullet," I said.

"When did it happen?"

"Last spring sometime," I said carefully. The time, the date, the place are as indelibly inked on my soul as the scar is on my flesh.

"Did you catch him?"

"Who?"

"The man who shot you."

"It was a woman. She's dead."

"Oh."

"Do you mind turning out the lights?" I asked. I didn't want to talk anymore. The conversation was circling too close to my own hurt. It was one thing to help Ginger with hers. Dealing with my own was something else.

The light snapped off. I could feel Ginger settling on her side of the bed. I groped under the bed and located my .38. Once it was within easy reach, I lowered my pillow, resting on it as if it were full of thumbtacks or nails.

"Beau?"

"Yes."

"Could I just lie next to you? I need an arm around me. Someone to hold me."

Tentatively, I held up the covers. She slid across the bed and nestled into the crook of my arm. I inhaled the fragrant perfume of her freshly washed hair. I felt the curve of her hip next to mine, the gentle swell of her breast under a layer of covers. For a long time we were quiet. I think I was holding my breath.

"Beau?"

"Yes."

"What are you thinking?"

"I'm trying to remember which of the Ten Commandments says 'Thou shalt not covet thy neighbor's wife.'"

"Do you?"

"Do I what?"

"Covet me?"

Right then I realized the Garden of Eden was a put-up job. "Yes."

Her hand flitted across my chest, her touch inflaming every strained nerve in my body. She pulled herself up until she lay on my chest, her lips grazing mine.

I was conscious of the tantalizing feel of silk against my skin, the musky odor of a woman's awakening body. She kissed me, cautiously, as though unsure of my response. I wasn't sure either. I waited long enough to be sure lightning still didn't strike, then I pulled her to me, my mouth seeking hers, finding her hungry, willing, eager.

She guided my hand through the cleft in her gown. Her breast was taut and expectant beneath my cupped fingers. I sampled her ear and traced the slender curve of her neck with my teeth and tongue. She gasped, and her body arched as gooseflesh swept across her skin beneath my fingertips.

She slipped from my grasp. I heard her impatiently cast off the silken barrier of gown. My Fruit of the Loom hit the floor as well. Ginger came back to me naked, sleek, and ready. Beyond pleasure, she sought only release.

She slid her body onto mine, moisture finding moisture, need finding need, plunging me deep within her. I grasped her slim waist, raising her, lowering her, hearing her sharp intake of breath each time I probed closer to home, each time I led her to the brink then drew her back, offering and withholding the final gift.

"Now," she whispered. "Please."

When the flood came, it engulfed us both. We surfaced in a quiet pool, spent and out of breath. "That was wonderful," she whispered.

"I'll bet you say that to all the guys," I teased.

She was suddenly subdued. "There's only been one other," she said. "He's never been this good. Ever."

"Flattery will get you everywhere." I drew her into my arms, cradling her head on my shoulder. "Are you going to shut up and go to sleep? It's late. The desk clerk is coming for the goddamn rollaway at eight in the morning."

"I'll be quiet," she said. "I promise."

She snuggled against me. We lay like that for a long time. Her breathing steadied and slowed. I listened as her heart beat next to mine, a thud followed by a smaller echo. Deliberately I tried to slow my breathing, hoping to God I wouldn't snore. Time passed slowly. I stared, sleepless, at the empty space above the bed, wondering how long it takes to learn to sleep double in a double bed, to misquote a familiar song. Probably a long time.

"Beau?"

"What now?"

"I can't do it."

"Do what?"

"Sleep like this. I don't know how to sleep with anyone but Darrell."

I pulled her to me, holding her for a moment in a crushing bear hug. I kissed the top of her forehead, then shoved her playfully toward the other side of the bed. "Go sleep over there, then, spoilsport."

"I'm sorry."

"Don't be. I understand."

And I did understand. Ginger Watkins had been caught up in the need to know she was still alive—a normal phenomenon in the aftermath of death, an instinctive affirmation of survival. If I hadn't been there, she would have found someone else. I just got lucky.

CHAPTER 8

THE TELEPHONE JARRED ME AWAKE AT SEVEN. "DETECtive Beaumont? Darrell Watkins is on the phone. He wants to speak to Mrs. Watkins. Should I put him through?"

I felt the unaccustomed warmth of a body snuggled close to mine. It took time to clear my head. I turned, and Ginger stirred, nestling comfortably against me. She had evidently moved there in the middle of the night, our sleeping bodies overcoming our conscious objections. "Sure, that's fine," I said into the phone.

With a noisy clatter I fumbled the phone back into place. "Ginger. Wake up. You've got a call."

Her eyes opened and focused on mine with a look of startled dismay. The phone rang again before she could say anything. I handed it to her.

"Hello?" Ginger said, her voice still thick with sleep. "Oh, hello Darrell." There was a long silence as she listened to what he had to say. Meanwhile, I lay naked under the covers, considering the best way to get to the bathroom while maintaining some degree of modesty.

"No. I haven't changed my mind," she said firmly. That galvanized me to action. I had no intention of eavesdropping on her domestic conversation. I groped on the floor, found the discarded roll-away sheet, and wrapped it around me. With clean clothes from the closet, I withdrew into the bathroom and took a bracing hot shower.

The water pounded me. Despite lack of sleep, I was invigorated, stimulated. Exhaustion, my constant companion for months, dissolved. I was incredibly happy, except for one small cloud on my horizon. Ginger might be remorseful.

I didn't want guilt or regret to tarnish what had happened between us, even if it was nothing more than the survivor's time honored, near-death screwing syndrome. Maybe that's all it had been for Ginger, but not for me. It had reawakened J. P. Beaumont's lost libido. I was glad to have the old boy back.

Humming under my breath, I emerged from the bathroom. Ginger sat on her side of the bed with her legs tucked under her. She was wearing the lush silk robe.

"Good morning," I said.

"Do you always sing in the shower?"

"Only when I'm happy," I told her.

"I see."

I looked at her, trying to assess the effect of her husband's phone call, hoping for some sign to indicate if she was glad to see me or if she wanted me to drop into a hole someplace. Her face remained inscrutable.

"Is Darrell coming up?" I asked, for want of something better to say.

"He wanted to, but I told him no. He thinks he can talk me into changing my mind. It won't work. I told him I'm staying here the rest of the weekend. I had planned to, anyway. There's no sense in going home just to fight."

"Will they cancel the workshop?"

She smiled mirthlessly. "Not even Trixie Bowdeen has nerve enough to go through with it after what happened to Sig."

"Who's she?"

"Chairman of the parole board."

"You don't like her much, do you."

"No," she responded.

With my hair combed and a splash of aftershave on my face, I surveyed the roll-away with an eye to making it look more like someone had slept in it and less as though a heavyweight wrestling match had occurred. I gathered up the sheets and blankets and started to put it to rights.

"Beau?"

Busy with the bed, I didn't look up when she spoke. "What?"

"Do you think badly of me?"

I abandoned the roll-away. "Think badly of you! Are you kidding? Why should I?"

"Because of last night. I didn't mean to . . . I—"

In two steps I stood beside her. "Look, lady," I said gruffly, placing my hand on her shoulder and giving her a gentle shake.

"It's the blind leading the blind. I was worried

about how you'd feel this morning, afraid you'd be embarrassed, think I'd taken advantage."

She reached out and took my hand. She kissed the back of it, then turned it over and moved it from her hairline to her chin, guiding my fingers in a slow caress along the curve of her cheek.

"I'm not embarrassed," she said softly. "Greedy, but not embarrassed." She allowed my hand to stray down her neck and invade the soft folds of her robe. She was wearing nothing underneath.

Her robe fell open before me. Our coupling the night before had been in pitch-blackness. Now my eyes feasted hungrily on her body. She was no lithe virgin. Hers was the gentle voluptuousness of a grown woman, with a hint of fullness of breast and hip that follows child-bearing. A pale web of stretch marks lingered in mute testimony.

My hand cupped her breast. It changed subtly but perceptibly. The nipple drew erect, the soft flesh taut and warm beneath my fingers. She caught my chin in her hand and turned my face to hers until our lips met. "Please, Beau," she whispered, her mouth against mine.

I shed my clothes on the spot while she lay naked before me, tempting as a pagan sacrifice offered to me alone. My fingers and tongue searched her body, exploring her, demanding admittance. She gave herself freely, opening before me, denying me nothing. She took all I had to give and more, her body arching to meet my every move. A final frenzy left her trembling against my shoulder, my face buried in her hair.

"It wasn't an accident, was it?" she said, when she could talk.

"What wasn't an accident?"

"Last night."

"I don't understand." I was mystified.

"While you showered, I was wondering if last night was an accident or if it could have been that way all along."

I raised up on one elbow to look at her. Her face was serious, contemplative.

Understanding dawned slowly. No one had ever before made love to her like that. Darrell Watkins had never tapped the wellspring of woman in her—not in eighteen years of marriage. I kissed her tenderly. "That's the way it's supposed to be."

"The bastard!" she said fiercely. "The first-class bastard! I'll take him to the cleaners."

I had unwittingly unleashed Hurricane Ginger into the world. "Maybe he doesn't know any better." I inadvertently defended him, and she gave me a shove that sent me sprawling from the bed onto the floor.

"He's been giving it away to everyone else. By God, it's going to cost him." Angry tears appeared on her cheeks.

The phone rang on the other side of the bed. I scrambled to reach it. "This is the desk. Can I come get that roll-away now? I'm almost ready to leave."

I cleared my throat. "Sure. Anytime. The bed's all ready to go." I spoke casually, all the while motioning frantically to Ginger. She hopped out of bed and made a beeline for the bathroom.

"By the way," I continued, stalling for time, "before you come, would you ask the dining room to have my usual table set for two? We'll be down for breakfast in a few minutes. I don't want to wait in a crush of reporters."

"No problem," Fred replied.

I rushed back into my clothes and made the room as presentable as possible. I went so far as to beat an indentation in the pillow on the roll-away. I also did my best to straighten one side of the king-size bed.

Ginger's transformation was speedy. Dressed, brushed, and wearing a subtle cologne, she emerged from the bathroom well before the clerk arrived. She may have worn some makeup other than a dash of pale lipstick, but I couldn't tell for sure. She looked refreshed and beautiful. Smiling, she surveyed my clumsy efforts to conceal our activities. Walking to the far side of the bed, she expertly straightened the bedding.

"Whose reputation are you trying to protect?" she asked.

"All of the above," I told her.

"I see."

The desk clerk knocked. We managed to fold up the roll-away contraption and move it out of the room.

"Hungry?" I asked after Fred was gone.

"Famished," she replied.

"Let's go do it, then," I told her. We walked through a quiet Rosario morning. The only noise was an occasional squawking gull. No one else from her group seemed to be up, although several of the dining room tables were occupied. The hostess led us directly to my preferred table, one by the window overlooking Rosario Strait.

"Morning, folks," said the same cheery waiter

who had served us the night before. "What can I get you?"

"The works," I told him. "Eggs over easy, hash browns, toast, juice, coffee."

He looked questioningly at Ginger. "I'll have the same," she said with a smile.

My water glass had a narrow sliver of lemon in it. I speared the lemon with my fork, then offered it to Ginger across the table. Puzzled, she sat holding it.

"What's this for?" she asked.

"To wipe that silly grin off your face," I replied. "People might get suspicious."

She laughed outright, but soon a cloud passed over her face. "I believe," she said thoughtfully, "I'm beginning to understand what Sig meant."

Outside our window the sky directly overhead was blue. As we watched, a thick bank of fog marched toward us, rolling across the water, obscuring the strait beyond the resort's sheltered bay.

We were well into breakfast when, over Ginger's shoulder, I saw an obese but well-groomed woman pause at the dining room entrance, survey the room, then make her way toward us like a frigate under full sail. She wore a heavy layer of makeup. Her fingers were laden with a full contingent of ornate rings. A thick cloud of perfume preceded her.

"Ginger." Her voice had a sharp, school-marmish tone. Ginger started instinctively, then composed herself.

"Good morning, Trixie."

The woman stopped next to our table and appraised me disapprovingly. "I went by your room several times last night and this morning, but you weren't there." She paused as if waiting for Ginger to offer some kind of explanation. None was forthcoming.

"Trixie, I'd like you to meet a friend of mine, J. P. Beaumont. Beau, this is Trixie Bowdeen, chairman of the parole board."

"Glad to meet you," I said.

Trixie ignored me. "Have you gotten word that the meeting's canceled?" she asked coldly.

Ginger countered with some ice of her own. "I think that's only appropriate."

Trixie forged on. "We're all leaving this morning. Do you need a ride back to Seattle?"

"No, thanks. I can manage."

"All right." Trixie turned her ponderous bulk and started away. Then she stopped and returned to our table. "Under the circumstances, it's probably best if you don't go to Sig's funeral."

All color seeped from Ginger's cheeks, but she allowed herself no other visible reaction to Trixie's words. "Why not?" Ginger asked.

Her question seemed to take Trixie aback. "Well, considering . . ." Trixie retreated under Ginger's withering gaze, turned, and in a rustle of skirt and nylons, left the room.

Ginger carefully placed her fork on her plate and pushed it away. "Can we go?"

I took one look at her face and knew I'd better get her out of there fast. Trixie Bowdeen had just layered on the straw that broke the camel's back.

CHAPTER 9

THE FASTEST WAY OUT OF THE BUILDING WAS DOWN THE back stairs and out past the long, narrow, bowling-alley-shaped indoor pool. By the time we reached the terrace outside, Ginger's sob burst to the surface. She rushed to the guardrail and stood leaning over it, her shoulders heaving, while I stood helplessly to one side with my hands jammed deep in my pockets so I wouldn't reach out to hold her.

I've never seen fog anywhere that quite compares to Orcas Island fog. One moment we stood in the open; the next we were alone in a private world. As the fog swept in, Ginger faded to a shadow. I moved toward her, grasping her hand as the building disappeared behind us. She was still crying, the sound strangely muffled in the uncanny silence.

Pulling her to me, I rocked her against my chest until she quieted. I continued to hold her, but I also glanced over my shoulder to verify we were still invisible to the dining room windows. She drew a ragged breath.

"Are you all right now?"

She nodded. "I am. Really."

"That was an ugly thing for her to do."

"Trixie enjoyed passing along Mona's message." There was a shift in Ginger's voice, a strengthening of resolve. "I've got to resign. Without Sig, I can't stand up to those people. They're all cut from the same cloth."

Ginger broke away from me and moved along the terrace, running her hand disconsolately along the guardrail. I trailed behind her, at a loss for words, wondering what made her think Trixie had served as Mona's emissary.

"The fog feels like velvet," Ginger commented. "I wish I could hide in it forever and never come out."

"That's not the answer."

"Isn't it? When you're drunk you don't feel the hurt."

"What are you going to do?" Her remark had sounded like a threat to start drinking. If she was truly a recovering alcoholic, a drink was the last thing she needed.

"It's okay. Don't worry. I'll go to a meeting. There's one in Eastsound tonight."

"What meeting?"

"An A.A. meeting. Whenever Sig and I were on the road, we went to meetings together. We planned to go to this one tonight. I don't remember where it is."

"Can I come?"

Ginger stopped and faced me, looking deep into my eyes before she shook her head. "It's a closed meeting, Beau, not an open one where everyone is welcome. I'll go by myself. If I'm not going to Sig's funeral, it'll be my private remembrance for him."

She made the statement with absolute conviction. I couldn't help but respect her desire to have a private farewell for the man who had pulled her from the mire. We didn't discuss it again. The subject was closed.

The fog lifted as quickly as it had come. I moved discreetly away from her. "You're one hell of a woman, Ginger Watkins, I'll say that for you." She gave me a halfhearted smile and started toward the building.

"Are you sure you want to go in there? There's probably a whole armload of reporters having breakfast by now. The murder of a public official is big news."

She stopped, considering my words. "Reporters? In there?" She nodded toward the dining room overhead.

"The desk clerk told me last night that some of them stayed over. I know for a fact Maxwell Cole did."

"He was that funny-looking fat man you were talking to in the lobby when I came back from being fingerprinted? The one who was supposed to meet Don Wilson?"

"One and the same."

"Who does he work for?"

"The *P.I.* He writes a crime column."

She paused thoughtfully. "Is that all he's interested in? Crime?"

I couldn't see where the discussion was going. "Why are you asking?"

She grinned impishly. "I told you I'd get Darrell, starting now. I'll file on Monday, but it'll hit the papers Sunday morning. The only reason they want me to reconsider is to keep it quiet until after election day. Believe me, Darrell doesn't want me back. Now, where do I find what's-his-name?"

"Max? Probably under a rock somewhere."

"I mean it, Beau. I want to talk to him."

Hell hath no fury, and all that jazz. I figured Darrell Watkins deserved just about anything Ginger could dish out. "Go on into the Moran Room and wait by the fireplace. I'll see if I can find him and send him there. I'm also going to have your things moved to another room for tonight, if you're going to stay over."

"Why? Can't I stay with you?"

I shook my head. "Discretion is the better part of valor, my dear. You can sleep wherever you damn well please, but you'd better have a separate room with your clothes in it or you'll get us both in a hell of a lot of trouble."

"Oh," she said. "I guess I should've thought of that."

Maxwell Cole was eating breakfast. Talking to him was tough because all I could see was the blob of egg yolk that dangled from one curl of his handlebar mustache. "Ginger Watkins wants to talk to you," I said.

His eyes bulged. "No shit? Where is she?"

"In the Moran Room, just off the lobby, waiting."

Cole lurched to his feet, signaling for the waiter to bring his check. "Hey thanks, J. P. I can't thank you enough."

Max persists in calling me by my initials. My real name is Jonas Piedmont Beaumont. Mother named me after her father and grandfather as a conciliatory gesture after my father died in a motorcycle crash before he and Mother had a chance to tie the knot. It didn't work. Her family never lifted a finger to help us. She raised me totally on her own. They never forgave her, and I've never forgiven them. It's a two-way street.

I shortened my name to initials in high school. In college people started calling me Beau. Except for Max. He picked my initials off a registration form, and he's used them ever since, mostly because he knows it bugs me.

"How about if you drop the 'J. P.' crap, Maxey? That would be one way of thanking me."

With a hangdog expression on his face, Max followed me out of the dining room to the crackling fireplace in the Moran Room. Afterward I stopped at the desk to reserve a new room for Ginger. Just as I finished, someone walked up behind me and clapped me on the shoulder. It was Peters.

I shook his hand. "Huggins got ahold of you, then?"

"No. I came because a little bird told me." Peters grinned. Then in a lower voice, "What the hell are you doing packing hardware? You're supposed to be on vacation."

"It's a long story," I said.

"I'm sure it is. The ferry was crawling with deputies. They're handing out copies of Wilson's picture to everyone who gets on or off the boat. What's up?"

Peeking around the corner, I could see Ginger

and Max in deep conversation. I had noticed a small, glass-walled conference room just off the dining room. I asked to use it. Once inside, with the doors safely closed against unwanted listeners, I told Peters all I knew. Maybe not quite all. I left out a few details. He didn't have any business messing around in my personal life.

Peters shook his head when I finished. "I wouldn't be in Huggins' shoes for all the tea in China. If this thing gets blown out of proportion, lots of political heads could roll. Homer Watkins isn't a lightweight."

"How come you know so much about him?"

"There's enough in the papers that you can piece it together. Your problem is, you only read the crossword puzzles. Crosswords do not informed citizens make."

"Leave me alone. They're nothing but propaganda."

"Let's don't go into that, Beau. I like current events. You like history. I like sprout sandwiches. You like hamburgers. Neither of us is going to change."

I reached for the file folder Peters held in his hand. "Wait a minute. I'm supposed to give this to a Detective Huggins. You're not the investigating officer."

"For God's sake, Peters," I protested. "Don't be an ass. I'm the one who called and asked for it, remember?"

"Captain Powell gave me specific orders that the report goes to Huggins. You're on vacation. Powell doesn't want you screwing around in somebody else's case."

"I'll be a sonofabitch," I said.

Peters ignored my outburst. He had joined forces with the captain and the chaplain to corner me into a "vacation." He, more than the rest, understood my loss. "How're you doing, Beau?" he asked solicitously, changing topics. "You're looking better, like you're getting some rest."

I smiled to myself, considering my total sleep from the night before. I decided against depriving Peters of his illusions.

"Sleeping like a baby," I said, grinning.

Huggins showed up about then. He saw us through the plate-glass windows and knocked to be let in. I introduced him to Peters. Within minutes the table was strewn with the grisly contents of the envelope. Maybe Peters couldn't give them to me, but nobody told Huggins not to.

The pictures were there—the senseless slaughter, the bloodied house. Denise Wilson had fought Lathrop. She hadn't died easily. She had battled him through every room before it was over. The pictures sickened me, as did Lathrop's smirking mug shot. There was no picture of Donald Wilson in the file. Without Maxwell Cole's contribution, we would have been up a creek.

"We're screening all the people on the ferries. We'll be talking to employees and guests here today," Huggins told us. "Someone will have seen him. You don't just appear and disappear like that unless you're a goddamned Houdini."

"He's not at his house?" I asked. Huggins shook his head. "Is there any other way to get here besides a ferry?" I continued.

"There are float planes and charter boats. We're

checking all of them, but it doesn't look to me as though he has that kind of money. He came over on the ferries, I'm sure of it, and we've got those babies covered."

Peters smiled. "You've heard that old joke going around Seattle, haven't you?"

"What's that?"

"What does a San Juan County police officer use for a squad car? A Washington State Ferry with blinking blue lights."

Huggins glared at him. "Very funny," he said, "but we do a hell of a good job around here."

Every once in a while Peters pulls a stunt that convinces me he's not nearly so old as his years. Then there are times when he's as wise as the old man of the sea.

This wasn't one of those times.

CHAPTER 10

I CALLED RALPH AMES, MY ATTORNEY IN PHOENIX. Along with the car, I inherited Ames from Anne Corley. In six months' time, he had become an invaluable friend over and above being my attorney. I called him at home.

"What're you doing?" I asked.

"Cleaning the pool," he replied.

I have little patience with people who own pools or boats. They're both holes you pour money into. Not only that, it's a point of honor to do all the work yourself, from swabbing decks to cleaning filters.

"Did you ever consider hiring someone to do it?"

"No, Beau. I don't jog. Cleaning the pool makes me feel self righteous."

"To each his own. What are you doing tomorrow?"

"Flying to Portland. Didn't Peters tell you?"

"Tell me what?"

"We have a custody hearing in The Dalles on Tuesday. Keep your fingers crossed."

Peters was at war with his ex-wife. She got religion in a big way and went to live with a cult in Broken Springs, Oregon, taking their two little girls with her. Peters wanted them back. Ames took the case, joining the fray at my request and on my nickel. What's the point in having money if you can't squander it?

"That closemouthed asshole. That's good news."

"So what do you want, Beau? This is my day off. It is Saturday, you know."

"How about flying into Sea-Tac today instead of Portland tomorrow? I'm up on Orcas Island. There's someone here I'd like you to meet. I told her you'd take a look at her situation."

"Which is?"

"Divorce. Messy. With political ramifications. Looks like collusion between her husband and her father-in-law to toss her out without a pot to piss in."

"Are you giving my services away again, Beau?"

"I care enough to send the very best."

He laughed. "All right. I'll see what I can do. Let me call you back."

I gave him the number. As I hung up, Ginger appeared at my elbow. "Who was that?"

"Ames, my attorney from Phoenix, remember? I told you about him. I asked him to come talk to you."

"Here? On Orcas?"

"Sure."

"But you said he was in Phoenix."

"He is. He was coming up tomorrow, anyway. He's trying to get a reservation for this afternoon."

"From Phoenix?"

"If you're going to file on Monday, you need to talk to him tonight or tomorrow."

"How much is it going to cost?"

"Nothing. He'll put it on my bill."

I correctly read the consternation on Ginger's face. "How do you rate?" she asked. "I thought you were just a plain old, ordinary homicide detective. How come you have a high-powered attorney at your beck and call?"

"It's a long story," I said. "I came into a little money."

"A little?" she echoed.

"Some," I conceded.

"I see," Ginger said.

"You done with Cole?" I asked, changing the subject.

"He's one happy reporter." She grinned. "That story will make Darrell's socks roll up and down. It should hit the paper tomorrow."

"What did you say?"

"Enough. I named names. At least a few of them. A private detective had already checked those out. Darrell will come across as an active philanderer. Hot stuff."

We left the lobby and walked toward the new room where housekeepers had moved Ginger's things. "What do you think Darrell will do?" I asked.

She gave a mirthless laugh. "He'll huddle with Homer and the PR man. The three of them will decide how to play it. Name familiarity is name familiarity. They may get more press if they do an active denial. They'll take a poll and decide."

"That's pretty cold-blooded."

"Um-hum."

"But how are you going to feel with your personal life splashed all over the front page?"

We reached the building where her new room was. Ginger stepped to one side, waiting for me to open the door. The eyes she turned on me were luminously green and deep.

"I just found out about personal," she said softly. "None of that is going in the paper."

There was a tightening in my chest and a catch in my throat. Mr. Macho handles the compliment. I tripped over my own feet and stumbled into the hallway. I found her room, unlocked the door, and handed her the key.

"Are you coming in?"

The invitation was there, written on her face, but I shook my head. "Ames is supposed to call my room. I'd better not."

"Does that mean I can't see you? Have I been a bad girl and you're sending me to my room?" she teased.

"No. Let me see what's happening as far as Ames and Peters are concerned. Maybe you and I can go on a picnic."

"Terrific. I'll change into jeans."

"Wait a minute. I said maybe."

She looked both ways, up and down the hall, then gave me a quick kiss on the cheek. "Please."

"Well, all right, now that you put it that way."

Smiling, she disappeared into her room. I returned to mine. I had gotten a second key for Peters, and he was there waiting when I arrived.

"Who's your roommate?" he asked casually as I flopped onto the bed. "Her makeup case is still in the bathroom."

I wasn't any better at sneaking around than Ginger was. I made a stab at semi-full disclosure. "Ginger Watkins stayed here last night. Didn't I tell you?"

Peters' eyes narrowed. "I don't think so."

"There weren't any more rooms, and she couldn't go back to hers. Whoever got in had a key."

"Right." Peters nodded complacently, humoring me.

"We got a roll-away. She's married, for chrissake!"

"Okay, okay," he said. "Have it your way. What's the program?"

"You didn't tell me Ames has a court date in The Dalles."

"Small oversight." Peters grinned. "So we're even. What's going on?"

"I asked Ames to come up here tonight. I'm hoping he can help Ginger with her divorce."

"And you still expect me to fall for that crap about a roll-away bed?" He laughed.

As I threw a pillow at him, the phone rang. It was Ames. "I get into Sea-Tac at five-fifty. Can someone meet me?"

"We'll flip a coin," I told him. "One of us will be there. What airline?"

"United."

"Okay. I'll book rooms here."

"Rooms?"

I glared at Peters. "Peters snores," I growled into

the phone. "I sure as hell don't want him in my room, and you won't want him in yours, either. Besides, they've just had a bunch of cancellations. I know rooms are available."

"Rooms," Ames agreed.

Peters and I flipped a coin. He called heads, and it was tails. I figured it was my lucky day. Considering the ferry schedule, he didn't have much time to hang around. I called the desk and reserved two more rooms. Up at the far end of the complex. By the tennis courts. Adjoining.

I was still on the phone when someone knocked. Peters went to the door.

"My name is Ginger Watkins. Is Beau here?"

Peters stepped to one side and rolled his eyes at me once he was behind her. She wore a full-sleeved apricot blouse and a pair of tight-fitting Levi's that did justice to her figure. With a jacket slung nonchalantly over one shoulder, Ginger was a class act all the way.

"This is Detective Ron Peters," I said, "my partner on the force in Seattle."

"I'm pleased to meet you." Her smile of genuine goodwill had its desired effect.

Peters' appraising glance was filled with admiration. "Pleasure's all mine," he murmured.

Ginger turned to me. "Did I leave my calendar here?" she asked. "It isn't in the room, and I checked with the maids. They said they moved everything."

"I haven't seen it. When did you have it last?"

"I don't remember. I may have taken it with me when I went to meet Sig. It's got the address for the meeting tonight. I'm sure someone else can tell me where the meeting is, but I keep all kinds of phone numbers in the calendar. It would be hard to replace."

"Could you have left it in the car in Anacortes?"

She considered that possibility. "No," she said. "I don't think so."

I picked up the phone and called the desk to ask if anyone had turned in the missing calendar. No one had.

"Come on," I said when I got off the phone. "We'll walk Peters to his car. He's just leaving for the airport."

"You are?" she asked. "You barely got here."

"I did," Peters agreed sullenly, "but shore leave just got canceled."

Peters took off in his beat-up blue Datsun. Ginger and I diligently searched the meeting rooms, the dining room, the bar, and the lobby to no avail. The calendar wasn't there.

Rosario is nothing if not a full-service resort. While we were busy, the kitchen packed us a picnic lunch, complete with basket and tablecloth. Ginger's enthusiasm was unrestrained. She practically skipped on her way to the parking lot. A genuine Ford Pinto, white with splotches of rust, was parked next to my bright red Porsche 928. As I went to unlock the rider's side, Ginger assumed I was going to the junker. She started for the rider's side of that one, stopping in dismay when I opened the Porsche.

She came around the Pinto grinning sheepishly. "Isn't this a little high-toned for a homicide cop?"

I placed the picnic basket in the back and helped her inside. "Conspicuous consumption never hurt anybody," I said.

With a switch of the key, the powerful engine turned over. When she was alive, Anne Corley drove the car with casual assurance. I always feel just a little out of my league, as though the car is driving me.

"Have you seen Moran State Park?" I asked. Ginger shook her head. "Why don't we try that? This late in October it isn't crowded."

"You're changing the subject, Beau," she accused.

I feigned innocence. "What do you mean?"

"Tell me about the car," she insisted.

And so I told her about the car. About finding Anne Corley and losing Anne Corley. One by one I pulled the memories out and held them up in the diffused autumn light so Ginger and I could look at them together. We drove and walked and talked. We climbed the stairs in the musty obelisk without really noticing our surroundings. It was my turn to talk and Ginger's to listen.

By the time I finished, we were seated at a picnic table in a patch of dappled sunlight with the food laid out before us. There was a long pause. "You loved her very much, didn't you?" Ginger said at last.

"I didn't think I'd ever get over her."

"But you have?"

"I'm starting to, a little."

"Meaning me?" From someone else, that question might have sounded cynical, but not from Ginger.

I nodded. "Today is the first I've felt like my old self. Peters attributed it to my getting enough sleep."

"That shows how much he knows."

"He's young. What can I tell you?"

"And I'm the first, since Anne Corley?"

"Yes."

"And I was good?" It was a pathetic question. She was looking for the kind of reassurance most women don't need after age eighteen or so.

We were alone in the park. I came around the table and sat behind her, my hands massaging her tight shoulders, rubbing the rigid muscles of her neck. Her body moved under the pressure of my kneading fingers, relaxing as stiffness succumbed to the balm of human touch.

"You were terrific," I whispered in her ear.

She turned to me, two huge teardrops welling in her eyes. "That was stupid. I shouldn't have asked."

She leaned against me, and I continued to rub her neck, feeling her tension soften and disappear.

"No one's ever done that to me before," she said.

"Done what?"

"Rubbed my neck like that."

I kissed her forehead. "All I can say, sweetheart, is you've been married to a first-class bastard."

Unexpectedly, she burst out laughing. I don't think anyone had ever referred to Darrell Watkins in quite those terms in her presence. She turned her neck languidly from side to side like a cat stretching in the sun. "That felt good," she murmured.

We repacked the picnic basket. "Could I stop by your room for a little while before I go? The meeting doesn't start until eight."

"Sure," I said. "By the way, how do you plan to get to that meeting?"

She clapped her hand over her mouth. "I forgot. I don't have my car. I can probably catch a ride with the van that goes to the ferry."

"Don't be silly. Take the Porsche," I said.

"I couldn't do that."

"Oh yes you can."

It was almost our first quarrel, but finally she knuckled under to my superior intellect and judgment. Besides, I had the clinching argument: by taking my car, she wouldn't have to leave nearly so early. She capitulated. Who says women can't be swayed by logic?

And hormones. And expensive toys.

CHAPTER 11

WE TOOK A MEANDERING ROUTE BACK TO ROSARIO. AT one point we paused, laughing, at a large hand-painted sign on a ninety-degree curve that said, "Slow Duck Crossing."

"Does that mean the ducks are dumb, or are you supposed to slow down?" Ginger asked.

"Possibly a little of both," I observed, braking to negotiate the narrow corner.

A flurry of yellow slips of paper awaited us at the desk. The first, a message from Huggins, was jubilant. A ticket-seller at the Anacortes ferry terminal remembered Don Wilson as a mid-afternoon walk-on passenger. The evidence was speculative and purely circumstantial, but that gave Wilson opportunity. He already had motive.

Huggins' second note was more ominous. Results of the autopsy were in. Larson's cause of death was a blow to the base of the skull with a blunt object. He was dead before he hit the water. The cut on his forehead had occurred after he was dead. The news hit Ginger pretty hard. In addition, her room key had not been found among Sig Larson's personal effects.

A message from Peters said he and Ames were skipping dinner in order to make it back to Orcas. Since the food on the ferries wasn't fit to eat, he advised me to make dinner reservations for after their arrival.

Ginger passed me her own fan-fold of messages, enough to form a formidable canasta hand. Darrell Watkins had called every half-hour. Homer Watkins had called several times. All of the messages, with increasing urgency, said for Ginger to call back.

She returned the calls from my room. I think she wanted the moral support of my presence. She spoke with Darrell first. He had learned of the impending column in the *P.I.* and wanted her to retract it. She was adamant. She would stand by every word of the story as written. He threatened to come up. She told him not to bother, that nothing he could say would make her change her mind.

The call to Homer was much the same. His attempts at browbeating also came to nothing. I wondered if either of them recognized a subtle shift in her from the day before, an undercurrent of gritty determination. J. P. Beaumont, posing as Professor Henry Higgins, heard the difference and gave himself a little credit.

Nonetheless, the phone calls had a subduing effect on our high spirits. I think we had intended to take advantage of each other's bodies before Ginger left, to recapture the magic of commingled enjoyment to last us until she returned from her meeting. Instead, we sat in my room without even holding hands, talking quietly as the sun went down.

I can't remember now what we talked about. We ranged over a wide variety of topics, finding surprising areas of common interest and knowledge. For someone with little formal education, Ginger was a widely read, challenging conversationalist.

I invited her to join Peters, Ames, and me for dinner after the meeting. She waited until the very last minute to leave for Eastsound, delaying her departure so long that she finally decided to change clothes after the meeting. She was clearly torn between wanting to go to the meeting and wanting to stay with me. I could probably have talked her out of going had I half tried. Out of respect to Sig Larson, I didn't make the attempt.

I walked her to my car. "Be careful," I said. "That's a hot little number."

She smiled. "I've driven one before."

"What time will you be back?"

"Ten. At the latest."

"I'll make reservations for then," I told her.

"Kiss me good-bye?" she asked.

I looked around. The parking lot was deserted. As near as I could tell, all the media types, including Maxwell Cole, had abandoned Rosario on the heels of the rest of the parole board, but years of being a cop have made me paranoid about reporters. I gave her a quick, surreptitious kiss. "Give old Sig a hail and farewell for me too," I said huskily. I had a lot to thank him for.

"I will," she whispered and was gone.

I went into the bar. Barney smiled when he saw me. "Find that calendar yet?" he asked, bringing me a McNaughton's and water.

"Not yet."

"You get what you needed from that fat slob last night?"

"Yeah," I answered. "Thanks."

"All those yahoos went home this morning," he continued. "They were a bunch of animals, especially that creep, what's-his-name . . . Dole?"

"Cole," I corrected. "And yes, he is a creep."

I drank my drink, aware of how much better I felt. Unburdening myself to Ginger had somehow lifted the pall that had paralyzed me since Anne Corley's death. I set down my empty glass and pushed back the stool.

"Only one?" Barney asked, surprised.

"Later," I told him. "I've got places to go, people to meet."

In actual fact, I went back to my room for the second shower and shave of the day. I dressed carefully. I wanted Ginger to see me at my best, wearing one of the hand-tailored suits Ames had insisted I purchase.

At nine forty-five I went back to the lobby. "Oh there you are," the desk clerk said. "I just this minute had a call for you." He handed me a slip of paper with Homer Watkins' name and number on it.

"He called for me, not Mrs. Watkins?" I asked.

"He was very specific," the clerk assured me. I walked to the pay phone and dialed the number. He answered on the second ring.

"This is Detective Beaumont," I said curtly into the phone.

"It's good of you to call," he said. His voice was smooth as glass, with the resonance of an old-fashioned radio announcer. It was a long way from our first telephone conversation. "I talked to a friend of yours today, a Maxwell Cole. He's under the impression that you have some influence with my daughter-in-law."

"That's correct," I replied. It was also something of an understatement.

"I thought you should be advised that Ginger has been somewhat unstable of late."

"Ginger Watkins' mental health is none of my business," I said.

"I couldn't be happier to hear you say that. She's been under a great deal of stress and can't be held responsible for her actions."

"What are you driving at?" I demanded.

"That's all I wanted to discuss," he said. "I have another call." Having another call on a second or third line constitutes a high-tech version of the brush-off. I put down the phone.

I went into the Moran Room to wait for Ames and Peters. The ferry was due in at nine-thirty, so I expected them at Rosario right around ten. I waited in front of the massive marble fireplace with its cheerful fire.

Ralph Ames was laughing as he came into the lobby. He and Peters were having a good time. I met them at the door. We left word for Ginger, and the three of us went on into the dining room. It was late, and the room was almost empty. We sat at a candlelit table and had a drink.

"You breaking training?" I asked as the waiter handed Peters a gin and tonic.

He raised his glass. "Just this once." He grinned.

We were so busy talking and catching up that I didn't notice the time. At ten-thirty the waiter suggested that if we wanted to eat before the kitchen closed, we'd better place our order. Suddenly I wasn't hungry. I told Peters and Ames to go ahead and order, that I'd wait for Ginger. I excused myself and went to the lobby, where I had the desk clerk call Ginger's room. No answer.

When Fred shook his head, I felt a sickening crunch in my stomach. "Something may have happened to her," I said. "Would you let me check her room?"

After the roll-away bed escapade, he could hardly say I had no business doing so. He put a Back in a Minute sign on the desk, and we hurried to Ginger's room. It was empty, undisturbed.

Back in the Mansion, I checked the dining room. Ames and Peters were happily working their way through salads, but Ginger was nowhere in sight. I went to the pay phone and dialed the sheriff's substation at Eastsound.

The dispatcher answered eventually, her response to my question short and to the point. There had been no reports of any traffic accidents. I tried to fend off rising panic. "Do you know any of the people who go to the Saturday-night A.A. meeting in Eastsound?" I asked.

"Yes, but I can't give out those names. It's confidential."

"Get one of them to call me back, then. It's urgent."

"I'll see what I can do."

I paced the floor in tight circles, trying to hold

panic in check. When the phone rang, I pounced on it like a cat attacking a paralyzed mouse.

"My name is James," the voice on the phone drawled. "You wanted to talk to someone from A.A.?"

"Yes, I did. Did you go to the meeting tonight?"

"'Course I did. I was one of the speakers."

"Was there a woman there, a woman in a pale orange blouse and Levi's?"

"Sorry, mister, I can't give out that information. Whoever joins our fellowship is strictly confidential. That's why people feel safe in coming."

"You don't understand," I said desperately. "She left here at twenty to eight, going to the meeting. She hasn't come back. All I want to know is whether she made it that far."

There was a long pause. "No," he said.

"No *what*? No, you won't tell me?" I wanted to reach through the phone line and throttle him.

"No, she wasn't there. I woulda remembered someone like that. It was only locals tonight. No visitors."

Cold fear rose in my stomach, my throat. "Thank you," I managed, depressing the switch on the phone. I released it and redialed the substation. The dispatcher was annoyed.

"You'd better get ahold of Huggins over in Friday Harbor. Tell him to call Detective Beaumont. We've got trouble."

Hal called me back within minutes. "What's up?"

"It's Ginger. She's disappeared. She went to a meeting tonight and never got there. I've checked. The meeting was over at nine. She's still not back."

"It's almost eleven!"

"I know," I responded bleakly.

"What kind of car?" he asked.

"A Porsche 928. Red."

He whistled. "No shit? A Porsche? What's the license number?" I gave it to him. "Okay," he added, "I'll be there in half an hour," he said. "Where are you—Rosario?"

"Yes."

"I'll come straight to the docks. I'll call the dispatcher and have her send Pomeroy. I think he's on duty tonight." He paused. "Why'd you let her go by herself, Beau?"

I winced at his implied accusation. I had already asked myself the same question. "She wanted to."

"Oh," he said.

It wasn't a very convincing reason, not then, not now.

With leaden steps I walked back to the dining room to let Ames and Peters know that Ginger Watkins wouldn't be joining us for dinner. Not then. Not ever.

CHAPTER 12

THEY FOUND THE PORSCHE AT SEVEN SUNDAY MORNING in the pond by the Slow Duck Crossing sign. I stood to one side, watching the tow truck drag my 928 from the muck. Ginger, still wearing her apricot blouse, lay dead inside.

Huggins opened the door, and water cascaded out, leaving her body slumped over the steering wheel. Pomeroy gave me a half-smirk as I walked over to look inside and make positive identification. I nodded to Hal and walked away as the lab crew surrounded the car.

Peters was down the road, pacing the blacktop. "From the looks of it, she ploughed into the water full throttle and never tried to stop."

He was voicing my own thoughts. I said nothing.

"Is there a chance she passed out?"

"No," I said quickly. "Absolutely not."

Peters eyed me questioningly. "Why not?"

"She didn't drink."

Huggins left the car and came over to where we

were standing. "Watkins is on his way," he said. "It'll be a madhouse when he gets here. I understand he's got a whole press entourage."

"Great," I muttered.

"Did you see anything along the road?" Huggins' question was addressed to both Peters and me. Peters pointed. "There's a place back there where she laid down a layer of rubber. Looks like she floorboarded it from a dead stop." The three of us walked back to the place Peters had indicated. Huggins examined the mark, then nodded in agreement. He looked at me.

"Suicide, you think?"

"No way!" I declared vehemently. Huggins and Peters exchanged glances.

"We were going to have dinner," I continued. "She was looking forward to it." My rationale landed with a resounding thud, convincing no one, not even me.

As soon as I saw Darrell Watkins, I recognized him. I had indeed seen pictures of him. Politicians are never as tall or as good-looking as their publicity shots make them seem. Darrell Watkins was no exception. He was three or four inches shorter than I am, maybe five-ten or so. His face boasted classically handsome features topped by dark brown wavy hair, but a hint of potbelly protruded over his belt. A little too much of the good life showed around the edges.

Beside Darrell walked a taller, distinguished looking man with a shock of white hair. There was a definite family resemblance. Homer Watkins, although pushing seventy, carried himself with the easy grace of an aging athlete. His son might have gone to seed, but not Homer. I looked at them with the kind of curiosity one reserves for snakes in a zoo. They didn't look like evil incarnate, but they had made Ginger Watkins' life hell on earth.

Huggins walked forward to greet them, waving back the crush of newsmen, photographers, and cameras that swirled around them. Ginger would have been offended that the aftermath of her death created a media event that would give her candidate/widower hours of free broadcasting coverage and hundreds of newspaper column-inches all over the state. I thought I was going to be sick.

"Hey, Beau, are you all right?" I had turned my back on the mêlée and was walking away. Peters followed.

"I've got to get out of here," I groaned. "I can't stand this bullshit."

I continued walking. Peters worked his way back through the crowd to redeem his car. I was several hundred yards down the road by the time he caught up with me. He pulled alongside. "Get in, Beau. Don't be a hard-ass." I was too sick at heart to argue.

"The press was handling Watkins with kid gloves," Peters said apropos of nothing.

I glowered at him. "What did you expect?"

Peters shrugged and broke off any further attempt at conversation. In the silence that followed, I tried to come to terms with what had happened. How could Ginger Watkins be the lifeless form slouched in my car? And what could I have done to prevent it? And where the hell was Don Wilson?

Ralph Ames waited for us in the driveway outside the Mansion. "I heard," he said as I dragged myself out of the car. "Is there anything I can do?"

"Not unless you can figure out a way to bring her back." I choked out the words and beat it for my cabin, leaving Peters and Ames standing there together. I didn't want to talk to anybody or hear any mumbled words of sympathy. I didn't have any right to sympathy. That was Darrell Watkins' exclusive territory.

I threw myself across the bed, aware of a faint trace of Ginger Watkins lingering in the bedclothes. I wanted to lock it out of my consciousness, but at the same time I wanted to hold onto it.

There was a gentle tap on the door. Ames came into the room, alone. He sat down on one of the chairs beside the table. For a long time he sat there without speaking. "You can't blame yourself," he said at last.

"Why not? I never should have let her go alone."

"It's not your fault."

I wanted to bellow at him, to rant and rave and vent my anger and frustration. "It is! Don't you see that it is?"

Ames remained unperturbed. "It was an A.A. meeting, is that right?"

"Yes," I said wearily.

"How long had it been since she quit drinking?"

My anger boiled back to the surface. "She wasn't drunk, and she didn't commit suicide. Doesn't anybody understand that, for God's sake?"

He ignored me. "It's possible, Beau. She had lost a good friend the day before—"

"Goddammit, Ames, I'm trying to tell you.

Something happened between us. She didn't want to die."

Ames studied me carefully. "I see," he said slowly. He rose to his feet. "I'm sorry, Beau. I didn't know." His quiet understanding rocked me. Hot tears rose in my eyes. I didn't bother to brush them away. Ames paused in the doorway. "It's still not your fault," he added.

The hell it's not, I thought savagely as the door closed behind him. Wilson was here all the time, and I let her walk right into his trap.

I don't know how long I lay on the bed. Long enough to get a grip on myself. Long enough to know that if I walked outside I wouldn't embarrass myself and everyone around me.

I had been awake all night. Exhaustion claimed me, and I slept. In a dream Don Wilson and Philip Lathrop were together, both locked in the same cell. Armed with a gun, I tried to shoot them through iron bars. Each time I pulled the trigger, nothing happened. They laughed and pointed, both of them, together.

I woke in a sweat. Peters was sitting in the chair by the window. Ginger's chair.

"Bad dream?" he asked.

Not answering, I heaved my feet over the edge of the bed and sat there with my face buried in my hands, hoping the whole thing was a nightmare. It wasn't. Ginger Watkins was dead.

"They've released your car," Peters said.

I felt as if I'd been shot. "They've what?"

"Released the Porsche," Peters repeated. "Had it towed into Ernie's Garage in Eastsound."

"That's impossible! Murder was committed in

that car. No one should go near it until the crime lab has gone over it with a fine-toothed comb."

"They've gone over it, all right. Not with a fine-toothed comb. The consensus is that she went drinking instead of to her meeting. They're treating it as a DWI, calling it an accident, pending the outcome of the autopsy. They found an empty vodka bottle in the car. The San Juan County Sheriff's Department says it can't afford to be responsible for a car like that. Too valuable."

I got up and went into the bathroom, where I splashed my face with cold water. My square-jawed reflection in the mirror was haggard, drained. When I came out of the bathroom, Peters hadn't moved.

"It wasn't an accident," I said.

"How are we going to prove it?"

It took a few seconds for the meaning of his words to sink in, to understand that I wasn't in it alone, that Peters would help—and so would Ames, for that matter. But even though his "we" eased my burden, the question remained: How would we prove it?

"Drive me to Eastsound," I said. "I want to talk to the mechanic."

"Huggins says he's tops."

"Sure he is. In a backwater like this, you can just bet they've got a top-drawer mechanic. He's probably one step under highway robbery."

We got into Peters' Datsun. He managed to drive us to Eastsound without having to pass the duck pond. "Are you going to tell me what happened?" Peters asked.

"No." My answer was abrupt. "Not now."

Peters deserved better than that. We had been partners for almost a year. He, more than anyone, had seen me through the Anne Corley crisis. I had learned to respect his quiet reserve and to tolerate his health fetishes. In the world of partners, alfalfa sprouts are a small price to pay for someone you can count on.

He didn't take offense. He brought our discussion back to the Porsche. "Huggins says Ernie can dry it out. If he gets to work on it fast enough, he might be able to prevent it from mildewing."

"So by releasing the car, Hal thinks he's doing me a favor?" Peters nodded. "God damn him," I said.

Ernie's Garage wasn't tough to find. It's the only one in town. I walked into the clapboard building, wondering for a moment if anyone was there. "Just a sec," an invisible voice called.

A mechanic's dolly wheeled out from under an upraised pickup. On it sat a man with his left leg missing below the knee and his left arm missing below the elbow. Where his hand should have been, a complicated metal gripper was strapped to his arm with a leather gauntlet. The gripper held a small wrench. Ernie Rogers had bright blue eyes, a curly red mustache, and a shiny bald spot on the back of his head. "How'do, mister," he drawled. "What can I do for you?"

"That's my car over there," I said, pointing. The Porsche huddled in a darkened corner of the garage.

"She's a pretty little thing." He clucked sympathetically. "Too bad about what happened."

"Huggins says you can dry it out and get it working. That true?"

He nodded, removing the wrench from its gripper and wiping his metal hand on greasy pants in the typical mechanic's gesture. "It'll cost you," he said. "How long you had 'er?"

"About six months."

"Ever done any major repairs on a Porsche?" Ernie asked. He was still sitting on the dolly, squinting up at me.

"No," I said. "Never have."

"I gotta take the whole damn thing apart, clean it with solvent, dry it, and put it back together."

"How much?"

"Six or seven grand."

In the old days, that's how much I would have spent on a brand-new car. Luckily, these weren't the old days. "How long will it take?"

"Depends on how soon you want me to start. Should do it as soon as possible if you want to save the interior. It'll take time—a couple weeks, maybe. I gotta get the money up front, though. Know what I mean?"

In the old days I never would have had a checking account with ten thousand dollars in it, but Ames had made me open a market-rate account. I pulled the checkbook out of my jacket pocket and wrote out a check for seven thousand dollars, payable to Ernie's Garage. I handed it to him. He looked at it, folded it deftly with one hand, and stuck it in his overall pocket.

"Thanks, Mr. Beaumont. That your phone number on the check in case I need to get ahold of you?"

"Yes. Keep track of your expenses. The insurance company will reimburse me."

Peters and I started toward the door. "I'm sorry about the lady in the car," Ernie said. "She wasn't your wife or anything, was she?"

"No," I said. "We were just friends."

The lie came easily. Ginger had said the same thing about Sig Larson. I wondered if she had told the truth.

CHAPTER 13

PETERS STOPPED AT THE FRONT DESK AND BOUGHT A paper. He showed me Sig Larson's picture on the front page. "Max's interview with Ginger should be there," I told him.

He flipped through the pages and double-checked the index in the bottom corner of the front page, looking for Cole's City Beat column. "It's not here, Beau," he said. "I looked."

"But he said it would be in today's paper."

"So he lied," Peters said. "What else is new?" Peters sorted through the paper and removed the crossword puzzles, setting them aside for me to work later. "I'm going up to my room to get some rest," he said. "Ames wants to go back to Seattle on the seven-forty ferry tonight. You're welcome to ride along."

"Let me think it over, Peters. I can't quite see the three of us crammed in that Datsun, but—"

"Don't look a gift horse in the mouth," he told me. "It's a hell of a long walk from Anacortes to Seattle."

I accompanied Peters as far as his room. When he went inside, I knocked on Ames' door. Ralph was sprawled on his bed with the contents of a briefcase strewn around him. "Working on Peters' case?" I asked. He nodded. "Are we going to win?"

He looked at me squarely. "Maybe. Maybe not. Our best bet is to work out a negotiated settlement instead of going to court."

"Will they settle?"

He shrugged. "Justice is blind. Money talks. They'll settle if the price is right."

"It pisses me off to think of donating money to that ranting, chanting asshole." It was my money. Although I was willing to do whatever was necessary to buy Peters' kids a chance at a normal childhood, it still made me mad.

Ames regarded me mildly. "You want to bail out?"

"Hell, no. I just don't like that guru making money hand over fist."

Shaking his head, Ames gathered up his papers and shuffled them into a neat stack. "What do you want, Beau?"

I eased myself into the chair by his window, aware that my back hurt. Despite the nap, fatigue railed at me from every muscle in my body. "I want to offer a reward."

"For what?"

"For information leading to the arrest and conviction of the person or persons who murdered Sig Larson."

He picked up a yellow pad and a pen and made several notes in his small, cramped handwriting.

"I can do that," he said. "From an anonymous donor, I presume?"

I nodded.

"How much?"

"Five."

"Thousand?"

I nodded again.

"Anything else?"

My mind started to click, like a car that has to be jump-started but runs fine after that. "What are you going to do, once you finish up in Oregon?"

"Go back to Phoenix. Why?"

"You told me I ought to do some investing, remember?"

He nodded. "What do you have in mind?"

"I understand there are a couple of condo projects in trouble in Seattle. Maybe now would be a good time to look into one of those. Would you mind sticking around and researching them?"

"Not as long as you're footing the bill." I got up to leave. "Are you coming back to town tonight?" he asked.

Pausing at the door, I considered my options. Riding with Ames and Peters would be physically uncomfortable but convenient. "No," I said, making up my mind, "I have some thinking to do. I'm better off here, away from everybody."

"And because you think Don Wilson is still on Orcas?"

He caught me red-handed. "So what?" I flared. "I'm on vacation. I can do as I damn well please."

"You don't have any objectivity in this case, Beau."

"Don't lecture me, Ralph. I'm your client, not some half-grown kid." I stormed from the room, slamming the door behind me, knowing he was more than half right.

I headed for the Mansion and the Vista Lounge. I wanted the taste of McNaughton's in my mouth, the feel of an icy glass in my hand. I almost ran over Maxwell Cole, who was about to climb into the hotel van in front of the building. I was surprised to see him. I thought he was already gone.

"What happened to your column?" I asked sarcastically. "Miss your deadline?"

"Deadline!" he echoed. "If you're talking about the piece I wrote yesterday, the one on Ginger Watkins, I didn't miss the deadline."

"So where is it?" I was looking for someone to bait, and Cole was a likely candidate. His handlebar mustache drooped lopsidedly, making him look more dreary than usual.

"They spiked the son of a bitch. The scoop of the year, and they spiked it!"

"Who did?"

"Beats the shit out of me. One minute it was in, the next minute it was out. My editor isn't talking."

The driver of the van honked. "Hey come on, man. Them ferries don't wait for nothing."

Cole scrambled into the van and settled in an aisle seat. The van pulled out of the gravel drive, leaving me lost in thought. It takes clout to spike a story, a hell of a lot of clout. I wondered who was flexing his muscle, Homer or Darrell, father or son, or father and son. It didn't matter. Whoever it was had robbed Ginger of her meager revenge, her sole token of defiance.

I charged into the lounge. It was deserted except for two slightly tipsy elderly ladies drinking sloe gin fizzes at a table by the arched windows. Barney folded a newspaper and shoved it under the bar as I sat down.

"McNaughton's?"

I nodded.

"It's too bad about Mrs. Watkins," he commented, placing the drink in front of me. "She seemed like a real nice lady, from what little I saw of her."

"She was," I agreed. I downed the drink and ordered another.

"Too bad about your car, too."

"Cars can be fixed," I said.

He grinned. "I guess old Ernie's in seventh heaven. Heard he's got himself a real-live Porsche to work on."

"You know him?"

"Hell, yes. Went to school together, kindergarten on. Ended up in Vietnam at the same time. Different outfits, though."

"That's where he lost his arm and leg?"

Barney nodded. "He doesn't let it bother him. Goes hunting every year, usually gets an elk. He's got a wife and two kids; another on the way."

"Is he any good?"

Barney grinned. "You'll have to ask his wife about that. He's not my type."

"As a mechanic, asshole. Is he a good mechanic?"

"He's good," Barney said seriously. "He'll put that car of yours back together better than it was before."

"Oh," I said.

A couple came in and sat at the other end of the bar. Barney left me to serve them. I sat there alone, nursing my drink, wondering where to start on a case that was not my case, on a murder that might be suicide or an accident, depending on your point of view.

In Seattle I knew what I'd do—sit down and try to pull together all the details on pieces of paper, set as many pieces of the puzzle on the table as possible, then move them around, trying to find a framework where they would fit.

Barney came back to me. "You want another?" he asked.

I looked at my glass. "Sure. Is that your paper under the bar?"

"It is, but you can have it. I'm done with it."

He pulled it out and laid it in front of me. I recognized Sig Larson's face looking up at me from under a screaming headline. I picked up the paper warily. I don't trust newspapers, don't like them, usually wouldn't be caught dead reading them; but this was different.

This time I was outside the official circle of information, and I needed a starting point. I was going to do something about Ginger Watkins' death, jurisdictions be damned. Sig Larson's death and Ginger's were inextricably linked. I intended to find out how.

I read every word of the laudatory obituary. A retired Eastern Washington wheat farmer, Lars Sigfried Larson had been widely respected. The article mentioned his volunteer work at Walla Walla and his involvement with Babe Ruth Baseball east of the mountains. It mentioned his widow, Mona, as well as his three grown children, married and scattered throughout the West. The funeral would be held in Welton on the banks of the Touchet River on Tuesday at two o'clock. The governor himself was expected to attend.

And so would J. P. Beaumont, I decided. I read on. The family requested that remembrances be sent to A.A. Even in death, Sig Larson didn't duck the issue of sobriety.

I had finished the article and was folding the paper when Peters came in and caught me. "What are you doing?"

"What the hell does it look like I'm doing? I'm trying to fold this goddamned newspaper."

"You haven't been reading it, have you?" Peters' eyes flashed with sly amusement. "You feeling all right, Beau? Maybe a little feverish?"

I stood up and struggled to return the newspaper to its place under the counter. When I flopped back down, Peters' grin faded. "Ames and I are getting ready to take off. Want to have a bite with us before we go?"

I signaled Barney for a new drink. When he set it in front of me, I raised the glass in Peters' direction in a sloppy salute. "Who needs food?"

"You're drinking too much . . ."

I cut him off. "Butt out, Peters."

Without arguing the point, he stalked from the bar. Misery does not necessarily love company. I made short work of that drink and the next one. Detective J. P. Beaumont disappeared with a subsequent dose of McNaughton's. All that remained was me, the man, or whatever bits and pieces were left of him.

"You're hitting it pretty hard, aren't you?" Barney asked, as he delivered my next drink.

"So what?" I returned. He handed me the glass, and I stared morosely into it. I swirled the amber liquid, listening to the crushed ice rustle against the glass.

Gradually, my carefully constructed defenses gave way. Pain leaked from every pore. Ginger's touch had reawakened that part of me that had died with Anne. Now Ginger's death released the grief I had kept so carefully bottled up inside me. It washed across me like a gigantic wave, choking me, drowning me.

The next thing I remember is Barney taking my last drink away and leading me, sobbing, from the bar. He got me as far as the door to my room before I was sick in a bordering flower bed.

It was still light when I staggered out of the bathroom and crawled into bed. I have a dim memory of Barney closing the curtains before he went outside and shut the door behind him.

CHAPTER 14

WHEN I WOKE UP, COLD SOBER, AT TWO O'CLOCK IN THE morning, I felt painfully alive again. I still hurt, but I had somehow bridged the chasm between the past and the present and was ready to go on. I had Ginger Watkins to thank for that, and there was only one way to repay her.

Ignoring my hangover, I rummaged around for paper, finally locating a fistful of Rosario stationery. I assigned each person a separate sheet of paper—Ginger, Sig, Wilson, Darrell, Homer, Mona. Under each name I noted everything I knew about them: things Ginger had told me, things I had heard from other sources. Maybe there's a better way of sorting out the players than by using paper and pencil, but I've never found one.

If I were keeping score, I'd have to say that Sig Larson dropped a few points in the process. I have an innate suspicion of perfection. Both Ginger's comments and the newspaper's undiluted praise made me wonder if the paragon had feet of clay. Being dead is only part of the qualifications for sainthood. Over and over, I recalled my off-hand denial to Ernie, "Just friends," and so was Sig to Ginger. Just friends, right? Like hell.

A twinge of tardy jealousy caused me to turn to Mona Larson's sheet. What about her? Ginger had dismissed her as a calculating bitch. What suspicious wife isn't a calculating bitch, especially if she has some reason, especially from the other woman's point of view?

I could see Mona Larson in my mind's eye, a woman from sturdy farm stock, someone well beyond her middle years who had stood by her man through thick and thin only to see herself losing him to an attractive younger woman. It would give the fruits of her labors a bitter aftertaste.

So, how jealous was Mona Larson? Enough to make her anger public by sending Trixie Bowdeen with the message for Ginger not to attend Sig's funeral. Where had Mona been when she was supposedly en route to Orcas? Huggins had been unable to locate her to notify her of Sig's death. It was an item that merited exploration, but it wasn't top priority. Not that many jealous spouses actually murder their spouses and their spouses' friends.

Friends. There was that word again. Even in private thoughts I tended to gloss over it. *Lover,* then. Ginger and I had been lovers, briefly. And maybe Sig and Ginger had been, too. But if so, Sig was just as bad as Darrell. Ginger hadn't faked her surprise or enjoyment, had she?

No. My ego wouldn't accept that, and no woman could be so unlucky as to have two men as insensitive and unfeeling as Darrell. No. My thoughts chased themselves full-circle. Ginger and Sig could not have been lovers.

What about Homer and Darrell? What did I know of them? Homer and Jethro, I thought. Between them they wielded a large amount of power. With it they had imprisoned Ginger. Neither had wanted to let her go; both had tried to get her to delay the divorce. I recalled Homer's resonant voice on the phone, explaining how erratic Ginger had been, trivializing her motives, warning me to disregard whatever she might say. And all the while Ginger had been dying, or was already dead.

Darrell. What about Darrell, the boozing, whoring scion of an old, established family? A scion who had fallen on hard times, whose wife had to go to work to keep the wolf from the door. I recalled Ginger's response to Hal's question about a contract on Sig's life. No money, she had said. Not no reason, but no money. And no justification, either, since Darrell himself had been screwing around for years. Darrell Watkins, one-man stud service, who never rubbed his wife's neck, who never . . .

I couldn't believe Darrell would have had the nerve to confront Ginger on infidelity. That caliber of double standard is fast approaching extinction. But where had Darrell Watkins been on Saturday night? It would be interesting to know, just for the record.

Ginger. Ginger laughing, crying, stretching her neck as my thumbs massaged the muscles of her shoulders. Ginger's face transformed by a pleasure she had never known or suspected. Remembering that hurt too much, so I stopped.

She had seemed totally carefree as she drove away, waving to me through the window of the Porsche. Respect for Sig had dictated that she go to the meeting and say good-bye, but she would have come back to me, to what I alone had given her. Of that I was sure. Who or what had stopped her? Not suicide. Not booze.

That brought me to the last sheet of paper. Don Wilson. Bereaved husband and father, plunged into the world of political activist, parading his grief on placards and sandwich boards, trying to get someone to listen, attempting to change the system that had robbed him of his wife and child. He had a point, but he had gone after the wrong people.

Why had he agreed to meet Max? Max said something was about to break. What, other than Sig Larson's head? Had the phony interview been a ploy, a device to guarantee press coverage? Maybe Wilson had believed that killing Sig and Ginger would give his cause the public airing necessary to bring it to the top of the silent majority's consciousness. As if they gave a damn.

But it's a long way from political activism to cold-blooded murder, and there was nothing to prove Wilson's conversion—nothing but motive and opportunity.

Wilson had come to Orcas Island. That much we knew—not beyond a shadow of a doubt, but with relative certainty. And, as near as we could tell, he had not left it, at least not by any of the regular routes. He could have hired a boat or a plane, but that was unlikely. It would be too obvious. Besides, Huggins said he had checked all charters and tracked down all private parties who had booked moorage.

Assuming Wilson was still on Orcas, where was he hiding? Did he have an accomplice? Was this the end of it, since Sig and Ginger's decision had placed Lathrop in the work/release program, or was the entire Washington State Parole Board in jeopardy?

Questions. Homicide detectives always have far more questions than they do answers. I analyzed the pieces of paper, pondering each word, poring over each scrap of information until I could have quoted it back verbatim. Hours later, eyes swimming with fatigue, I stumbled to the bed and fell across it, not bothering to undress or pull the covers over me.

Questions continued to buzz in my head. Who had known of the A.A. meeting besides Sig, Ginger, and me? And how would the killer have known she would be in my Porsche?

The human brain is the oldest and best random-access memory. I had almost dozed off when a single word roused me. Calendar. I sat up in bed. The meeting had been noted in her calendar, and the calendar was missing. In fact, it was the only item still unaccounted for in the aftermath of the break-in.

I groped through the darkness for the phone, knocking it to the floor. "What happens to your garbage?" I asked a startled Fred, who answered sleepily on the fourth ring.

It took him a couple of seconds to get his brain in gear. "It goes to the landfill," he mumbled.

"Do you have garbage cans? Dumpsters?"

"Dumpsters, one by each wing, and two here at the Mansion." Fred sounded more awake now. He was gradually becoming accustomed to my middle-of-the-night requests.

"When were they emptied last?"

"Friday afternoon, late. We're on a Monday / Wednesday / Friday schedule."

I banged down the phone and rummaged through my clothes for my most disreputable Levi's and the dung-colored sweater Karen's mother knitted for me the Christmas before we were divorced. I had sworn to wear that sucker out. This would finish the job.

I stopped by the desk and begged a flashlight from Fred. It was cold, and rain was falling as I started my five A.M. assault on Rosario's garbage dumpsters.

Those who think being a detective is romantic ought to try rummaging through three-day-old garbage with a raging hangover, flashlight in hand, in a driving rainstorm. Things happen to apple cores and orange peels and banana skins that can't be described in polite company. If I had known about garbage cans, maybe I would have taken my mother's advice and become a schoolteacher.

I started with the wing where Ginger's original room had been, searching through each carefully fastened black plastic bag. I did the same to the second-wing dumpster, and again found nothing. In terms of garbage, this was lightweight stuff—tissues and soda cans, discarded hairspray cans, and a couple of pornographic magazines. Clean garbage. No calendar.

The last two dumpsters were by the Mansion itself. They contained GARBAGE, foul-smelling foodstuffs that had sat around for several days and gotten surly. I took one whiff and almost gave up, but some of my mother's stubborn determination must have stuck. I dug in and got lucky. At the bottom of the first dumpster, I found it—a leather-bound, gold-embossed executive planner with Ginger Watkins' name imprinted on the front.

Carefully I laid the book to one side and re-filled the rancid container. After carrying the calendar back to my room, I stripped to the skin on the rainy porch, leaving my wrecked clothes by the door. I set the calendar on the floor just inside the doorway while I attempted to shower the odor off my body and out of my nose.

I came out of the shower wrapped in a towel and picked up the phone. I dialed Hal's number. On the third ring I realized it was only six o'clock. Homicide is always much more urgent when someone near and dear is dead.

"Guess what?" I asked when he finally answered.

"I give up," Hal mumbled groggily.

"I found Ginger's calendar, the one that was lifted from her room the other night."

"So big fucking deal. Do you know what time it is?"

"It was in the trash, down near the Mansion. You want to come out and pick it up, or should I bring it over to Friday Harbor myself?"

"Beau, give me a break, I didn't get to bed until three."

"Sorry, Hal, but I just found it. I thought you'd want to know."

"I'll pick it up later," he said grudgingly. "But it won't make any difference."

"What do you mean?"

He yawned, fully awake now. "Got the coroner's report just before I went to bed. Said her blood-alcohol reading was point-fifteen. She was dead drunk. Probably passed out cold when she hit the water."

"That's preposterous! It doesn't make sense."

"Of course it makes sense. Blood-alcohol counts don't lie. I'm telling you what they told me. It was an accident, and that's official."

I wanted to argue, but he wasn't having any. "The crime lab dusted for prints, enough to confirm that she was driving."

"You mean you're going to drop it just like that?"

"Look, Beau, we've already got one homicide. We don't need to change a DWI into homicide just for drill."

"But she wasn't drinking. She had nothing before she left here."

"You don't get a point-fifteen reading by osmosis. It was too much for her. The divorce, Sig Larson's death. She was despondent and slipped. It's the classic recovering-alcoholic story. She didn't live long enough to dry out a second time."

Ginger's words rang in my ears. "I won't go through that again. Ever." But I was the only one who had heard her make that categorical statement, the only one who knew that in twenty-four hours she had taken several giant steps beyond grief and found a reason for living.

"What was the time of death? Did they say?"

"Between eight-thirty and nine-thirty, give or take."

"I tell you, Hal, she had nothing to drink before she left here at twenty minutes to eight. How could she get that drunk in such a short time?"

He sighed. "You've been around boozers. With some of them, falling off the wagon is like stepping off a thirty-story building." Hal Huggins didn't budge. Neither did I.

"Do you want this calendar or not?" I demanded.

"I already said I'd come by later this morning and pick it up, but I'm not making any promises."

"Don't patronize me, Hal, goddammit. Will you have it analyzed or not? Don't pick it up just to humor me."

"For cripe's sake. I'll have it analyzed. Goodbye!" The receiver banged in my ear.

I looked at the calendar skulking by the door, its pungent odor invading the room. It made me wonder if I still wanted to be a cop when I grew up. I kept it in the room, odor and all. Considering the phone call, it didn't make much sense to keep it. I might just as well have pitched it outside into the drizzle, but I didn't.

I went to bed and tried to nap, without much luck.

CHAPTER 15

HAL HUGGINS WAS IN A FOUL MOOD WHEN HE SHOWED up an hour later. He called me from the lobby. "Bring that goddamned calendar down here and buy me breakfast, Beaumont."

Huggins was seated at a table before a steaming coffee cup when I ventured into the dining room. Grudgingly, he pushed out a chair for me. "I'm not very good company when I don't get my beauty sleep," he growled. "Where the hell is that calendar?"

I handed it to him, wrapped in a Rosario pillowcase.

"What do you expect to find in there?" he asked, nodding toward it.

"Prints, I hope. Especially on last week's pages."

He leaned back in his chair and glowered at me. "Let me ask you this, Beau. Do you think this calendar has anything to do with Sig Larson's death? The break-in occurred after he was already dead."

"No, but—"

"But what?"

"The meeting was listed in there, the one Sig and Ginger planned to attend together."

"Were you awake when you called me this morning?"

"Sure I was awake."

"I told you then and I'll tell you now, Ginger Watkins' death has been ruled accidental. We are not treating it as a possible homicide. Do I make myself clear?"

"Very. So you won't have the calendar analyzed?"

"I'll take it, just for old time's sake, but that's the only reason." Huggins glared at me, his face implacable.

"What are you so pissed about, Hal?"

"I'm pissed because I've got a homicide to work, and I'm shorthanded, and I didn't get enough sleep, and my neck hurts. Any other questions?"

"None that I can think of."

The waiter brought Huggins his food and took my order. Halfway through breakfast, Hal's savage beast seemed somewhat soothed. "You going back today?"

"Probably." Rosario had lost its charm. I wanted to go home and lick my wounds.

"You need a ride?"

"Naw. I can take the shuttle bus."

The waiter brought my coffee and freshly squeezed orange juice. "Find any trace of Wilson?"

Huggins shook his head. "Not yet. Looks like he stepped off the face of the earth once he got on the ferry."

"Maybe he did," I said. "Still no sign of him at his house?"

"Not a trace. King County has round-the-clock surveillance on the place. It doesn't make sense."

"Unless he's dead, too," I suggested.

Huggins' flint-eyed scrutiny honed in on my face. "He might be, at that," he said.

I didn't like the tone, the inflection. "Is that an accusation?" I asked.

"Could be," he allowed, "if I thought vigilante mentality had caught you by the short hairs."

"Look, Hal, I was only trying to help."

He nodded. "I'd hate to think otherwise, Beau."

It sounded like the end of a beautiful friendship. I tried to put the conversation on a less volatile track. "How'd she get the booze, then? It had to come from somewhere. It wasn't in the Porsche when she left here."

"When she left you," he corrected. "She might have gone back to her room and gotten it. She might have bought it on the way."

I was shaking my head before he finished speaking. Huggins' face clouded. "You're sure you never met Ginger Watkins before last Friday?"

"I'm sure," I answered, trying to keep anger out of my voice. From one moment to the next, Huggins and I shifted back and forth to opposite sides, like two kids who can't decide if they're best friends or hate each other's guts.

"Why's it so goddamned important to you that she wasn't drunk?" he demanded.

How does a man answer a question like that without his ego getting in the way? If she was drunk, then I'm not the man I thought I was. A psychiatrist would have a ball with that one. I know she was coming back. She and I had a date to screw our brains out after dinner. That one had a good macho ring to it. I had given her a reason for living. She wouldn't have thrown it all away. That dripped with true missionary fervor.

I said, "It's important to me, that's all."

"My mind's made up; don't confuse me with the facts, right?"

"Something like that."

"Beau—"

"Will you have the calendar analyzed?"

"I told you I will, but—"

"And you'll let me know what you find?"

There was a momentary pause. "I guess." He stirred his coffee uneasily, looking at me over the cup. "It's probably a good thing you're going home today. We might end up stepping on each other's toes."

"I take it that means you're firing me as a San Juan County deputy?"

He nodded. "Yup." He gave me a lopsided grin. "If it's possible to fire someone who's working for free." The tension between us evaporated. Huggins rose, taking his check and the calendar. I snagged the check away from him.

"It's on me, Hal, remember? Your beauty sleep?"

We shook hands. "No hard feelings?" he asked.

"None."

"All right then. I'll be in touch. If I were a betting man, I'd say there won't be a goddamned thing in this sonofabitch." He strode out of the dining room.

It's too bad I didn't take that bet, but hindsight is always twenty/twenty.

I went into the bar because I didn't want to go

back to my room. Without Ginger, my room seemed empty. Barney was industriously polishing the mirror.

"Morning," he said to my reflection. "Want a drink?"

"Just coffee," I replied. "I need to think."

He brought a mug and set it in front of me. "On the house," he said, refusing my money. Barney had a sense of when to leave people alone. He said nothing about my making an ass of myself. Instead he returned to his mirror and his Windex.

The question I had asked Hal was far more than rhetorical. He was right, of course. Blood-alcohol readings don't lie. No matter how much I wanted to deny it, Ginger Watkins had been drunk when she ploughed into the water. So where had she gotten the booze? From her room? A liquor store? Where?

"Hey, Barney," I said, "does Orcas Island have a liquor store?"

He grinned. "Hell, no. We're too small. We've got Old Man Baxter, though. He's the official agent. Lives up above Eastsound, about a half-mile beyond Ernie's."

"Did Huggins leave one of Don Wilson's pictures with you?"

"Are you kidding?" He reached under the bar and pulled out a whole handful. "Why, you want some?"

"One," I said. "I only need one." He handed me a picture. I pulled out a pen to write on the back. "Tell me again how to get there."

"Where?"

"Mr. Baxter's."

"Now wait a minute. You come in here, and I give you free coffee. Next thing I know, you want to go see our agent so you can mix your own drinks? No way! I'd lose one of my best customers."

"I promise I won't buy anything," I protested. "I just want to show him this picture."

"Well, in that case. . . . Go past Ernie's. It's the fourth mailbox on the left."

"Thanks, have the desk call me a cab, would you?"

"Why?"

"So I don't have to walk."

"No, I mean why do you want to see Baxter?"

"I want to know if either Ginger Watkins or this man bought something from him Friday or Saturday. Make the call, would you?"

Instead, Barney reached into his pants pocket and extracted a ring of keys. He tossed them across the bar, and I caught them in midair. "What's this?"

"It's the key to an old Chevy pickup parked over by the moorage. You're welcome to use it if you like."

It was a small-town gesture, one that caught me by surprise. When I thought about it, though, there's no such thing as auto theft on Orcas Island. I pocketed the keys. "Thanks, Barney. Appreciate it."

The pickup looked old and decrepit; but ugliness, like beauty, is only skin-deep. The engine ran like a top beneath a rusty hood. I drove into Eastsound, past Ernie's and stopped at the fourth mailbox on the left. The house was a picturesque gray-and-white bungalow that might have been lifted straight off Cape Cod. I knocked on the door.

Mr. Baxter himself opened it. He was a small man with a belly much too large for the rest of him. The living room of the house had been converted into a mini-display room, with a stack of hand-held shopping baskets sitting beside the door. The house had the smell and look of an aging bachelor pad—not much cooking and not enough cleaning.

"Help yourself," he said, motioning me inside.

I pulled Don Wilson's picture out of my pocket. "I didn't come to buy anything," I said. "I was wondering if you'd ever seen this man before."

He peered at the picture, then looked up at me. "You a cop?" he asked. His face was truculent, arms crossed, chin jutting. Mr. Baxter was a short man embattled by a tall world.

Huggins had pulled the plug on my unofficial deputy status. "No," I said. "The woman who died the other night was a friend of mine. I'm trying to find out what happened to her."

"Not from me you won't."

"I'm only asking if you recognize him."

"You ever hear of the confidentiality statute of nineteen and thirty-three?"

"Not that I remember."

"It says no liquor-store clerk tells nobody nothing, excepting of course federal agents checking revenue stamps. We can talk to them."

"All I'm asking is, Did you see him?"

"And if I give out information, they stick me with a high misdemeanor. Nosiree. I'm not talking to nobody."

I could see right off I wasn't going to change his mind. I left. Something made me stop at Ernie's. The doors of the Porsche were wide open, and the insides of the car were scattered all over the garage in a seemingly hopeless jumble. Ernie glanced up as I walked in. He was bent over the engine, a grimy crutch propped under his good arm.

"How'do, Mr. Beaumont. I was just gonna call you."

I figured it was time to jack up the price, now that the car was in pieces and I was a captive audience.

"Why?" I asked.

"You ever have any work done on the linkage?"

I shrugged. "No. Not that I know of."

He hopped away from the car to a nearby tool bench, picked up something in his gripper, and handed it to me. I looked down at two pieces of metal, slightly smaller in diameter than a pencil. "What's this?"

"That's the throttle linkage cable. Looks to me like it's been cut."

"What does that mean?"

"With that thing cut, Mr. Beaumont, all you have to do is put that baby in motion and you've got a one-way ride."

I looked down at the shiny crimped ends of metal. "It couldn't have broken in the accident?"

He shook his head. "No way."

"Mind if I use your phone?" I asked, keeping my voice calm. It was time for Hal Huggins to eat a little crow.

CHAPTER 16

HAL MARCHED INTO ERNIE'S GARAGE LOOKING THUN-derous. "What do you mean the linkage was cut?" he stormed.

Ernie pointed him in the direction of the tool bench where the two pieces of cable were once more lying in state. Silently Hal examined them, then he straightened. "How the hell could those crime-lab jokers miss something like this?"

"They were investigating an accident, remember?" I reminded him. "A DWI. Maybe even a suicide."

He glared at me. "That's no excuse."

"So where do we go from here?"

"Damned if I know." Hal settled on a bench near the door. "Not a chance of getting finger-prints now, either," he lamented.

Ernie, back under the hood, peered over his shoulder at Hal, grinning. "Only half as many as there could have been," he said.

Hal didn't bother to acknowledge Ernie's black humor. "Two homicides," he muttered. "Two goddamned homicides in as many days. Do you know how long we usually go up here without a homicide?"

"Did you tell anybody on the way over?"

"Hell, no. I tried to raise Pomeroy to come down to the dock and pick me up. I couldn't find that lard-ass anywhere. Luckily, somebody gave me a ride."

My mind was working. "Then the only people who know are you, Ernie, me, and the murderer."

"That's right. So what?"

"Let's keep it that way."

"What good will that do?" Hal asked.

"It'll give us a chance to investigate without the media breathing down our necks."

Hal nodded, slowly. "That does have some appeal." For a time we sat in silence. "How far could it have been driven like that, Ernie?" Hal asked finally.

Ernie answered without looking up from his work. "A couple hundred feet if the front end was aligned and it was on a straight stretch."

"What gear was it in?"

"Neutral when I got it, but I'm sure the tow-truck driver shifted it so he wouldn't tear up the transmission."

"Can you check with him?"

"Sure."

"And not a word of this to anyone," Hal admonished. "It's important."

Ernie straightened and favored Hal with a sly grin. "Had a feeling it was, or you wouldn't have been here in twenty-five minutes flat. Last time I seen you move that fast was at the Fireman's Picnic when a wasp was after you."

Hal laughed. "I set all-time world records with that sucker on my butt." The camaraderie was small-town stuff, foreign in a nice way.

"Don't worry. I'll keep it quiet." Ernie resumed working on the car, as though we were no longer there.

"What about Wilson?" I asked. "Any sign of him?"

Huggins shook his head. "We're looking, still keeping his house under surveillance, but so far nothing."

We rose and started toward the door; Ernie called after me, "By the way, Mr. Beaumont, maybe it won't cost you the whole seven grand after all."

Hal's eyes widened. "Seven grand?"

"Maybe six and a half." Ernie's head disappeared, dismissing us. Hal looked at me, stunned.

"Six and a half thousand? To fix the car?"

"It's a Porsche," I said. It seemed to me that no further explanation was necessary.

"How much they paying you these days? When I worked Seattle P.D., I was lucky to afford a lube and oil. Matter of fact, I still am. You into graft and corruption?"

"I happened into some money, Hal, that's all."

Hal glowered at me. "Some people have all the luck," he sniffed, walking outside. I followed.

"Where you going?" I asked.

"I'm looking for Pomeroy. He was supposed to come pick me up. I can't drive the goddamned police launch all over the goddamned island."

"Where do you want to go?"

"The duck pond, you asshole. Where else?"

That's how two homicide detectives, one legal and one not, returned to the scene of the crime in a bartender's borrowed pickup. It wasn't much, but it was a whole lot better than walking.

The place where the Porsche had laid down the layer of rubber made better sense now. The car had leaped forward from a dead stop. Even piecing that together didn't give us everything we needed to know. We gave up about mid-afternoon. I took Hal back to his boat.

"What are you going to do now?" he asked.

"Go home, I guess. Hanging around here won't do any good."

He sat in Barney's idling pickup, one hand on the door handle. "We'll get him, Beau. I promise." It was as close as Hal Huggins ever came to making an apology.

"Are you going to warn the rest of the parole board? What if he goes after the whole board, one by one."

Hal looked stricken. "I'll check it out," he agreed. "He could go through them like a dose of salts." He climbed from the pickup and headed for the dock.

Back at Rosario, I packed and checked out of my room. I had the desk clerk call for a float plane. I could have taken the ferry to Anacortes, but without a car, I'd still be a long way from Seattle. A charter pilot could drop me on Lake Union a mile or so from my apartment.

I dragged a newspaper along in the noisy little plane. I suffer from a fear of flying. There's nothing like reading a newspaper to make me forget that I'm scared. Newspapers always piss me off.

The editor opined that the tragic deaths of two members of the Washington State Parole Board over the weekend—one an apparent homicide and the other in a motor vehicle accident—pointed out the high cost of public service. He went on to say that Darrell Watkins was showing great personal courage in continuing to campaign in the face of the loss of his beloved wife.

Bullshit! There was no hint that the beloved wife, now deceased, would have filed for a divorce had she lived to Monday morning. In the editorial, Ginger's and Darrell's life had been a Cinderella story, poor girl marries rich boy and lives happily ever after. As far as Ginger was concerned, the fairy tale had suffered in translation. Somehow I had an idea that Maxwell Cole's interview would never see the light of the day. It wasn't just spiked, it was buried. For good.

The article on Ginger made no mention of drinking. The accident was described as a one-car accident on a narrow road. Darrell Watkins was quoted at some length. "I am going on with the race because I believe Ginger would want me to."

The unmitigated ass! Ginger had been wrong. Darrell Watkins had developed hypocrisy into an art form.

The float plane dropped me at a dock on Lake Union. Without luggage, I could have walked. With luggage, I called a cab. It was early evening when I got home—the city boy glad to be back in familiar territory, with the comforting wail of sirens and the noise of traffic.

My apartment is in the Royal Crest, a condo at Third and Lenora. *Condo* conjures images of swinging singles. There are singles here, all right, mostly retired, who do very little swinging. It's a vertical neighborhood where people bring soup when you're sick and know who comes and goes at all hours. I moved in five years ago on a temporary basis, hoping Karen and I would get back together. We didn't. Five years later, my escape hatch has become home.

In the elevator two people welcomed me back, and on the mat in front of my door I found a stack of crossword puzzles culled from various newspapers and left for me by my next-door neighbor and crony, Ida Newell. Yes, it was very good to be home.

I put my suitcases in the bedroom and looked around the tiny apartment with satisfaction. One of my first concessions to having money was to hire a housekeeper who comes in once every two weeks whether I need it or not. The house smelled of furniture polish and toilet-bowl cleaner. It was a big improvement over the old days when it smelled like a billygoat pen and I needed two hours' notice before I could invite someone up to visit.

The mail was mostly of the bill/occupant variety, although I noticed that some of the occupant stuff was a lot more upscale than occupant mail I used to receive. Somewhere there's a mass-mailing company that knows when you move from one income bracket to another. The whole idea makes me paranoid.

I thumped into my favorite leather chair, a

brown monstrosity that gives people with "taste" indigestion. I examined the bill from Rosario with its detail of all calls made from my room. I recognized most of them. Two of the numbers were unfamiliar. One had to be Homer's and the other Darrell's. I chose one at random.

Homer answered on the second ring. I didn't identify myself. "I'm a friend of Ginger's. I was calling to find out about her services."

"In keeping with Darrell's wishes, the services will be private."

"But I wanted—"

"I'm sorry. This is a very difficult time. Darrell wants to maintain a sense of dignity by keeping Ginger's funeral simple. Only family members and close personal friends. I'm sure you understand." He hung up without giving me an opportunity to explain why I thought I qualified as a close personal friend.

Remembering Ginger's description of how Darrell's campaign would handle news of the divorce, I understood all too well. A steering committee had decreed that Ginger's funeral should be handled with classic understatement and simplicity. Not too splashy. That would attract the sympathy vote.

I wanted to gag. Ginger had known news of the divorce wouldn't cost Darrell the election, but she had hoped to sting him with it. Instead, her death would provide the impetus for a come-from-behind victory. I wanted to protest to someone, but I didn't know who.

Restless, I walked two blocks to Avis and rented a car for the next morning. If I was going to make it to a funeral in Welton by two o'clock in the afternoon, I'd have to get an early start. My garage door opener was still with the Porsche on Orcas—probably wrecked, now that it had been wet. I parked the rented Rabbit on the street and went upstairs to get some sleep.

In a dream, Anne Corley and Ginger Watkins were together someplace. It seemed to be some kind of spa. They were both wrapped in thick white towels, with their hair hanging loose and wet. I came into the room. They waved at me and motioned for me to join them, but they were across a large room and between us lay a huge swimming pool. They motioned to me again, and I dove in, clothes and all. I tried to swim toward them, but the current was too swift. It caught me and carried me away, changing from a pool to a river. The dream ended with the sound of both of them laughing.

I awoke drenched with sweat. It was almost four o'clock in the morning. For a while I tried going back to sleep, but it didn't work. Remembering them both together haunted me. At last I got up and made coffee. The city was silent around me—not as silent as Orcas, but silent for the city. As I drank my coffee, I made up my mind that nothing would keep me from showing up at Ginger's funeral to offer my respects.

I consulted the map. I would go east on Interstate 90; but after Sig Larson's funeral, when I came back to Seattle, I would detour south to Centralia and find myself a Union 76 station. Ginger's father lived in Centralia. I was sure he would give me an invitation to the funeral if I explained to him that I was one of Ginger's old friends.

I filled a Thermos with the last of the coffee and headed out. I figured I'd have breakfast somewhere along the way.

CHAPTER 17

THE STATE OF WASHINGTON IS DIVIDED INTO TWO PARTS, east of the mountains and west of the mountains. They could just as well be separate countries.

West of the mountains is a fast-track megalopolis that is gradually encroaching on every inch of open space. East of the mountains seems like a chunk of the Midwest that has been transported and reassembled between the Cascades and the Rockies. It contains small towns, large farms, and the kind of vast horizons that brings to mind Robert Goulet's old song, "On a Clear Day You Can See Forever."

Welton is definitely east of the mountains. It's a tiny burg nestled in a hilly curve of the Touchet River, where two Walla Walla County roads meet in a casual Y that doesn't merit so much as a Yield sign, to say nothing of a blinking amber light.

Welton boasts a general store, a Grange Hall, a deserted schoolhouse, five or six dilapidated frame houses, and a double-wide mobile home perched on cement blocks behind the store. The Lutheran church burned down six years ago and has not been replaced. A sign on the light post next to the gas pump announced the schedule for the Walla Walla County Bookmobile. Next to it, another handbill posted notice of Sig Larson's funeral.

The gas jockey at the Texaco Station/General Store, a toothless old geezer named Gus, informed me that Lewis and Clark's party had once camped overnight on the river, supposedly somewhere near where the Grange Hall now stood. As far as he knew, Sig Larson's funeral was the biggest event to hit town since then.

"It isn't ever' day we have this kinda excitement around here," he commented as he scrubbed the rented Rabbit's windshield and checked the oil. "We're gonna shut 'er down and go over to the Hall for the funeral. Least we can do for old Sig, that's for sure."

"He lived around here?"

"Not anymore. Sold out a couple years back when that there wife of his decided Welton warn't good enough. Talked him into one of them high-falutin condanubians over to Lake Chelan. T'was a shame, a dad-gummed shame, if you ask me."

"But he'll be buried here?"

"First wife's buried here, you know. Think the kids had something to do with bringing him back. Son John's a bigwig lawyer down to California. He's the one took it on hisself to see things got done right."

"So Mona's Sig Larson's second wife?"

Gus snorted and spat a brown stream of tobacco juice over his shoulder. "She was already hanging round while Elke—that was Sig's first wife—was dyin' in the hospital over to Spokane."

"I take it you don't like Mona much."

He nodded sagely. "That's for sure," he said. "You can say that again."

Gus wore the logger trademark of mid-calf Levi's held up by a pair of bright red suspenders. Finished with my car, he stood with both thumbs stuck through his suspenders and surveyed the scatter of cars parked haphazardly around the Grange Hall. "Heard the governor hisself is coming. Wonder if ol' Mona'll get herself all gussied up or if she'll show up on that there motorcycle of hern."

Motorcycle! That hardly tallied with the white-haired, displaced-homemaker farm wife I had imagined Sig Larson's widow to be—someone wearing an apron who baked her own bread and canned her own tomatoes.

A mobile television unit bearing a Spokane station's call letters and logo lumbered past us and parked under a tree near the Grange Hall. "Don't that just beat all?" Gus asked. "All them television cameras and ever'thin', just for Old Sig's funeral." He spat again in disbelief.

As we watched, a helicopter dropped noisily from the sky and landed on the weedy playfield of the abandoned schoolhouse next door. Governor Reynolds stepped out, ducking under the blades, accompanied by none other than Homer Watkins himself.

Seeing Homer there was something of a shock. Ginger had implied that highly placed family connections had resulted in her appointment to the parole board, but seeing Homer with the governor brought the reality home.

"I'd better get going," I told Gus. I hurried to the Grange Hall and took an unobtrusive seat in the next-to-last row of ancient folding chairs. From there I could see who came and went without being observed.

I had stopped in Kenniwick and bought a huge bouquet of flowers, which now sat prominently displayed near the foot of Sig Larson's coffin. I had signed the card from "A Friend" and let it go at that. The flowers were a remembrance from Ginger to Sig through me. If Ginger and Sig were flapping around upstairs somewhere, then they both knew what I meant. If they weren't, it didn't matter anyway.

Unlike Lewis and Clark's historic visit, Sig Larson's funeral was immortalized by the press, the same teeming mob that had invaded Orcas Island. They were joined by troops from Spokane and Tri Cities as well. A full contingent of the Fourth Estate was there, jockeying for position and camera angle, elbowing one another out of the way.

It was simple to divide the guests into two parts: the plainly dressed quiet folk who had probably been lifelong friends and neighbors of Sig and Elke Larson, and the public officials and anxious candidates whose attendance was calculated to pick up a little free publicity over and above the paid political announcements.

The entire front row, on both sides of the aisle, was marked Reserved. As the pianist attempted a frail, halting prelude on an old upright piano, a group of six handsome young people, three couples in their late twenties to early thirties, was ushered to the front row. I surmised they were Sig's children and their spouses. Gus had told me there were two Larson boys and one girl, all married. They sat together on one side of the front row, leaving two places open next to the aisle.

The surviving members of the parole board, five of them, straggled down the aisle behind Trixie Bowdeen like a bunch of dazed sheep. Next came Governor Reynolds and Homer Watkins.

There was some confusion about seating arrangements as they reached the front row. Homer and Governor Reynolds held a hurried, private consultation before both men crossed the aisle to speak solemnly with the young couples. Then they rejoined the parole board.

Darrell Watkins was notable only in his absence.

The room filled quickly, until every chair was taken and people stood two-deep in the back of the room. It was then Mona Larson staged her grand entrance. She wore a black dress with a bold V neckline and a flared skirt over a pair of high-heeled black boots. Her hair, black and glossy, hung straight to her shoulders, with a fringe of bangs that made her look far younger than I had expected. Her tiny waist was encircled by a wide turquoise and silver belt. A weighty squash-blossom necklace with matching earrings completed the ensemble. It wasn't exactly mourning, but it made the point. It was also very striking.

A murmur rustled through the room. Mona strode down the aisle, well aware of the sensation she caused. At the front of the room she paused momentarily to get her bearings, then she turned her back on Sig Larson's children and took the empty seat next to Governor Reynolds. Another flurry of comment whispered through the hall.

From the back of the room it looked more like a shotgun wedding between feuding clans than the funeral of a highly regarded public official. Mona Larson was behaving badly by Welton standards, and it was clear she didn't give a damn.

A minister took his place behind the podium. "Dearly beloved," he intoned, "we are here this afternoon to say good-bye to our dear friend Lars Sigfried Larson . . ." The cameras whirred and the circus got under way.

I don't remember much about the service. As far as I was concerned, I was there on official/unofficial business. I kept my eyes open in case Wilson thought Welton far enough away from Orcas that he could afford to turn up and savor his handiwork. Murderers do that in a kind of cutthroat one-upmanship, but Don Wilson was nowhere to be seen.

At the end of the service, the reverend announced that the Ladies Aid would be serving a potluck lunch, and all were welcome to come back to the hall after interment in the cemetery beyond the school.

The pallbearers hoisted the coffin. Mona Larson, followed by the governor and Sig's children, led a slow procession out of the hall, across the road, and into the cemetery. A man sat smoking on an idled backhoe near the fence, waiting to perform his essential role in the process. Once Sig's coffin was lowered into the grave, Mona turned and left the cemetery alone. Without speaking to or acknowledging anyone, she climbed into one of three waiting limousines and left Welton with an air of regal contempt.

Gus hobbled up next to me. "Ain't she somethin'?" he demanded, with just a hint of awe. "Actin' like she's the dad-gummed Queen of Sheba."

The press corps descended on the food like an army of ravenous ants. I spied Maxwell Cole packing around a paper plate piled high with ham and scalloped potatoes, but I managed to avoid him. The local folks clustered around the Larson children, expressing condolences, relieved now that Mona's abrupt departure had reduced the tension.

Homer Watkins materialized at my elbow. "I understand you're J. P. Beaumont. Aren't you the one I talked to on the phone the night Ginger died?"

I wondered who had squealed on me, but with Max in the room, it wasn't hard to figure it out. "Yes," I said.

"Tragic, tragic," he murmured.

"It is, isn't it," I agreed. "I was a little surprised there was no mention of the impending divorce in the paper."

His eyes hardened. "She told you about that?"

"We talked," I replied noncommittally.

"She wouldn't have gone through with it. She had been under a great deal of stress. I'm sure once things settled down, she would have been fine."

"Fine or quiet?" I asked.

One eyebrow arched. He stepped back half a pace.

"Darrell didn't come?" I asked. The question was more to irk him than to have an answer.

Homer replied nonetheless. "He didn't feel up to it. Good day, Mr. Beaumont. I won't trouble you further."

As people lined up for second and third helpings, Governor Reynolds raised his hand for attention. "I'd like to make an announcement," he said. The media folks abandoned their plates and hustled off in search of equipment. Reynolds moved to the front of the room.

He put on his glasses and read from a prepared text. "This has been a sad occasion for the State of Washington. Sig Larson was a public servant, and he was murdered in the course of that service. He paid with his life. We have reason to believe that his death was related to his being on the parole board. Consequently, as of today, I am placing all members of the parole board under the protection of the Washington State Patrol. That is all."

There was a momentary lull after he finished speaking, then a rush of comment. Reporters attempted to call questions to him from the floor, but he turned away. Reynolds and Homer hurried out of the building. People followed them upstairs and outside, but they dashed to the waiting helicopter without speaking to anyone. With the governor gone, people moved back into the basement, where Trixie Bowdeen assumed the role of spokesman.

"Were you aware the governor was taking this action, Mrs. Bowdeen?"

"Yes," she said. "Each of us has been assigned round-the-clock protection, starting today."

"Is there any idea who the killer or killers might be?"

"No comment."

"How does your husband feel about your having a round-the-clock bodyguard?"

"Fortunately, he's not the jealous type." Trixie Bowdeen flashed what was supposed to be a charming smile. Her quip was greeted by general laughter. I didn't laugh. Governor Reynolds had not specifically mentioned Ginger's death, but I was sure Huggins had notified him regarding the changed status of the investigation. In any event, the protection was probably a good idea.

I left the hall and was halfway across the road when Maxwell Cole called my name. "Hey, J. P."

I turned to find him huffing behind me, carrying a plate of half-consumed pumpkin pie. "What do you want?"

"Any line on Wilson?"

I kept my expression blank. "No," I said. "Nobody's seen him."

"How come Ginger Watkins was driving your car?"

"None of your business," I snarled, walking away.

He trotted after me. "I heard her blood-alcohol count was point-fifteen, but she was supposed to be on the wagon."

"Shut up," I said savagely.

He shut up, but only momentarily, "Do you know anything about the governor's victim/witness protection program? Is Reynolds going to drop that idea? That's what Wilson was after."

I stopped in my tracks. "What do you mean?"

Cole looked a little reluctant, as though he had said more than he intended. "Wilson expected an announcement that day at Rosario."

"From the governor's office?"

"That's what he told me on the phone."

"This is the first I've heard anything about an announcement," I said, turning to walk away.

"But, J. P.—"

Ignoring him, I walked back to the gas station where I had left the Rabbit. I climbed in and drove to where two uniformed limo drivers stood smoking under a tree. I rolled down the window. "Did that other driver say where he was taking Mrs. Larson?" I asked.

One looked at the other, who shrugged. "The Red Lion in Pasco, I think," he said. "You know where that is?"

"No," I replied, rolling up the window and putting the Rabbit in gear, "but I'll bet I can find it."

CHAPTER 18

I DROVE THE FORTY MILES INTO PASCO THINKING ABOUT Ray Johnson. Ray and I were partners on the homicide squad for eleven years before he took off to become Chief of Police in Pasco. That's what happens to longtime Seattle P.D. folks. They get tired of the rat race and go looking for some one- or two-horse town where they can settle down and not have to look at the slice of life that turns up dead or drunk or both in Seattle's parks and alleys.

Ray had abandoned ship almost ten months earlier, and I had started working with Peters. It takes time to adjust to a new partner, but in the course of that ten months so much had happened that now it seemed Peters and I had been together for years, and Ray Johnson was ancient history.

Ten months is a long time to go without seeing an old friend, and I decided I'd eat a chiliburger and down a whole pot of thick coffee with Ray Johnson before I left town. For old time's sake.

Without having Peters lecture me on the evils of the caffeine or red meat.

The sign at the Red Lion in Pasco said, "Welcome Mary Kay." I mistakenly thought Mary Kay was a waitress or barmaid who had returned for a visit.

That shows how wrong you can be.

The Red Lion in Pasco, like Red Lions everywhere, is built on the kind of grand scale that says, "Conventions welcome; all others enter at your own risk." As I drove up, a car pulled out of a parking place directly in front of the lobby. I grabbed the spot, feeling smug. Getting out of the Rabbit, I noticed that the car next to me, and two on the other side of that, were all recent-model pink Cadillacs. They had matching bumper stickers which read, "Ask me about Mary Kay."

Still musing about that, I entered the lobby. A huge banner solved the mystery. Stretched across the lobby, it proclaimed, "Welcome Mary Kay Cosmetics." A regional sales convention was in full swing, and the hotel was thronged with troops of motivated, energetic ladies, all dressed in pink, who periodically burst into disturbingly impromptu choruses of company songs. I should have recognized it as an omen and realized I was headed for trouble.

A harried desk clerk managed to find me a room. Once safely shut away, I picked up the phone and asked for Mona Larson. "I'll ring," the operator told me.

"Hello." The voice was low and husky. For a second I thought I was talking to a man.

"Mona Larson, please," I stammered.

"This is she."

"My name is Beaumont. I'm here investigating a homicide. I need to talk to you."

"How the hell did you find me? That's why I didn't go home. I'm sick of being hounded."

"I'm a detective; that's how I found you. But it's only me. I've ditched the press."

Her tone mellowed a little. "That's a relief. Those bastards have been driving me crazy."

"Would you care to have a drink . . . coffee?"

"I could use a drink. Where are you?"

"In my room. I can meet you in the coffee shop or the bar." Sig Larson didn't drink. Maybe Mona didn't either. It was best to offer the lady a choice.

"All right. It'll take me a few minutes. I'll meet you in the bar. How will I know you?"

"From the looks of the lobby as I came in, I'll probably be the only man in the place."

She laughed. "You'll be the onion in the Mary Kay petunia patch."

She was right. Walking into the Starlight Lounge unnerved me. It was cocktail hour. All the old jokes about salesmen on convention came to mind and did a flip-flop. Saleswomen were just as bad. They sat in groups of twos and threes, giving me a clothes-stripping once-over. Other than the bartender, I was the only man in the room.

I had barely sat down when a woman in her mid-forties sidled up to my table. "Care for a drink?"

I looked around in consternation, hoping she wasn't talking to me. She was. Her face was a paper-smooth mask, eyes shadowed with a disconcerting blend of several different colors. Her lips, darker on the outside than on the inside, made me wonder what a two-toned tube of lipstick looked like.

"Sorry," I answered. "I'm meeting someone."

"Too bad," she said with a wink. She returned to her table while the bartender appeared at my elbow. "Drink, fella?"

"A McNaughton's and water," I said. He paused to wipe the table. "This is a little weird," I commented under my breath.

He laughed. "You think it's bad now, wait until nine o'clock when they're all on their lips."

The bartender returned to the bar. I sat there, conspicuously alone, waiting for Mona Larson. At Welton she had looked quite bizarre, but now I was anxious to see her. Mona's dramatic clothing would be a welcome contrast to the unrelenting pink, her disdain an antidote to the uncomfortable attention I was receiving at the moment.

Mona rescued me, all right. She had changed her black dress for a black, zippered jumpsuit. Her hair had been pulled up to the top of her head and stuck there with an unlikely comb. A few loose tendrils of hair trailed softly down her neck. Still wearing several pounds of silver and turquoise, she sauntered into the bar with a feline grace that disposed of the pink ladies once and for all.

"Mr. Beaumont?" she asked, extending her hand.

I half rose in greeting. Her handshake was firm, her dark brown eyes straightforward. "Don't bother getting up," she said, sinking gratefully into a low-backed chair opposite me.

"Thanks for saving my bacon," I said.

She glanced around the room disdainfully. "From what? These horny broads?" She turned to me and grinned. "You look like you can take care of yourself."

From what Ginger had said about Mona Larson and from what I had seen at the funeral, I was prepared not to like her, but her manner had a disarming forthrightness about it, and very little of the grieving widow.

"Sorry it took so long," she apologized. "I had a phone call. Are you from Orcas?"

The bartender brought my drink and took her order for Chivas on the rocks while I contemplated my situation. I was in no way from Orcas, and as a Seattle homicide detective, I had no business asking her anything at all.

I took a sip of my drink. "No. I'm from Seattle."

"I didn't know Seattle was involved in the case."

"We are now," I said.

"Do you have a card?"

There are times when I think I'll just stick my little toe in some water. Before I know it, I'm in over my head. I reached into my pocket and pulled out my leather cardholder. I handed her one of my business cards, which she examined without comment and put into a zippered pocket on the leg of her pants. Her fingers were long and slender, but the nails were close-cropped.

"So what do you want to know?"

"How well did you know Ginger Watkins?"

"Well enough."

"What do you mean?"

"We were shirttail relatives. Homer and Sig's first wife were brother and sister. Our families had some business dealings together."

So that was the connection. I had wondered about it.

"Were you and Ginger friends?"

"No."

I waited, hoping she'd expand on the subject. She didn't. "You and Darrell, then?"

"Darrell Watkins is an asshole," Mona said. "He's why I was late. He called from Seattle while I was at the funeral, wanted to explain why he wasn't there. As if I give a rat's ass." She extracted a pack of cigarettes from another zippered pocket. I hurried to offer her a light. She leaned back inhaling.

"Did you know Ginger was going to get a divorce?"

"You bet. I called Darrell to tell him."

"Why?"

She regarded me coolly. "Look, Mr. Beaumont, I played that side of the fence once. You're married to a jerk. Some nice guy sympathizes, listens to you, tells you what a bad deal you've got. First thing you know, you ditch the jerk and marry the nice guy. That's the name of the game, survival of the fittest."

"You think Ginger was trying to pack Sig off?"

She blew a languid cloud of smoke. "Not on

purpose. She was so fucked up, she probably didn't know she was doing it. They were nice people, both of them."

I tried reconciling Mona's words with the person who had forbidden Ginger to attend Sig's funeral. It didn't add up. "Why didn't you want Ginger to come to the funeral?"

"Who said?"

"That's what I understood," I replied. "It came from someone, maybe Trixie Bowdeen."

"That cow? All she does is make trouble. She minds everybody else's business. Ginger could have come if she wanted to. It wouldn't have bothered me."

She glanced away from me, angrily swiping a tear. Pain lurked behind Mona Larson's tough exterior, under the brittle wit.

"You loved him very much, didn't you."

She looked at me, her eyes bright with tears. "That's not how they see it in Welton," she said. "I'm the gold digger who married Sig Larson for his money. What a laugh!"

"Did you?" Mona's manner encouraged a direct approach.

She didn't deny it. "There's not much left," she countered.

"The money from the farm?"

"Gone. He left me a mortgaged condo on Lake Chelan, plus my share of the Seattle project, whatever that's worth. I own my Harley free and clear, and that's it, except for my jewelry." She fell silent. I felt sorry for her. Ginger Watkins' calculating bitch wasn't nearly as ruthless, close at hand.

"You work on the Harley yourself?"

She cocked her head. "What made you ask that?"

"Your nails are a whole lot more serviceable than the rest of the nails in this room, like maybe they get a little grease under them on occasion."

"Good guess," she said.

"What do you know about Don Wilson?" I asked, switching topics.

She looked me straight in the eye. "I told him if he called again I'd file a complaint."

"For what?"

"Telephone harassment. I knew all about his wife and kid, but he'd call in the middle of the night, making wild threats. He finally stopped."

"When?"

She thought. "A month or so ago, maybe longer."

"He threatened Sig?"

"Constantly."

"What did he say?"

"That he'd make Sig pay."

"Did Sig do anything about it?"

"Mostly he laughed it off. Initially he tried reasoning with the guy, but you can't talk to someone like that. They won't listen." She paused. "Do you think he did it?" The question was quiet. The noise of the room ebbed and flowed around us.

"It looks like it, at least for now."

She signaled the bartender for a drink. When he brought it, she lit another cigarette. "It's funny. Sig was so glad to get the appointment to the board. He thought, with his experience at Walla Walla, he could help; that he'd make a real contribution." She stopped, words giving way to reflection. It was an awkward silence.

"I understand Sig didn't drink."

She took a sip from her Chivas. "He wanted me to quit, too. There's nothing like a reformed drunk." She gave me a forlorn smile. "I would have, eventually." There was another long pause. She needed comforting and I was at a loss.

"Would you like to have dinner?" I asked at last.

She shook her head. "Not now, maybe later. I have some things I need to do first."

"How long will it take?"

"An hour or so. I'll give you a call when I finish."

She jotted my room number on the back of my card, and returned it to her pocket. We talked a while longer before she got up to leave. She held out her hand. "It was nice meeting you, Detective Beaumont. I'll see you later."

I watched her walk away, striding purposefully out of the room, a lady with places to go and people to see. It was only after she was out of sight that a wave of concern washed over me. I left money on the table and hurried after her, but she was nowhere in sight. I found a house phone and dialed her room. It rang and rang, but there was no answer.

Stopping by the desk, I asked what kind of car Mona Larson had registered. The clerk didn't bother to look at her card. "She's the one with the Harley, mister." He grinned. "Doesn't seem possible someone her size could handle one of those suckers."

I roamed through acres of parking lot to no avail. Finally I went back to my room and tried calling Ray in Pasco. No answer. I tried Mona's room several times as well, but there was still no answer. Giving up, I turned on the movie channel. I don't know when I fell asleep.

CHAPTER 19

A SHARP RAP ON THE DOOR JARRED ME AWAKE. FLIPping off the droning television set, I opened the door to find two uniformed police officers standing in the hallway.

"Are you J. P. Beaumont?" the first one asked, stepping uninvited through my open door. He wore gold-rimmed glasses and chewed a cud of gum with unbridled enthusiasm.

"Yes. What do you want?"

The second officer was heavyset: not fat, but with a definite paunch. "You know a lady named Mona Larson?"

"Yes, I do. What's up?"

"When's the last time you saw her?"

"I don't know. What time is it?"

The one in glasses looked at his watch. "Eight-thirty," he said, wrapping the gum around the tip of his tongue and giving it a small, interior pop.

"I saw her about six-thirty. She said she had some things to do."

"Did she say what?"

I shook my head. "No. What's going on?" I kept asking the question, but they disregarded it.

The heavyset one pulled a business card out of his inside jacket pocket and turned it over, examining both sides. I recognized it as one of my own. "Says here you're Detective Beaumont. You here in Pasco on official business?"

A twinge of uneasiness warned me something wasn't right. "No," I said after a pause. "I was at a funeral in Welton this afternoon and decided to spend the night."

"Sig Larson's funeral?" There was an unpleasant undertone to his question.

"Yes. As a matter of fact, it was."

The gum-chewer wandered over to the window. "Mind if we have a look around?"

"No. Yes. What's this all about?" I demanded, getting my back up.

"He asked you nice like," the heavyset one warned. "Now, can we look around or not?"

I retreated to the bed and sat down, more than half angry. Obviously there was some mistake. They had no business pushing me around like a common criminal. I wanted to get to the bottom of whatever it was. "Go ahead," I said, managing to control myself.

Glasses searched the whole room—under the bed, in the closet, in all the drawers, in the bathroom—while Fatso kept an eye on me, all the while fingering his nightstick. "No luggage?" Glasses asked when he finished.

"I didn't plan to spend the night."

"No, I suppose not."

"Are you going to tell me what's going on?" I

felt as though I had fallen into a bad dream where things happen and no one tells you why. There wasn't much I could do about it. It was two against one. They were calling the shots.

"You got anyone who'll say where you were between six-thirty and now?"

"I already told you. I've been right here at the hotel, mostly asleep. Now tell me what the fuck is going on!"

Glasses rolled his eyes. "Isn't that what they all say, Willy? I was asleep the whole time. All by myself."

Willy grinned. "That's what they say."

"Now wait just a goddamned minute. You'd better tell me what's happening."

"You want to tell him, Joe?" Willy asked.

"Naw, you go ahead. Since he's so anxious to hear."

"Well sir," Willy said, savoring the words, "it's about this lady we found along the road a little while ago. Victim of a hit-and-run. She had your card in her pocket with a room number written on the back."

"Mona?" I asked. "Is she all right?"

"Didja hear that!" Joe exclaimed. "She's dead as a doornail, and he wants to know if she's all right. You'd better move on over to the wall. Put your hands above your head."

For a second I sat there, too stunned to move. Mona too? I had just had a drink with her, talked to her. We were going to have dinner. Willy took a menacing step toward me. "He said move."

I was in no position to argue. I did as I was

told. Willy patted me down. Removing my jacket from a chair, he discovered my shoulder holster underneath. "Why, looky here, Joe." Willy tossed my .38 to Glasses. "Read him his rights." Willy pulled a pair of handcuffs out of his pocket and held them in front of me. "Turn around, buster," he ordered. "You're under arrest."

"What the hell do you clowns think you're doing?"

"Clowns, Joe. You hear that? This renegade big-time cop from Seattle thinks we're a couple of clowns."

"You have the right to remain silent—" Joe began.

"You guys have to be shitting me. Ray Johnson used to be my partner—"

"You have the right to an attorney—"

"And your uncle George sits on the Supreme Court. Right, funnyman?" Willy sneered.

"Anything you say may be held—"

"I said turn around," Willy repeated, his words taking on an ominous edge. I turned. The handcuffs snapped shut behind me. "Did you hear your rights now, Mr. Beaumont?" He gave the cuffs a sharp yank, making sure they were fastened securely.

"I heard them."

"Did you understand them?"

"Yes."

He spun me around so I faced him. "We wouldn't want any question of abrogating your rights, now would we?"

"You asshole—" I began.

He grabbed me by the shoulder and shoved me toward the door. "Where are your car keys?"

"Find them yourself," I snapped.

"Here they are, Willy," Glasses called from the dresser.

"Bring 'em. We'll check out the car on the way." They led me handcuffed through the front lobby of the Red Lion, where several dozen women watched in openmouthed wonder.

I've arrested plenty of people in my time, but being arrested was an entirely new and painful experience. Handcuffed wrists in the small of the back make you feel humiliated and trapped and scared and guilty, even if you're not. I wanted to hide my face in my hands, to shield myself from gaping, prying eyes. I couldn't, not with my hands cuffed behind me.

I had parked the Rabbit near the front door. Now it was nowhere to be seen.

"Where is it?" Willy demanded.

"I don't know. It's gone. Somebody moved it."

Glasses and Fatso nodded at each other knowingly. "Sure they did," Willy said. "What kind of car is it?"

"A Rabbit, a red, rented Rabbit."

"Sounds about right," Willy said. "Bring the car, Joe. We'll drive around through the parking lot and see if Mr. Beaumont here can remember where he left it. Musta been driving in his sleep."

Maybe the reason cops hate reporters and vice versa is that we're so much alike. The same kind of questioning minds end up in both professions.

The difference lies in what we do with the answers.

It came as no surprise that the same thought process that had brought me to the Red Lion in search of Mona Larson would do the same for a reporter. Fate alone dictated that the reporter should be Maxwell Cole. He arrived just as Willy shoved me into the backseat of a patrol car, blue lights flashing. Cole almost walked past us, but then he spied me. "J. P.," he yelped. "Hey, what's going on?"

I prayed we'd leave right then, but we didn't. Joe meandered through the well-lit parking lot, searching for my car. By the time we located the Rabbit in the back row of the lot, a noisy cortege of people had formed behind us. "That's it," I said, nodding toward the Rabbit.

Joe left the patrol car idling and sauntered over to it. Through the open door, I could hear a chorus of questions. Glasses ignored them. He knelt in front of the car and examined the front bumper, then he stopped long enough to peer into all the windows. He hurried back to the patrol car. "Hand me the pliers, Willy."

With my key, Glasses unlocked the door on the rider's side. He used the pliers to lift the latch and open the door. I was grateful for that. At least he wasn't disturbing my evidence. He leaned into the Rabbit, then straightened and came back to the patrol car. "Call for a backup, Willy. Tell them to get someone to impound the car while we drag our friend here off to jail."

"Why? What have you got?"

"Remember the desk clerk told us she was wearing a bunch of Indian jewelry?"

"Yeah."

"Looks like it's all there, and the front end is smashed all to shit."

"That's impossible! I tell you, I've been asleep in my room since seven o'clock."

"We've got you dead to rights, mister," Glasses said.

"I swear I didn't do it."

"Save it for the judge," he said.

We waited in the car interminable minutes until a second patrol car with flashing blue lights and a wailing siren worked its way through the onlookers.

By the time we got to the station, there was a crowd of reporters milling outside, with Maxwell Cole leading the pack. Many of the out-of-town newsies had decided to stay over, thus gaining admittance to the third media event of the day. When Willy opened the door, I didn't want to get out. My mouth was dry; my knees shook, not with fear so much as helpless rage and indignation.

"Get out," Willy commanded.

I didn't, couldn't. Willy grabbed me by the shoulder and bodily pulled me from the car. Again I wanted a shield, a sack, a cloak of invisibility—anything to lock out the eyes and the cameras and the voices and the nightmare. Willy and Joe herded me into the station and handed me over to a woebegone detective named Barnes.

Barnes struck me as a detective's detective, an old-time cop who used common sense as opposed to some computerized procedural manual. He brought me a Styrofoam cup of bitter coffee. "They read you your rights?" I nodded. Over his voice, in the background, I could hear the demanding questions of the reporters who were laying siege to the Pasco City Police Department.

Barnes cocked his ear as if listening to the uproar outside. "You want to tell me what happened?"

How could I tell him what happened when I didn't know? Mona Larson was dead, but I didn't know how or why or where. "Where do you want me to start?"

"How long did you know Mrs. Larson?"

"I just met her this afternoon."

"At her husband's funeral?"

"No, later, when she came back to the hotel, after the funeral."

"You followed her?" It was a leading question.

"Yes."

"You went to her room?"

"No. I called her, from my room. We met for a drink."

"Why?"

"To talk."

"About?"

"Sig, her husband."

"You knew him, then?"

The questions were getting worse. So were the answers. "No. Not until after he was murdered."

Barnes' eyes glittered with that now-we're-getting-somewhere look. I recognized it. I've used it myself during interrogations. "After?"

"I heard a woman screaming from my room at

the Rosario Resort on Orcas Island. I checked it out and found Ginger Watkins with Sig Larson's body. I've been working unofficially with Hal Huggins, the detective from Friday Harbor. Call and ask him. It's the San Juan County Sheriff's Department."

"I probably will give him a call," Barnes said reasonably. "After we finish here. So you met Mrs. Larson for a drink, in the bar?"

"Yes. I think it's called the Star Light Lounge."

"And you talked about?"

"I don't remember exactly . . . her marriage, Welton, her stepchildren. Lots of things. Then she had to leave."

"Did you go with her?"

"No."

"Follow her?"

"No. I told you, I went back to my room for a nap."

"Come on, Detective Beaumont. Let's get to the bottom of this. Did you and Mrs. Larson quarrel about something?" His position solidified. Up till then, I had answered his questions in a warily cooperative fashion, but something in his manner shifted, warning me. Before, I had believed we were on the same side. It was now clear that we weren't.

"Where's Ray Johnson?" I asked.

"The Chief? What business is that of yours?"

"Call him," I said flatly. "Ray and I used to be partners on the force in Seattle."

I could tell my words made some impact. Barnes got up and walked across the room, hands deep in his pockets. "Mrs. Larson was deliberately run down by a man driving a red car. Witnesses saw a Rabbit leaving the scene. Aren't you driving a red Rabbit?"

I didn't answer. He walked back across the room and looked down at me accusingly. "So what have you got against the parole board, Detective Beaumont? Did they let out a crook you thought should have stayed locked up?"

"I'm trying to tell you—"

"You've been on the scene of two recent homicides before this one." He picked up a newspaper that had been lying facedown on his desk. "Not only that, Mrs. Watkins died in your car, a red Porsche. How come you like red so much?"

"Call Ray Johnson, for chrissake! He'll vouch for me."

"The chief is unavailable. He and his wife are celebrating their twenty-fifth wedding anniversary with a second honeymoon in Spokane. I'm not calling him for anybody."

"What about Hal Huggins, the detective over in Friday Harbor?" I struggled to restrain my temper.

Barnes smiled indulgently, as if I were a not-too-bright kid who had screwed up some simple directions. "If you want to call somebody, I'd suggest you call your attorney, not a character witness. You want to use the phone?"

"No, I don't want to use the phone. I want out."

His smile disappeared. "I don't believe you understand, Mr. Beaumont. You're being booked on an open charge of murder."

The words filled the room, sucking out the atmosphere. It was suddenly difficult to breathe.

"You're right," I said, caving in, "I want to use the phone." I tried Peters first. No dice. He was in The Dalles, with Ames, for the custody hearing. I didn't know where they were staying.

It's easy to panic in a situation like that, to decide that you're totally isolated and there's no way to get help. I finally dialed Ida Newell's number, collect. Ida, my next-door neighbor, is a retired schoolteacher, the proverbial little old lady in tennis shoes. She collects crossword puzzles for me and mothers me as much as I'll tolerate. It was ten-thirty, but she stays up late to watch the news.

"Why, Beau," she said pleasantly, once the operator connected us. "Where are you?"

I didn't entirely answer that question. "I need your help, Ida. I've got to get in touch with my partner and my attorney. I won't be able to call out after this. Could you please find them and give them a message?"

"Certainly." Thankfully, she didn't ask any questions.

"Their names are Ron Peters and Ralph Ames. They're staying somewhere in The Dalles."

"Where?"

"I don't know."

"Look here, Beau, if you don't know where they're staying, how do you expect me to find them?"

I wanted to bully her to action, but I fought to keep impatience out of my voice. "They'll be at the best hotel or motel in town. Try the phone book, the Yellow Pages."

Ida sounded dubious. "If I find them, what do I say?"

"Have Ames call me." I glanced at Barnes, who nodded reluctantly. I read her the number off the phone.

"That's all?"

"Tell him it's urgent."

"Well, all right."

"Thanks, Ida. You've no idea how much I appreciate this."

I put down the phone. Twenty minutes later, after fingerprints and a mug shot, I was locked up in a cell. Out of deference to my being a police officer, they gave me a private cell.

It was small consolation.

CHAPTER 20

I SLEPT. I DON'T KNOW HOW, BUT I DID. MAYBE WHEN you're up against something you can do absolutely nothing about, sleep is Mother Nature's balm for the insoluble problem. I slept, blissfully ignorant of what went on around me. Everyone told me about it. Later.

Through the wonders of modern telecommunications, old J. P. Beaumont hit the eleven o'clock news on every major television station in the Pacific Northwest—Spokane, Seattle, Portland, and Boise. The lead story was all about Seattle's rogue cop being booked into Pasco City Jail on an open charge of murder. It made for very splashy journalism and pushed Sig Larson's funeral back to just before Sports.

As far as the press was concerned, my guilt was a foregone conclusion. Not everyone had access to the kind of material Maxwell Cole did. They had to content themselves with only the immediate story. Max sat down and composed an in-depth piece that he transferred by modem to the *P.I.* in downtown Seattle. He dredged it all out of his fertile memory—the kid in the alley when I was a rookie, Anne Corley, Ginger dead in my Porsche. His column would have done the *National Enquirer* proud.

I slept.

Peters saw the story on a Portland station in The Dalles. He dialed Ames' number and found it busy. Ida Newell had just reached Ames at the Papadera Inn, The Dalles' only Best Western motel. Peters came to Ames' room while Ralph was still talking to Ida. Before the news was over, Ames and Peters were checked out of their rooms and driving hell-bent-for-leather to Tri Cities.

I sawed logs. It's called the sleep of the just.

In the bridal suite of Spokane's Ridpath Hotel, Evie Johnson fell asleep while Ray congratulated himself on his performance, not bad for twenty-five years of marriage. He could still hold his own in the bedroom department.

With Evie drowsing contentedly beside him, he switched the TV on low. He'd watch the news for a couple of minutes. He woke Evie scrambling out of bed. She sat up as he pulled on his clothes.

"Where are you going?" she demanded.

"I've gotta go, hon," he said. "You stay here. I'll leave the car so you can come home tomorrow."

"Why? What's wrong?"

"Someone back home lost his marbles and arrested Beau for first-degree murder."

"Can't you call?"

"I can't knock heads over the phone."

By the time Ray was ready, Evie had called the airport and discovered that the last plane for

Tri Cities left at ten fifty-five. She dressed quickly, throwing things into the suitcase. "I'll go with you," she told him. "There's no sense in staying here alone."

And still I slept.

San Juan County Sheriff Bill Yates woke Hal Huggins out of a sound sleep. "What the hell is going on?"

"How should I know?"

"I rented a float plane. He'll put you down on the Columbia. Get over to Pasco and find out."

So Hal Huggins, too, began a midnight trek to Tri Cities while I slept on, dreaming I was slicing off one of Maxwell Cole's gaudy ties with a huge pinking shears. No wonder I didn't want to wake up.

Ray hit town first. He came roaring into the jail, waking everybody, including a couple of drunks in the next cell who complained bitterly about being disturbed. "Why the hell didn't someone call me? I could have told you . . ." he shouted over his shoulder as he came down the hall. I could see Barnes hovering at a discreet distance.

"Come on, come on," he growled as the jailer fumbled with the key. "Open up, you nitwit!"

I swung off my cot and slipped into the plastic slippers that had replaced my shoes. I was wearing a bright orange jail jumpsuit that was more than slightly too short in the crotch and, as a consequence, more than moderately uncomfortable.

"Where the hell are his clothes?" Ray rumbled at Barnes. "Go get 'em."

Barnes disappeared down the hall. Ray hurried into the cell as the door opened. "Are you all right, Beau?"

"Sure, Ray. I'm fine. It was a mistake, that's all."

"Why the hell didn't you call me?"

"They said you were celebrating your twenty-fifth anniversary and couldn't be disturbed."

"I'm disturbed, all right! You can bet your ass I'm disturbed!"

Ray hustled me down the hall and into a restroom where Barnes brought me my clothes. "How did you hear about it?" I asked.

"It was on the news. At eleven."

"Where, in Spokane?"

"That's where I saw it, but I'll bet it was all over. You should see the mob of reporters outside right now. The place is crawling."

"Great," I muttered. "That's just great."

He led me into his office, a place not much bigger than the cubbyhole the two of us had shared in the Public Safety Building in Seattle. This one boasted a polished wooden desk, not the institutional gray/green metal of Seattle P.D.

"Where is Evie?" I asked. "I'll bet she's pissed."

Ray grinned. "She was until she found out it was you. She drove back with me. Evangeline always had a soft spot in her heart for you, Beau. There's no accounting for taste. You hungry?" he asked.

Once he reminded me, I was actually far beyond hunger. "Starved," I told him.

He picked up the phone and dialed a number. I heard a phone ringing somewhere outside. "Go pick up a couple of chiliburgers from Marie's," he barked into the phone. "Tell her they're for me, with extra cheese and onions. And make a new pot of coffee. We're going to be a while."

He leaned back in his chair and folded his hands across his gradually widening girth. "What the hell is going on?"

Partway into my story, there was a knock on the door. A pretty young woman entered, carrying two steaming platters of chiliburgers. She left us with them and went out, returning with two freshly brewed cups of coffee. "Thanks, LeAnn," Ray murmured as she set a mug in front of him. LeAnn flashed him a shy smile.

"See there?" He grinned once the door closed behind her. "Around here I get some respect."

The two platters contained burgers smothered with thick chili, melted cheese, and chunks of chopped onions. Ray took a bite, followed by a sip of coffee. "Reminds me of the Doghouse," he said. "Sometimes I really miss that old place."

The Doghouse is a restaurant a few blocks from my condo in Seattle. Ray and I frequented it the whole time we were partners. I go there less often now that Peters and I work together.

I was ravenous. We had barely made a dent in the two platters when we heard a commotion outside. Ray's phone rang. "What is it?" He listened, then held the phone away from his ear and covered the mouthpiece.

"Somebody named Ames. Says he's your attorney."

"Ames! Ida must have found him."

"You want to see him?"

"Sure."

"And a guy named Peters?"

"Him too."

LeAnn opened the door. Ames strode purposefully into the room, talking as he came. "Look here, Chief Johnson, I demand to see my client at once!" Ames stopped abruptly when he spotted me sitting with a plate on top of Ray's desk scarfing down chiliburger as fast as I could shovel. Peters, directly behind Ames, almost rear-ended him.

"What the hell!" Peters exclaimed. The looks on their faces would have been comical if they hadn't been so serious. They had broken speed laws in two states, driving through the night to rescue me from jail, only to find me happily chowing down with the Chief of Police.

I stood up, wiping my mouth with a napkin. "Ralph, I'd like you to meet my former partner, Chief Ray Johnson. Ray, this is Ralph Ames, my attorney, and my new partner, Detective Ron Peters."

"You guys hungry?" Ray asked, indicating the half-consumed chiliburgers. "We could order a couple more. It would only take a minute."

Peters stifled a shudder of disgust and shook his head. Ames said a polite "no thank you" and got straight to the point. "What's going on?"

So I started the story again, from the beginning. I had reached almost the same point where Ames and Peters had made their entrance when the phone rang again. "No lie? He's here?" Ray said. "Send him in."

Hal Huggins came in. Ray showered him with the effusive cordiality one reserves for a late arrival at a class reunion. Once pleasantries were exchanged, the story reverted to square one. I was beginning to wish I had taped it on the first go down so I could turn on a machine and listen to it, rather than repeating it again and again. When I finally finished, there was a long silence.

Huggins spoke first. "I didn't figure him to be that smart," he said.

"Who?" I demanded. Obviously, Huggins knew something the rest of us didn't.

"Wilson. Don Wilson."

"Why him?" Peters asked.

"The calendar," Hal answered. "Ginger Watkins' calendar. Beau found it in a garbage can up at Rosario Sunday night. Wilson's prints are all over it."

"Where'd you get a copy of his prints?" I asked.

"From the F.B.I. Wilson served in the army."

Ray looked dubious. "How'd you get an F.B.I. report back so fast? Those things take months."

"You forget. Parole board members are political appointees. Governor Reynolds placed a call to the White House, and the F.B.I. found his prints in short order."

"So it is Wilson after all," I mused.

"Looks that way," Huggins agreed. "I'm getting a search warrant today." He turned on me. "You're sure he wasn't at the funeral?"

"I'm sure. Believe me, I looked."

Huggins was thinking aloud. "I wonder if we could request any of the television videotape and have someone go over it looking for him."

"Could be," Ray agreed. "Some of them are pretty good about it."

Hal continued. "He had to be there, must have followed you to the Red Lion. He saw you meet

Mona Larson and decided to add one more notch to his scorecard. And frame you in the process."

I thought back on my drive into Pasco. I could remember no cars on the road behind me, but I hadn't been looking. I shook my head. "I didn't see any," I said. "But why frame me? It doesn't make sense."

"Muddy the water a little," Huggins suggested. Peters nodded in agreement.

"Had you told anyone that you planned to stay overnight in Pasco?" Ray's homicide instincts were still good, even though he had kicked himself upstairs.

"No. How could I have told someone? I didn't make up my mind until I was almost here and decided to see you."

"Either he followed you or knew where Mona was staying," Peters put in. "How did you find out?"

"I asked one of the limo drivers over in Welton."

"And they told you?"

"They didn't act as if it was any big secret."

The phone rang again. Ray answered. "Put it through," he said. He switched on the speakerphone on his desk.

"Is this Chief Johnson?" a voice asked.

"Yes."

"This is Lee Hawkins. I'm an aide to Governor Reynolds. We're just confirming that you have a suspect in custody in the deaths of Mona and Sig Larson."

"We do not have a suspect."

"But we were told—" There was a pause. "What

about Ginger Watkins? We understand her death has been reclassified as a homicide."

"I repeat. We do not have a suspect in custody. In fact, I'll be calling a press conference at seven." Ray paused, turning his chair to consult an old pendulum clock that hung on the wall behind him. In Roman numerals the clock said the time was six-eighteen. "I'll be issuing the Pasco Police Department's official apology to Detective J. P. Beaumont."

"But the paper said—" Hawkins began.

"The paper's wrong," Ray interjected. "They often are, you know. Detective Beaumont is not a suspect in any of the cases, and we have no one else in custody."

"But the governor is ready to announce that he is withdrawing protection from the parole board."

"He'd better retract that withdrawal," Ray said into the phone. "In fact, if I were him, I think I'd extend protection to all parole board family members as well."

I waved a hand to get Ray's attention. "Ask him about the victim/witness protection program."

Ray shot me a questioning look, then shrugged. "Someone here is asking about the victim/witness protection program." I mouthed my question to Ray, and he repeated it into the phone. "Someone wants to know when it will be ready."

Hawkins knew exactly what we were talking about. "Tell him not until the next legislative session convenes in January."

"Is that all you need to know?" Ray asked me.

I nodded. Ray put down the phone. "What's that all about?"

"Maxwell Cole said Wilson thought an announcement on that program was imminent."

"Doesn't sound like it to me," Ray replied, getting up and opening the door. "LeAnn, let the members of the press know that I'll be holding a press conference at seven A.M. In the city council chamber."

He turned back inside the room, grinning. "You know," he said, "I think I'm actually going to enjoy this one."

CHAPTER 21

WE DID ENJOY THE PRESS CONFERENCE. FOR ONCE WE caught the media absolutely flat-footed. When I walked to the podium with Ray, you could have heard a pin drop.

Ray Johnson went straight to the microphones as naturally as if he had been doing it all his life. In ten months he had indeed become a police chief rather than a homicide detective. He was totally at ease.

"Before I issue my statement, I want to introduce you to some guests. On my right is Detective J. P. Beaumont of Seattle P.D. Next to him is Ralph Ames, Mr. Beaumont's personal attorney. Next to him is Detective Hal Huggins of the San Juan County Sheriff's Department.

"What I have to say is short and sweet. The City of Pasco and its Police Department deeply regret that Detective Beaumont here was mistakenly arrested as a suspect in the murder of Mona Larson. We wish to express our sincere apology for any inconvenience this may have caused.

"We are pursuing several leads in the Larson case and are, in fact, working on a major suspect. I repeat, Detective Beaumont is not that suspect. My understanding is that, after consulting his attorney, Detective Beaumont has agreed not to press false-arrest charges against this jurisdiction. However, some legal action may be contemplated. I believe Mr. Ames will be speaking to that issue. Mr. Ames?" He yielded the platform to Ralph.

Ralph Ames looks unassuming. He dresses conservatively and well, but he's a real tiger in negotiations or in court. He stepped to the bank of microphones.

"Thank you, Chief Johnson. Yes, I have advised my client that false-arrest proceedings would be ill-advised. However, in the next few days we will be reviewing all media coverage of my client's arrest to determine whether we have grounds for defamation of character or libel suits in conjunction with media treatment of the incident. It's possible some of the reports were in fact libelous."

Ames sat down, leaving the hall in utter silence. I happened to be looking directly at Maxwell Cole when Ames made his pronouncement. Max blanched visibly, his complexion turning a pukey shade of green.

Ray resumed the microphone. "Any questions?"

There were none immediately. No one was eager to leap into the breach. Eventually, one brave soul near the back tentatively raised his hand. "Do you believe there's a connection between Mona Larson's death and that of her husband?"

I could see Ray's smile coming a mile away. "No comment," he said.

"I understand the governor has now extended State Patrol protection to all family members of the parole board as well as to board members themselves. Is that true?"

"You'll have to ask Governor Reynolds about that."

"Can you tell us why Detective Huggins is here?"

Ray turned to Hal. "Hal," he said, "would you care to answer that?"

We were having a good time. I could see Peters in the back of the room with a broad grin plastered across his face.

"No comment," Hal said.

That got the message across. The reporters could see we were having fun at their expense. There were no more questions.

"Well then," Ray announced, "I guess we're finished."

We left the council chambers together. Back in Ray's office, we couldn't help chortling. We milled around for a few minutes, deciding on the next move. Ames and Peters had been up all night; they were worn out. They wanted to use my room at the Red Lion for a nap. My rented car had been impounded, pending investigation. The crime lab agreed to release it to Avis when they were done with it.

Peters left Ames and me in the station lobby and walked two blocks to get his Datsun. For the first time I noticed how haggard and drawn Ames looked. He was weary beyond words. "You look like hell," I said.

"You wouldn't win any prizes yourself," he returned, his voice cracking with exhaustion, now that his press conference adrenaline had worn off. He flopped down in one of the brown leather waiting-room chairs, resting his head on the wall behind him.

"We lost." His voice was low. I almost didn't hear him. It took a minute for me to realize what he was saying. At last I tumbled. "The custody hearing?"

He nodded. "We got an old-fashioned, dyed-in-the-wool conservative judge who figures only mothers are fit to raise children. No matter what."

I dropped into the chair beside him, chagrined that I hadn't given the custody hearing a moment's thought. I had never seen Ames so down. He's usually the steady one, the eye of the hurricane.

"I'm sorry," I murmured. "How's Peters taking it?" I felt responsible. Peters had pretty much given up the idea of ever getting his kids back until I butted in, encouraged him to fight for them, and told him we'd turn the problem over to Ames. I had watched Peters' hopes rise as the custody hearing neared. Now all that hope had come to nothing.

"Not well," Ames said. He looked at me closely. "Have you ever seen those two girls of his?"

I shook my head. "He was divorced long before we started working together."

"They're cute as buttons, both of them, and they were ecstatic to see him."

"What happens now?"

"I don't know. I need to think about it. The New

Dawn attorney made a couple of broad hints, but I'm not sure he's on the level."

Peters pulled up outside and honked. We went out. Ames crawled into the backseat while I slipped into the front with Peters. While we had been involved with the reporters, his face had been animated, alive. Now a morose mask covered his handsome features.

"I'm sorry about the hearing," I said.

He put the car in gear. "Win some, lose some," he said, feigning nonchalance. It didn't work.

"But the girls are all right?" I insisted.

"Sure," he flared. "They can't have shots because shots show a lack of faith. They live on a diet of brown rice and fruit. Milk is a luxury. They have it once a week. On Sundays." Peters' anger played itself out. He fell silent.

"So what do we do now, coach?" I asked, turning to Ames in the backseat.

He shook his head. "I don't know. We took our best shot. I'll have to see what other avenues are open." Ames didn't elaborate, and silence lengthened in the little car.

"Thanks for coming to get me, you guys," I said. "Both of you."

"It's okay," Peters responded. "My turn will come."

Peters and Ames went up to my room to get some sleep. I was wide-awake. I went down to the lobby. On one of the lobby chairs I found an abandoned *P.I.* Curiosity got the better of me, overcoming my natural aversion to newspapers. I wanted to see what had made Maxwell Cole turn green when Ames mentioned libel suits. By picking up a discarded paper, I could read the column without giving them the satisfaction of paying for it.

Max used the words "rogue cop" over and over. He might have coined the expression himself. The story didn't contain much that was different from the other garbage he's written about me over the years, except for the Mona Larson allegations.

I had a feeling this was one instance where Max's retraction would receive prominent coverage. If I were in his shoes and thought Ralph Ames was coming after me with a libel suit, I'd be looking for cover.

I did pick up one other piece of useful information from reading the newspaper. Ginger Watkins' funeral would be held on Thursday afternoon. No time or place was given, but included in the brief announcement was Ginger Watkins' father's name. He was listed as a resident of Centralia. Tucking that tidbit away in the memory bank, I worked the crossword puzzle in ten minutes flat. For me, that was something of a record.

My presence in the lobby created a continuing stir. Mary Kay ladies sporting May Kay nametags and Mary Kay faces wandered by, staring openly. When I finished the puzzle, I approached the desk and asked if I could use a house phone to bill some calls to my room. The clerk, a sweet young thing with long blond hair, dropped her pen when I announced who I was.

"I'll have to check," she stammered, retreating into a back office. She returned a few minutes later. "Mr. Dixon says that will be fine," she gulped.

I smiled. "If anyone asks, tell them I was framed."

She nodded, wide-eyed, and said, "Thank you." She was so flustered she forgot to tell me to have a nice day.

I gave the hotel operator my room information, and asked Centralia Information for Tom Lander's number.

"The number is 763-4427."

I hung up and dialed. There was no answer. I dialed Information again. I'm a longtime believer in the old phone-factory adage, "Let your fingers do the walking," except mine walk straight to directory assistance. This time I asked for a Union 76 station. Again I dialed.

A man answered, an older man whose voice was deep and whose speech was slow. "Tom's Seventy-six. Tom speaking."

"My name is J. P. Beaumont. I'm a friend of Ginger's. I wanted to let you know how sorry I am."

"Thanks." There was a pause. I could hear him struggling to gain control. "It was your car she was driving, wasn't it?" he asked.

I was surprised that he recognized my name. "That's right," I told him. "I understand the funeral is tomorrow afternoon."

"Yes," he said. "Two o'clock."

"I tried calling Darrell but was told the services will be private. I was sorry to hear that. I'd very much like to attend. Do you think that's possible?"

"Far as I'm concerned. I don't know where those characters get off making it private. Funerals should have lots of people. It shows folks care."

"Where is it? The paper didn't say."

"Two o'clock in the Congregational Church downtown. In the chapel."

"Could I come as your guest?"

"Sure."

"I'll meet you at the church. About one forty-five."

"How will I know you?"

"I'll be able to find you," I told him.

"If anybody tries to stop you, tell 'em Tom Lander said you could come."

The next call was to a florist in the Denny Regrade near my apartment. I ordered a bouquet of flowers for Ginger Watkins from Sig Larson. While I was at it, I called a Pasco florist and ordered flowers for Mona Larson, too. I told the clerk to check with the Pasco Police Department to see where and when they should be sent.

She took my credit-card number and wanted to know what to put on the card.

"Sign the card 'A friend,'" I told her, and let it go at that. I hoped like hell it would be the last batch of flowers I'd be ordering for a while.

CHAPTER 22

IT WAS POURING RAIN THE MORNING OF GINGER WATkins' funeral, the kind of hard, driving rain that demands umbrellas and confirms for unfortunate tourists that everything they say about Seattle's weather is true.

I rummaged through a closet searching for my one battered umbrella, a fold-up relic with two broken ribs and a bent handle. I hardly ever use it. Seattle's rain is usually no more than a misty drip, a dry drizzle that seldom merits use of what Seattleites fondly refer to as "bumbershoots," otherwise known as umbrellas.

Ames settled into the Westin Hotel. He had work to do and didn't want to be disturbed. Peters went back to the department where one of our Battered Wife/Dead Husband cases was about to come to trial. He spent the day locked up in a series of depositions.

J. P. Beaumont, still on vacation, was left to his own devices. I stopped by to thank Ida Newell for tracking down Ames and Peters.

"I was glad to," she assured me. "Why, the way they wrote you up in the paper was criminal. Are you going to sue them? They deserve it, especially that columnist fellow."

"Ames is looking into it," I told her. "I will if he tells me."

Later, I went to get a haircut. Virgil has been my barber ever since I moved to the city. I've followed him from his first little hole-in-the-wall shop to gradually more prosperous surroundings. Now he's located in an attractive brick rehab on the corner of Third and Vine.

Busy, Virgil waved me into a chair to wait. "It's about time you came in here," he griped. "Saw you on TV, and I says to Betty, I says, wouldn't cha know he'd go and get himself on TV when he needs a haircut? Pray God he doesn't tell who cuts his hair, know what I mean?"

I knew exactly what he meant. I was long overdue. Getting haircuts was one of the things I had neglected in the previous months of malaise.

Virgil finished with a retiree from the Grosvenor House and beckoned me into the chair. "Saved all those articles from the paper for you," he said. "Figured if you was out of town, you might not get 'em, you know?"

"Thanks, Virgil."

"Understand your car got wrecked, too."

"They're working on it up at Orcas. I guess it'll be all right, eventually."

He clipped away, humming a country-western tune under his breath. I know enough about music to know he hummed very badly. When he finished, it was only eleven. I walked over to Seventh and stopped at the Doghouse, more for the company than the coffee. Doghouse regulars greeted me as a celebrity. After all, the idea of a cop gone bad is a real attention-grabber. I sat in a back corner booth and did some serious thinking.

About Sig and Ginger and Mona. I had never met Sig while he was alive, but his death had profoundly affected me. Ginger and Mona I knew briefly, only a matter of hours, before they too were dead. The three deaths plagued me, weighed me down. I kept going back to Mona and Ginger. Different, yes, but both young and vital, and both cut down. Something about the two of them nagged at the back of my mind, but I couldn't put my finger on it. The harder I tried to capture it, the more elusive it became.

The fingerprints accused Don Wilson, but where was he? How was he outmaneuvering all efforts to find him? Was he operating alone or with help? These were questions without answers; or if the answers were there, I couldn't see them.

I ambled back to my apartment and made myself a peanut butter sandwich. Sometimes, out of respect for Peters, I occasionally add sprouts to the peanut butter, but the plastic bag of sprouts in the vegetable drawer of my refrigerator had deteriorated to a vile greenish goo. With the sandwich and a glass of milk, I settled in my recliner and dialed the San Juan County Sheriff's Department.

I more than half expected to be told that Huggins was in Seattle attending a funeral. Instead, he answered.

"Hal? Beau here. You coming to Seattle for Ginger Watkins' funeral?"

"I was going to ask you to go, Beau. I'm up to my neck around here. Think you can swing it?"

"Sure. Homer tried to keep me away, saying Senator Watkins wanted a small, private ceremony, but I got my name on the guest list anyway."

"How'd you manage that?"

"Her father invited me. As his guest."

Hal clicked his tongue. "Homer won't like that." I was sure that was true.

"I take it you've had a couple run-ins with the old man?"

"Like running into a brick wall. I've tried to talk to the husband, and he's stonewalled me at every turn."

"Homer has?"

"Yes, goddammit. Homer."

"Any word on Wilson?"

"Hell no."

"Keep me posted if you hear anything, Hal."

"Sure thing. The search warrant didn't come through yesterday. I'm hoping for this afternoon. And Beau?"

"What?"

"You do the same. If anything turns up at the funeral, give me a call."

I dressed and walked down Fifth to University. The Congregational Church is located at the corner of Sixth and University. The tiny chapel at the south end of the building pinch-hits as a downtown Catholic chapel for weekday noontime business Masses. Ecumenism is alive and well and living in Seattle.

Taking up a position in the lobby of the Park Place building across the street, I watched as people arrived or were dropped off at the church. The first black limo accompanied by two state patrolmen deposited Homer and his illustrious son, Senator Darrell Watkins. The second limo, also with an armed guard, brought Governor Reynolds.

When the third, unattended by official motorcycles dropped off an older, nondescript man who paused uncertainly on the sidewalk, I left my vantage across the street and approached him.

"Are you Tom Lander?" I asked.

"Mr. Beaumont?" he returned, his tone doubtful.

"Yes." Relief passed over his face. We shook hands. He looked down at his old-fashioned suit and dusted an imaginary fleck of lint from his arm.

"Big cities make me nervous," he said uncomfortably.

Homer materialized out of nowhere. "Hello, Tom," he said, elbowing me aside. "They're ready for us now." He scowled at me, trying to place me. "This is a private service, Mr.—"

"Beaumont," I supplied.

"It's all right, Homer," Tom said. "He's with me."

Homer Watkins gave Tom a constrained nod. "Very well," he said, walking stiffly toward the church. Tom Lander and I followed. The chapel couldn't have held more than forty people. An usher showed Tom to a front-row seat, while I took one near the door.

As people came in, I realized Peters would have recognized the political personalities from their pictures. I was an outsider, with no program or scorecard. My only hope of identifying the various guests was to lay hands on the guest book in the vestibule.

I did recognize the parole board, however. Led by Madame Bowdeen, they appeared far more nervous than they had been in Welton. Pressure was taking its toll. Had I been in their shoes, I would have been nervous, too. Looking around, however, I could have assured them with reasonable accuracy that Don Wilson was nowhere to be seen.

A young, bearded minister conducted the service in a smooth, professional way, telling us that Ginger Watkins was a person who had found herself in service to others. His comments made me hope that maybe he had at least a passing acquaintance with the lady.

As the eulogy began, my eyes were drawn to Darrell Watkins' heaving shoulders. He sat in the front row head bowed, silent sobs wracking his body. Next to him Tom Lander reached over and laid a consoling hand across his grieving son-in-law's shoulder.

I can stand anything but hypocrisy. Darrell was making an obvious play for sympathy, and Tom Lander fell for it—comforting the asshole who had screwed around on his daughter the whole time they were married, who had never bothered to give her the smallest satisfaction in lovemaking, who had kept her locked in a confining, stifling marriage, trotting her out on command when his rising political star demanded the display of a pretty wife.

It put a lump in my throat to realize I had given Ginger more pleasure by accident than that whining bastard had in eighteen years of marriage. I didn't hear the rest of the service. I seethed, watching Darrell's bitter, remorseful, crocodile tears. Too little too late. When the pallbearers carried the white coffin out the door, Darrell followed, his face contorted with anguish, supported on one side by Homer and on the other by Tom.

"That son of a bitch," I muttered to myself. I don't think anyone heard me.

Outside, people milled on the sidewalk, waiting for the funeral cortege to form and lead us to Woodlawn Cemetery. I paused as long as I could over the guest book, mentally noting as many names as possible. Then I waited by Tom's limo, expecting to tell him good-bye. Instead, he asked me to come along, to ride to the cemetery with him.

I didn't particularly want to go, but it was hard to refuse the old man. He was so isolated and alone that, in the end, I went.

We rode in silence. I was still seething over the funeral, and Tom seemed lost in thought. I stayed in the car during the graveside ceremony, refusing to be an audience to any more theatrics on Darrell's part. I used the time to jot down as many names as I could remember from the guest book.

Once we started downtown, I had myself fairly well in hand.

"What now?" I asked, initiating conversation.

Tom shrugged. "Darrell said I was welcome to come over to the house, but I don't know. I don't feel comfortable with all those mucky-mucks."

"Do you know most of those people?" I asked.

"No."

"How about a cup of coffee before you decide?"

He seemed to welcome the delay. He nodded. "That would be real nice."

The limo driver raised a disapproving eyebrow when I dismissed him, telling him to drop us at the Doghouse. I knew Tom would be far more at home there than in the rarefied atmosphere of the Four Seasons-Olympic or the Westin. He settled gratefully into a booth and smiled when the waitress, calling me by name, brought a coffee pot with the menus.

"I guess even big-city folks can be friendly," he said.

"This is my neighborhood, Tom. I live just a few blocks from here."

We both ordered coffee. I watched Tom shovel three teaspoons of sugar into his cup. "How did you know Ginger?" he asked, stirring absently.

"I only met her the day before she died," I said quietly, "but she helped me, more than I can say. She talked me through a problem I had been avoiding for months. I had to go today. I owed her."

"Ginger was like that," he said. He smiled sadly. "Always ready to help the other guy, always a friend in need. She was the kind of kid who dragged home broken-winged birds and expected me to fix them."

He paused. "They mostly died," he added. He stared disconsolately into his cup. "Did you know about the drinking?" he asked.

His question jarred me. "Yes."

"I thought she had beaten it. Sig Larson helped her. What made her start again?"

"I don't know." I didn't have a clue. I ached for him as he pondered Ginger's death. His child's death. Why had she died drunk? Someone had neglected to tell him that her death had been re-classified as a homicide, and I figured it wasn't my place to tell him. That was up to Hal Huggins.

"There was some gossip about them, you know," Tom continued, "Sig and Ginger. But I never put any store in it. Ginger wasn't like that."

"No," I agreed. "I'm sure she wasn't." The topic made me very uneasy. "Did you know she in-tended to file for a divorce?"

"She wouldn't have," he answered with firm conviction. "She might have threatened, to get Dar-rell to shape up, but she wouldn't have left him. We Landers hang in there. It's a family tradition."

I wanted to say that Ginger had hung in there more than long enough but I didn't. That would have been kicking him while he was down. Be-sides, it would have given away too much about Ginger and J. P. Beaumont. Better to let sleeping dogs lie. As far as Tom Lander was concerned, Ginger Watkins and I had been just friends. Noth-ing more.

"Do you want to go to the house?" I asked.

"Would you come along?" he countered.

He needed an ally, and I was it. "Why not?" I

said, rising. "Between the two of us, we should be able to handle that bunch."

We took a cab to the motel where Tom was staying, then we drove to Darrell Watkins' Capitol Hill mansion in a GMC pickup with "Tom's Union 76" emblazoned on the door.

CHAPTER 23

THE WATKINS MANSION SITS ATOP CAPITOL HILL WITH a spectacular view of downtown Seattle and Puget Sound. At the base of the hill, Interstate 5 bisects the city. As we rounded the circular driveway and drove past a gurgling fountain, I could imagine Homer and Darrell sipping cocktails and watching the freeway turn to a parking lot each evening as commuters tried to go home.

"Who lives here?" I asked.

"Homer used to," Tom said, "but now he's moved into a condominium."

"This is where Ginger lived, then?"

"For about a year," Tom answered.

The mansion itself was a spacious white colonial, set in a manicured, parklike setting. By the time we arrived, the drive was already teeming with a variety of trendy late-model vehicles. Ginger had described the last few years as a struggle for financial survival. That was why she had gone to work for the parole board. These surroundings gave no hint of encroaching poverty.

"They bought this from Homer?"

Tom shrugged. "Ginger never talked to me about their private affairs. They used to live over there someplace." He gestured down the back of Capitol Hill. "Nice enough place, if you didn't need to find it in the dark."

We rang the bell, setting off a multinote chime. A uniformed maid opened the door. "Yes," she said in a truculent manner designed to frighten off gate-crashers.

"Tom Lander."

"Oh, yes, Mr. Lander." She stepped back, opening the door in welcome. "You're expected."

We entered a foyer with an intricate parquet floor and a magnificent chandelier that hung from a vaulted ceiling far above us. Polished mahogany handrails lined a circular staircase. From behind a closed door to our left came a murmur of voices. "This way, please," the maid told us.

As the door opened, we heard a small burst of laughter from a group of people gathered near a fireplace at the opposite end of an enormous room. To one side an arched doorway led into the dining room where a lavish buffet supper lay spread across a gleaming tabletop.

A scatter of twenty-five or thirty fashionably attired people chatted amiably over drinks and hors d'oeuvres. It would have made a wonderful cocktail party. Any relation to a funeral was purely coincidental.

Our host was nowhere in sight, but Homer

broke away from the congenial group and came to meet us, a careful smile displayed on his face. "I'm glad you decided to come, Tom. You too, Mr. Beaumont. Care for a drink?"

"I'll have a beer," Tom said.

"McNaughton's and water," I answered. Homer nodded to the maid, and she disappeared.

Gravely solicitous, Homer guided Tom toward the fireplace. I trailed behind. "Let me introduce you to some of the folks, Tom. There wasn't enough time at the church."

Several of the names were preceded by "Representative" or "Senator." Clearly this was more a gathering of Darrell's peers than it was one of Ginger's friends. I tried keeping track of names, attempting to remember only those I hadn't already gleaned from the guest book.

Senator George Berry and Representative Dean Rhodes. Ray Johnson always told me that the secret to remembering names was creating colorful word pictures using the names. I had seen him do it for years. I made a stab at it.

Rhodes and Berry. I imagined several roads and saw them intersecting at one giant strawberry. Representative Doris Winters. I covered the strawberry with a giant load of winter snow. Berry, Rhodes, Winters. So far, so good. Representative Larry Vukevich. Shit. Vukevich! Race car driver. Okay. Vukevich racing past the berry. Senator Toshiro Kobayashi. I gave up.

The maid handed me my McNaughton's. I wandered away from the introductions to a chair beside a leaded-glass window. I needed Peters. He'd know all those people. The room was stifling. I belted that drink and ordered another when the maid walked past again.

The door at the end of the room opened, letting in a welcome rush of cool air. Darrell Watkins—accompanied by a handsome, smiling young brunette—entered the room. Tom's back was to the door. Homer, facing both Darrell and Tom, gave an almost imperceptible shake of his head over Tom's shoulder. Darrell caught the warning and spoke quietly to the woman, who melted smoothly into the crowd.

So this was the tender blossom, the competition Ginger had talked about, already marking her territory and claiming her prize. I downed my second McNaughton's and sauntered over to where the brunette had settled on a green velvet love seat. She crossed her legs, revealing a rather lengthy stretch of shapely thigh.

"Would you like a drink?" I asked.

She smiled up at me. "Sure. Vodka tonic."

I found the maid and placed the order. "It's for the young woman over there, I forget her name."

"Miss Lacy," the maid supplied helpfully.

"I'll have another McNaughton's," I said, returning my glass. Casually I meandered back to the sweet young thing on the love seat. "My name's Beau," I said. "You're Miss Lacy?"

"Darlene," she replied, smiling.

"Glad to meet you, Darlene. Mind if I sit down?"

"No." She moved to make room, demurely covering some of the visible thigh. "Are you a lobbyist?" she asked.

"No, I'm a friend of Ginger's."

"Oh," she said, a trifle too quickly.

I don't believe any of Ginger's friends had been expected.

"It's too bad about Ginger," Darlene continued. "I didn't know her personally, but everyone says she was a very nice person."

"She was," I replied.

The maid brought the drinks. Darlene sipped hers, eyes holding mine over the top of her glass.

"What do you do?" I asked.

"I'll go to Olympia in January. I'll be on staff, either with the lieutenant governor's office or the senate. It doesn't matter to me." She laughed. "A job's a job."

Homer caught sight of us sitting together and hastened toward the love seat. "Mr. Beaumont, I didn't mean to ignore you. Would you care for a sandwich, deviled eggs, salad?"

"No, thanks. I was just chatting with Miss Lacy here. She was telling me about her new job. Sounds like a good deal to me." I managed a hollow grin, hoping it adequately expressed my feelings on the subject.

"Have you met Darrell?" Homer asked.

"No," I replied. "Haven't had the pleasure." I took another belt of McNaughton's—for luck, maybe. Or maybe because the room was uncommonly hot and I was very thirsty. I set my empty glass on a polished table and followed Homer to where Darrell was waxing eloquent with the lady from my memory word picture. Snow, I decided fuzzily. That was her name.

Homer caught Darrell's attention. "Darrell, this is Mr. Beaumont. It was his—"

Darrell turned toward me, his smile turning sallow. "Oh yes, Mr. Beaumont. I hope your Porsche isn't ruined."

"No. It'll be fine. It takes time. I wanted to express my condolences," I said.

"Thanks," he said, his face assuming the grieved air that had offended me at the funeral. "So nice of you to stop by." I resisted the temptation to smack that phony look right off his face. Homer steered Representative Snow away from us, leaving Darrell and me together. Darrell signaled the maid for two more drinks. "It's scary," he said, turning back to me. "First Sig, then Ginger, now Mona."

I was sure he knew all about Don Wilson. Considering the family's close ties to the governor's office, that was hardly surprising.

"I hope to God they catch that guy before he gets anyone else," Watkins continued.

"Me too," I said. "We usually do, sooner or later."

He gave me an appraising look. "We? Is Seattle P.D. involved too?" he asked.

"No, not officially. I'm here because Ginger and I were friends." The maid broke in to deliver drinks. My series of McNaughton's had come in rapid enough succession that I was getting a little buzz.

"I don't recall her mentioning your name." It did my heart good to note the subtle shift in Darrell's manner, a wariness. I was something he didn't expect. How about that! Maybe Ginger had some secrets too, asshole. How d'you like them apples? The thoughts bubbled unspoken through my new glass of McNaughton's.

"You can't tell about women," I said jokingly. "Ginger and I go back a long way. We ran into each other up at Orcas by accident; but then, life is full of little surprises, right?"

"Right," he replied lamely.

The door opened, and a new trio of people entered. Darrell excused himself to greet them. The room had grown more crowded. There were far more people sipping drinks than had been at the chapel earlier.

The coffee, the McNaughton's, and the water asserted themselves. Searching for a restroom, I wandered into the kitchen, slipping through the swinging door when a maid carried a new tray of deviled eggs into the dining room.

The kitchen, massive and polished, was a combination of old and new. An ancient walk-in refrigerator covered one wall while, on the other side of the room, a long commercial dishwasher steamed under the hand of a heavyset woman rinsing a tray of plates. On a third wall sat a huge eight-burner range, while the middle of the room held a sleek stainless steel worktable laden with food. The woman looked up from the dishwasher and saw me at the doorway. "Can I help you?" she demanded.

"I'm looking for a restroom."

"No restrooms here," she stated flatly. "Upstairs. On the right."

Chastised, I retreated the way I had come, threading my way through the chatting guests to the foyer and up the stairs. A dizzying trip up the circular stairway convinced me I had had too much to drink. The first likely-looking door I found was locked. I tried the next floor. Bingo.

I had already flushed and was splashing my

face with cool water in an effort to sober up when I heard voices in the hall outside. I'm sure it never occurred to anyone that a guest might have ventured all the way upstairs in search of a restroom. I opened the door and stepped into the hall. "It looks great, Darrell," a voice was saying from a room farther up the corridor. "The fact that it was private makes it that much better."

"That's what we pay you for, Sam." I recognized Darrell Watkins' voice. "That's what a campaign manager is supposed to do."

"Name familiarity's way up, up five points over last week. That's a tremendous change this late in the campaign. I'd say you have it in the bag."

"I'd better get back downstairs. Leave that paper up here when you go," Darrell said. "We wouldn't want Tom to stumble across it before he leaves."

I was standing outside the door when Darrell Watkins stepped into the hall. He almost ran over me.

"You son of a bitch!" I muttered.

"What are you doing up here?"

"Taking a leak," I said.

"I think maybe you'd better go, Mr. Beaumont."

"I'll go when I'm good and ready, asshole."

Another man appeared behind Darrell, a young blond man in casual clothes who looked as if he had just stepped out of a racquet club advertisement. Behind both of them stood the newly hired Darlene Lacy.

"Who's this, Darrell?" the other man asked.

I answered. "The name's Beaumont, Detective J. P. Beaumont, Seattle P.D." I was riding a boozy wave of moral indignation. "So you ran a poll, did you?" I sneered. "Figured the voters would like it better if you made it look quiet and dignified. That's how Ginger said you'd handle the divorce, too."

"I don't know what you're talking about."

"Oh yes you do. You got the newspapers to bury the story, but Ginger was filing on Monday morning."

"Shut up," Darrell said.

"I won't shut up. How much does it cost to buy the press?"

"You're drunk, Mr. Beaumont. You'd better leave."

"I'm more pissed than I am drunk."

"Get out," he snarled. He moved toward me, reaching out to put a hand on my shoulder.

"Get your hands off me!" I flung him away. What happened next was in slow motion. I reached for him, wanting to grab him by the shoulders and shake his teeth out. Instead, I lost my balance and slipped, shoving him backward toward the stairs. He fell, catching his face on the heavy mahogany ball at the top of the handrail. When he straightened, blood spurted from his nose.

"I said get out!"

"I'm going."

"What's happening up there?" Homer called from below.

Darrell held a hanky to his nose. "Nothing," he replied. "Mr. Beaumont here has had one too many."

I charged down the stairs, shoving my way past Homer in the foyer. The air outside the house was sharp and cold, with a stiff breeze blowing off the water. It cleared the smoke-laden air from my lungs and cut through the haze of McNaughton's in my head, enough so I was shocked by what I had done. Taking a drunken swing at Darrell Watkins would add credence to the J. P. Beaumont legend—the hotheaded, killer-cop myth promoted by Maxwell Cole and his cohorts.

I took a deep breath of the biting, cold air. "You're not doing a whole hell of a lot to live it down," I told myself aloud.

A horn honked beside me, startling me out of my reverie. Tom Lander's GMC pulled up beside me. Tom leaned over and rolled down the window. "Get in," he ordered.

I did.

"What happened back there?" he asked, putting the pickup in gear.

"I had to get the hell out of there. They were driving me crazy."

"Me too," he said, accepting what I said at face value. "Where to?"

I directed him to my building at Third and Lenora. I didn't invite him up. I was sure he'd be reading all about it in the morning edition, and I didn't feel like doing any explanations beforehand.

"Thanks for coming along," Tom said as I opened the door to get out. "I'm glad at least one of Ginger's friends was there."

Nodding in agreement, I climbed out onto the sidewalk, then I reached back into the truck to shake his hand. "Your daughter was a very special lady, Tom. I'm sorry she's gone."

"Thanks," he said. He drove away without further comment.

Words are never enough in a situation like that. Actions were what was needed. I turned and walked into the lobby of the Royal Crest.

By then I was stone-cold sober.

CHAPTER 24

FRIDAY MORNING. MY LAST DAY OF VACATION, AND I was hung over as hell. It seemed like all I had done was drink and go to funerals, a regular bus-man's holiday. I called Ames to invite him to breakfast. Reluctantly, he agreed.

"I'm very busy, you know," he said crossly as we picked up our menus. "I'm working on the condominium thing, and I'm still negotiating with New Dawn. What do you want?"

"Well," I parried, "as my attorney I thought you ought to know I was in a mild altercation with a Washington State senator last night. Bloodied his nose, probably blacked his eyes. . . . Accidentally," I added.

Ames put down his menu. "This is a joke, right?"

"Wrong. No joke."

"Maybe you'd better tell me about it."

For an answer, I handed him a copy of a newspaper. Ames read silently:

"In a private funeral ceremony attended only

by family and close friends, State Senator Darrell Watkins said a tearful farewell to his wife Ginger yesterday afternoon.

"Mrs. Watkins, a member of the Washington State Parole Board, died in a one-vehicle accident on Orcas Island, Saturday, October 25. Her funeral services were delayed to allow fellow board members to travel to Welton for the funeral of another board member, Sig Larson, who was the victim of a homicide the previous day.

"Initially thought to be the underdog against longtime incumbent, Lieutenant Governor Rod Chambers, Sen. Watkins has seen his political base increase even as he has faced personal tragedy. Public-opinion polls now show him running neck and neck with Lt. Governor Chambers.

"A Watkins family spokesman said services for Mrs. Watkins were kept private to avoid a 'sensationalizing press from taking advantage of an unfortunate situation.'

"Senator Watkins, in a terse statement issued late last night, said that he is canceling all campaign appearances for the remainder of the week."

Ames looked up from the paper. "Don't I remember reading that it was his wife's wish that he continue with the campaign? When did you break his nose?"

"Last night. After the funeral. I'll bet he's not a pretty sight this morning."

"No wonder he canceled his public appearances."

"That sorry son of a bitch deliberately staged a 'private ceremony' in order to gain the sympathy vote." I relayed to Ames the conversation I had overheard.

"This the first you've been around politics?" Ames inquired dryly. "That's how it works. Will he bring charges?"

"I don't know. That's why I called you."

"Were there any reporters there at the time?"

"You mean when he fell? Not that I know of."

"I'm surprised they're downplaying it like this. By all rights, you should be plastered all over the front page for the second time this week."

"Maybe I just got lucky," I suggested.

Ames shook his head. "I doubt it. They probably won't go for criminal charges, but my guess is we'll be hearing from their attorneys. They'll sue for damages."

"Wonderful," I mumbled.

"Considering their financial situation, they'd be crazy not to."

"What do you mean?"

Just then the waitress brought our food and put it in front of Ames. He had taken a file folder out of his briefcase. He sighed, put the folder down, and picked up his fork. "You know which of the condominium projects are in trouble, don't you?"

"I wasn't asking about that. You said it wouldn't make sense for them not to sue me."

"Beau, listen to me. I'm trying to explain. The two that are in trouble are Belltown Terrace and Waterview Place. Belltown Terrace is theirs. Scuttlebutt says the project will go on the auction block by the end of the year unless they pick up some new capital. They might go for a fat out-of-court settlement in order to pick up some quick cash."

"Slow down. You're talking about two different things."

"I'm talking money."

"Look, Ralph, if they're going bankrupt, then I'd better not get involved. I didn't realize they were almost to sheriff's-sale time."

Ames looked at me sadly and shook his head. "You haven't been listening."

"Yes, I have. Why would I want to buy a unit from someone who's about to go belly-up? More specifically, why would I want to buy in a building owned by someone who's about to sue me?" Waiting for Ames' answer, I chased a slippery chunk of egg across my plate with a piece of whole wheat toast. Peters had convinced me to give up white bread, not cholesterol.

"A unit!" Ames exploded. "Who's talking about a unit? I'm talking about the building. You said you wanted to invest. It would be a great write-off. You rent the units for five to seven years; then go in, do some remodeling, and sell them. It's a heck of a good deal."

I put down my toast. I put down my fork. "You were supposed to be looking for a condominium for me to buy."

"The penthouses in Belltown aren't sold. You could live there, but in order to keep our noses clean with the IRS, you'd have to pay rent back to the corporation."

"Ames, I can't buy a whole building."

"Well, not by yourself. I can get you in with a syndicate. I know of one in the market for just this kind of deal, five of you altogether. What do you think?"

I didn't know what to think. I knew my inheritance was considerable, but I still hadn't gotten a handle on the magnitude of it. I kept trying to get my arms around it.

"You do what you think is best," I said to Ames. "You know a hell of a lot more about this stuff than I do, but I can't see myself doing business with Homer and Darrell Watkins, especially after last night."

"Forget last night. We'll be dealing with the bank, not Homer and Darrell. The FDIC is ready to eat the bank alive if they don't get out from under this loan. Want to go over the financial papers?"

I shook my head. "That's your job."

Ames patted his mouth with his napkin and returned the file folder to his briefcase. "Very well," he said, rising. "I've got to run. I'm expecting a call from The Dalles."

"How's that going?" I asked.

He shrugged. "I'm not talking. I don't want to get Peters' hopes up, but it's not a dead issue."

He left me in the restaurant. After I paid the bill, I walked down Second to Belltown Terrace. It was a twenty-story building with a small grassy courtyard setting it back from the street. The sign said "Model Open," so I went inside. A real estate lady came down to meet me. She showed me through the entire project, from the indoor pool and exercise room to the outdoor racquetball court and running track. A gas barbecue grill sat on a small patio near the party room.

I lost the barbecue and also my only form of cooking expertise when Karen and I split up. The number of decent barbecued ribs I'd had since then could be counted on one hand. I decided that if Ames could negotiate my way into the building, it might not be such a bad idea.

Taking the woman's card, I promised to call her once I made up my mind. Back on the street, I dealt with the problem of my last day of vacation. The bug was on me. Jurisdictions notwithstanding, I had to do something.

I didn't bother going back to Avis. Considering my track record, they wouldn't be eager to rent me another car. I tried Hertz instead. I drove north on I-5 and took the Lynnwood exit. Using the phone book, I located Don Wilson's address. When I got there, I found that both the front and back doors were secured with police padlocks. Huggins had made the place off-limits. A quick check of the neighborhood showed no surveillance vehicles.

Wilson's house was set back by itself on a wooded lot. The nearest neighbor was a good half-block away in a tiny clapboard cottage. I walked to it and knocked. After a time the door inched open the length of a security chain.

"Yes?" a woman's voice demanded.

I held one of my cards up to the door so she could see it. "I need to ask a couple of questions about Mr. Wilson."

"You and everybody else," the woman grumbled, but the door closed long enough for her to unfasten the chain. "What do you want to know?"

The woman was more than middle-aged, with a white apron spread across an ample figure. With an exasperated glare, she pointed her index finger at her ear and made several quick circular gestures.

"What else do you want to know?"

"Crazy enough to kill someone?"

"Wouldn't you be if you was him? You know what happened to his wife and kid."

"When did you last see him?"

"Look," she said, "I'm trying to cook dinner. I don't have all day. I already said this once. Do I have to say it again?"

"It would help," I said.

She sighed. "Well, follow me into the kitchen, then—before I burn it up." Opening the door wide, she motioned me inside. I followed her into a small kitchen where she was peeling vegetables for what looked like a stew. "Last I saw him was Friday morning. He was unloading signs from his car."

"Unloading?"

"That's what I said. Unloading. Packing them into the house."

It struck me as odd. If he was on his way to Orcas to demonstrate, he should have had his signs along. "Why?" I said, more to myself than to the woman.

"How should I know?"

I spent a while longer in the steamy kitchen, but other than stoutly defending Don Wilson's right to go off the deep end, the woman told me nothing more of consequence. I drove back into Seattle with the unsettling feeling that I knew both more and less than I had known before.

By the time I got home, late-afternoon sun had broken through the clouds. I called Peters at the Department.

"How's it going?" I asked.

"I hate depositions," he answered.

"What are you doing tonight?"

"Oh, I don't know. I thought I'd hang around here long enough to wait out the traffic." Friday afternoon rush-hour traffic is worse on Seattle's two floating bridges than it is during the rest of the week, as weekend travelers join regular commuters trying to cross Lake Washington to get to the suburbs and beyond.

"Why don't you stop by and have dinner? Maybe Ames could join us."

"What kind of food?" Peters asked.

I hadn't planned that far in advance. "I don't know."

"Tell you what," Peters offered. "I'll stop by the market and pick up something."

He didn't fool me for a minute. That way he could control the menu. "Sure," I said. "That'll be fine."

Hal Huggins called right after I talked to Peters. "Where've you been? I've been calling all afternoon."

"Out," I said without explanation. "What do you want?"

"We searched Wilson's house," Huggins said. "All his picketing stuff was there—the signs, the brochures, the petitions. Nothing out of the ordinary except one thing."

"What's that?"

"He left a half-chicken thawing on the counter, like he planned to be home in time for dinner. And he didn't leave food out for his cat. By the time we got there, the cat had helped himself to the chicken."

"Smart cat," I said.

"Get serious, Beau. What does that say to you?"

"He didn't expect to be gone long."

"Yeah," Huggins agreed.

We talked a few more minutes before my Call Waiting signal buzzed me to say Peters was downstairs. He carried a box of marinated vegetables, a pound of cooked spinach tortellini, and some fresh sole that he proceeded to bake in my oven. Ames turned us down cold, so it was only Peters and I who sat down to a gourmet dinner overlooking Seattle's nighttime skyline. Peters glanced at his watch as we finished eating.

"I'd be lucky to be home now, even if I left right at five. It takes an hour on Fridays. Longer if there's an accident on the bridge."

"Why don't you move downtown?" I asked.

A shadow crossed his face. "I keep thinking I'll get the girls back. You can't raise kids in the city."

I told him then about what I had seen at Belltown Terrace—the running track, the pool, the facilities. "You could raise kids there," I told him, "and not have to spend half your life commuting in a car."

"I don't have the kids. . . . Probably never will," he replied bitterly. "Besides," he added, "I don't have that kind of money."

Respecting Ames' wishes, I said nothing about continuing negotiations in The Dalles.

Our evening was pleasant. I told Peters about

the reception at the Watkins mansion, including my taking a swing at Darrell Watkins. I tried unsuccessfully to recall the names of some of the people there. Vukevich was the only one I could remember for certain. "There was a Representative Snow, I think, and maybe somebody named Lane."

Peters shook his head. The names didn't sound familiar. So much for using word pictures to enhance my memory. You can't teach an old dog new tricks.

CHAPTER 25

Ernie Rogers called at six forty-five Saturday morning. The car was ready; would I like him to bring it to Seattle?

"Sure, but—" I thought about the Porsche and wondered how he'd handle it. Ernie heard the pause and understood it.

"My wife will drive," he said.

"Well, sure. Do you know your way around Seattle?"

"Some."

I gave him directions, describing the electronic gate into the garage on Lenora at the base of the building. "The Genie may not work now that it's been wet."

"It should," Ernie said. "I fixed it. We'll be there early afternoon."

"How will you get back to Orcas?"

"We're going to make a weekend of it. My mother-in-law is keeping the kids. We won't catch the bus back to Anacortes until Monday afternoon.

Jenny wants to do some shopping. We thought we'd turn this into a mini-vacation."

"Do you have reservations somewhere?" I asked.

"No, we'll check into a motel after we get to town."

"Do I owe you any more money?" I asked, wondering if I should be prepared to write another check.

"As a matter of fact," he answered, "you'll be getting back some change."

"I'll look for you when you get here," I said. "My parking space is number forty-eight. After you park, come on up to 1106. We'll go to lunch."

"Sounds great."

Peters called from home while I was drinking my second cup of coffee. He was reading his morning paper. "Somebody blabbed about the search warrant. I'll bet Huggins is pissed. The paper names Wilson as the major suspect in both Larson murders. Who's the leak?"

Peters and I had hammered away on Don Wilson's thawing chicken over drinks after dinner. "Does the article mention Ginger Watkins?" I asked.

"Not so far."

"I've gotta go, Peters." I hung up and dialed Hal Huggins' number in Friday Harbor. It was busy and stayed that way. I tried the Sheriff's Department. "I'm sorry. Detective Huggins is unavailable."

"This is Detective Beaumont from Seattle. I'll hold. He'll talk to me."

I was right. Hal came on the line a minute

later. "Sorry to keep you waiting, Beau. This place is a zoo. We've got reporters hanging from the ceiling fans. Somebody told them about the search warrant."

"Who?"

"How the hell should I know?"

"Pomeroy, maybe?" I asked. He was my first choice.

"I don't think so. I asked him. He denied it six ways to Sunday. I think he's telling the truth. Musta been somebody else."

A voice spoke to Hal in the background, and I heard his muffled reply. "Hey," he said into the phone. "I've gotta run. The press is eating me alive. I'll let you know if anything breaks."

I put down the phone and sat for a while. Eventually I called Ray in Pasco. He was at home. He sounded glad to hear from me.

"What did they find in the Rabbit?" I asked him after the niceties.

"Not in the Rabbit, on it. Mona's hair, and fibers from her jacket on the front bumper."

"No fingerprints?"

"Yours, smudged. Must have worn gloves."

"Great. Terrific. When's Mona's funeral?"

"It's over. Her brother brought in a bunch of Hell's Angels types from Idaho, cowboys on motorcycles. I went to the service. Except for the brother and his friends, no one was there."

At least I had sent flowers.

I made a late lunch reservation for the Space Needle. It's one of Seattle's best-known tourist attractions. The combination of food and view are unbeatable.

As I hung up the phone after making the reservation, I congratulated myself. It would be the first time I had visited the Space Needle since that night months ago when I went with Anne Corley. Maybe I was finally getting better.

I said a small thank-you to Ginger Watkins wherever she was.

Downtown is deserted on weekends. All the business people are home in the suburbs, mowing lawns and raking leaves. Farther downtown where the stores are, there are still crowds of shoppers, but not up in the Denny Regrade where I live. The flat stretches of the Regrade form a quiet village.

Actually, the Regrade used to be as hilly as the rest of Seattle, but sometime during the early nineteen-hundreds, a city engineer named R. H. Thompson got carried away with his work and decided to sluice Denny Hill into Puget Sound. He wanted flat, and he got it; only the Depression stopped him before he got started on Queen Anne Hill. That kind of nonsense wouldn't get past environmentalists today, but it did then. Now the Denny Regrade is flat as a pancake.

Expansion from downtown, also stopped by the Depression, left the Regrade as it is today, a neighborhood of condominiums and apartment buildings interspersed with offices and small businesses. New luxury high-rises and flea-bitten hotels coexist in relative harmony.

I opened the door to my solitary lanai and went out to soak up some quiet morning sun. I needed to think.

A couple of things were right at the top of my list. For one, why would the killer have carefully worn gloves to drive my car when he had blatantly left prints all over Ginger's calendar? Of course, he didn't expect the calendar to be found, but still, it was taking a hell of a chance.

And the half-chicken bothered me. My mother was a firm believer in "Waste not, want not." The idea of thawing meat when you had no intention of coming home didn't make sense. And how had he disappeared into thin air? And why had he unpacked all his protest materials before he left for Orcas?

Questions. Always questions with no answers. And reporters buzzing around with their own sets of questions, never having brains enough not to print everything they knew, or thought they knew.

Stymied, I went back inside to shower, shave, and dress. I was ready and waiting when Ernie and Jenny showed up at one-thirty. Jenny Rogers was a smiling woman, several years younger than Ernie. They were a matched set. Her flaming red hair and blue eyes made them look more like brother and sister than husband and wife. She had a pregnant shelf of tummy that could easily have held a coffee cup and saucer.

"Any trouble with the car?" I asked.

Jenny giggled. "Some," she replied.

I looked anxiously at Ernie, afraid something was wrong with the Porsche that he hadn't been able to fix. He grinned. "She had a hard time steering," he explained. "The baby kept getting in the way."

Sports cars are not necessarily built for pregnant drivers.

We decided to walk from my place to Seattle Center. I guess I had never noticed all the curb cuts in the sidewalks. Ernie wheeled along, easily keeping pace with Jenny and me.

They found the Space Needle enchanting. Jenny had never been there, not even on the observation deck. She was delighted with the revolving restaurant, exuberant about the food. Her enjoyment was contagious. We had a great time. Eventually, however, conversation turned to business. Ernie reached in a pocket and pulled out an envelope which he handed to me. In it was a check for five hundred dollars, made out in my name. "What's this?" I asked.

"The job didn't take nearly as long as I thought," he answered. "That's your change."

I remembered Barney at Rosario telling me that Ernie was the best. I had doubted it then, but now I believed it. I'd checked, and couldn't have gotten the work done nearly that fast or cheap anywhere else. Taking a pen, I endorsed the check back to Jenny Rogers and handed it to her.

She was stunned. "Why?" she asked.

"For driving the car back, saving me a day of traveling. And for the baby. Ernie said you wanted to go shopping."

She looked at him quickly, questioning whether she should accept it. He shrugged, and she put the check in her purse.

"Thank you," she said.

Ernie looked uncomfortable. He changed the subject. "Did you see the paper this morning?"

"I didn't see it, but I heard."

"The paper said it's because the parole board

let that Lathrop guy out and he killed Wilson's wife."

I shrugged. "Could be," I said.

"Well, they still shouldn't have fired Blia," Jenny said. Ernie shot a quick silencing glance in Jenny's direction. "Well, they shouldn't have," she insisted, with a defiant shake of her head. "It's not fair."

"What's not fair?"

"Blia Vang was a maid working at Rosario who got fired because she lost her keys. They said someone found them and used them to break into Mrs. Watkins' room."

I felt as if I had wandered into a conversation twenty minutes late. "Who's this again?"

"Blia Vang. A friend of ours." Jenny's blue eyes smoldered with indignation. "Somebody stole her keys, so they fired her."

"When?"

Ernie broke in with an explanation. "Blia worked the day that man was murdered. She left her keys on a cart, and someone took them. The hotel claimed she was careless and fired her."

My mind raced. Sig's key to Ginger's room had never been found, but the fact that the maid's keys had been stolen the same day was too much of a coincidence. My gut told me the missing keys were somehow related to the murder.

"Does Hal Huggins know?"

Ernie shrugged. "I don't know. She was too scared to say anything. The manager didn't find out until yesterday. When he did, he fired her on the spot."

"But has Hal talked to her?"

"I doubt it. She took off on the next ferry," Jenny interjected. "She would have been long gone before he knew."

I felt a mounting surge of excitement. Maybe she had seen someone in the hall, someone she could identify. "A material witness can't just walk away. She'll have to tell the authorities what she knows."

"She won't," Jenny said.

"She has to. She could be charged with obstruction of justice."

Jenny gave a sharp laugh. "Try explaining obstruction of justice to an Hmong refugee. That's why she ran away. She's scared. She almost died when they took her fingerprints. She won't talk to a cop."

"Does anyone know where she went?"

Jenny and Ernie exchanged glances. "Maybe," Jenny said reluctantly. "But I tell you, she won't talk to you or Hal either. She's scared."

It occurred to me suddenly that Jenny and Ernie Rogers seemed to be far more than casually involved. "Wait a minute. How do you know so much about her?"

Jenny looked shyly at Ernie. He answered with a mildly reproving glare. "We work with the refugees," he explained. "An Hmong saved my life while I was in 'Nam. I'm the one who got her the job at Rosario in the first place. I feel pretty bad about it. We both do."

I was like an old, flop-eared hound stumbling across a fresh scent. "Would you help me find her?" I asked, attempting to contain my elation. Their heads shook in silent unison.

"I'll get an interpreter," I argued. "I'd be off duty, no uniform, no badge. This could be important. She may have seen someone or something nobody else saw."

Jenny's manner softened when she understood I believed Blia innocent of any wrongdoing. Ernie remained adamant.

"There might be a reward," I added as a last resort.

"She won't talk to you," Ernie said. "Even if you find her, she won't talk."

"She would if you went along to translate," Jenny suggested. Ernie gave Jenny a black look, but his resistance was weakening. He sat for a long time, looking at me, weighing the pros and cons.

"You're sure she wouldn't get into any trouble?" he asked.

"I guarantee it."

"In that case," Ernie Rogers said gruffly, "I guess it couldn't hurt to talk to her."

CHAPTER 26

I COULD HARDLY WAIT TO GET HOME. JENNY HAD TOLD me there was a possibility Blia Vang was staying with relatives in Seattle. I wanted to start looking for her.

While Ernie waited in the cab, Jenny and I retrieved luggage from the Porsche. In the elevator, Jenny thanked me again for both the money and lunch. It made me uneasy. Being an anonymous benefactor is a hell of a lot easier than looking gratitude in the face.

"Buy something nice for the baby," I said, patting her tummy.

She smiled and stood on tiptoe, leaning over her pregnant belly to give me a peck on the cheek as the elevator door opened to let her off. She gave me the name of a motel near Green Lake in case I needed to get in touch with them.

Back in my apartment I called Detective Henry Wu, a third generation Seattleite of Chinese extraction. Hank came to homicide from the University of Washington with a major in police science and a minor in Far Eastern studies.

"Hey, Beau," he said, when I told him who was calling. "When you coming back?"

"Monday," I said. "But I need your help today. What do you know about Hmong refugees here in town?"

"A very tightly knit group," he replied. "They don't trust outsiders. With good reason, mostly."

"Do you have any friends there?"

"I've got an ear there," he allowed. "Not a friend. Why? What do you need?"

"There's a young woman, used to be a maid up at Rosario. Her name is Blia Vang. They fired her for losing a set of keys. I need to talk to her."

"What about? Is this official police business?"

"More like unofficial police business. Remember old Hal Huggins?"

"Sure."

"He's working a homicide on Orcas. This woman may have a lead for him. She took off before he could talk to her. Rumor has it she's in Seattle, staying with relatives. I've got an interpreter, someone she knows, a fellow named Ernie Rogers. I need to ask her a couple questions. Off the record. No badge, no uniform, nothing. There's even a reward, if that helps."

"Money isn't going to make a hell of a lot of difference if she has to talk to a cop."

"Don't tell her I'm a cop. Say a friend of Ernie Rogers needs to talk to her."

"I'll try," Hank agreed, "but don't hold your breath. Is that all?"

"Well, actually, there's one more thing."

"Shoot."

"My interpreter is in town until four-thirty Monday afternoon. That's when the bus leaves for Anacortes."

"Jesus Christ, Beau! This is Saturday."

"Call somebody. Leave a message. It's important."

"Right," he said sarcastically. "The Hmong all have phones and folks to take messages. I'll see what I can do."

"Thanks, Hank. I appreciate it."

I hung up. One of the hardest things about this business is waiting. You put an idea out into the ether, then you wait to see if anything happens. Television detectives notwithstanding, a lot of times nothing does.

On Saturday, nothing happened. I finally got around to unpacking the suitcases I had brought home and stashed in the bedroom without opening. On the table beside my recliner, I discovered the bill from Rosario. Ames had impressed on me the value of saving copies of all bills as potential weapons in future battles with the IRS. I stowed the bill away in a shoe box reserved for that purpose, your basic low-tech-filing system.

I tried Ames. Since it was cocktail hour on Saturday evening, I thought he might be persuaded into coming over. No dice. Claimed he was in the middle of something vital and couldn't take a break. More than a little put out, I walked across the street to the Cinerama and watched the original uncut version of *Oklahoma* for the seventh time.

Afterward, I went home, to bed but not to sleep.

Thoughts of Ginger Watkins and Mona Larson haunted me. There was a common denominator, but I couldn't put my finger on it.

It was after three when I fell asleep. The phone rang at six. It was Ames—bright, cheerful, energetic Ames—calling on the security phone from the lobby. "Let me in, Beau. I'm downstairs."

I staggered into the kitchen and started coffee. When I opened the door, Ames bounced into the apartment, brimming over with excitement. "I have the deal put together. The other syndicate members want to know if you're going to buy the penthouse before the purchase of the building, or if you want to rent it back." Words tumbled out in a torrent.

"In that case, you wouldn't be able to buy it outright for five years, but considering the tax write-offs on the building, you needn't worry."

"Wait a goddamned minute here, Ames! Do you mean to tell me you woke me up at six o'clock on Sunday morning because you put a real estate package together?"

Chastised, Ames accepted a proffered cup of coffee. "I had to wait for one guy's plane to land in Japan."

"Which building?" I asked. "The one with the barbecue?"

"Belltown Terrace," he said.

"Okay, that's the one with the grill. What's next?"

"Tomorrow I make them an offer."

I sat down opposite Ames with my own coffee cup. "I have a hard time seeing myself as a real estate magnate."

"It'll grow on you," he assured me, smiling.

"What do I do with this?" I asked, indicating the small apartment that had been my first and only haven after the painful split from Karen and the kids.

"Sell it, or keep it and rent it out. It's up to you."

I remembered when the mortgage on the unit plus the child-support I sent Karen had been an almost insurmountable problem every month. Things had changed. For the better.

I scrambled a couple of eggs while Ames fixed toast. I could summon no enthusiasm for this real-life game of Monopoly. Even though it was theoretically my money, I didn't feel any sense of its belonging to me—or of my belonging to it, for that matter.

"What's wrong, Beau?" he asked, finally noticing my genuine disinterest.

"Mona Larson and Ginger Watkins," I told him.

"What about them, other than the obvious?"

"Something bothers me, and I can't get a handle on it: some common denominator, besides Sig."

"They were both broke," Ames said.

"I beg your pardon?"

"They were both broke," he repeated. "Mortgaged up the yingyang. Belltown didn't work out the way they expected. First the cement strike caught them. When the units finally hit the market, they got clobbered by high interest rates.

"For a long time nothing sold. They all lost a bundle. The whole group mortgaged everything to pay the first segment of the construction loan last year, thinking they could hold out and make the money back through sales. The next segment is due the end of December. There's no way they'll meet it. If they could even pay the interest, they might forestall a sheriff's sale, but after looking at the PDCs, I don't think they can."

"PDCs. What are they?"

"Public Disclosure Commission statements. Elected and appointed state officials fill out financial disclosure forms showing their earnings and holdings . . . that sort of thing. They're a matter of public record. After looking them over, it's clear that the parole board income was keeping both the Larson and Watkins households afloat."

"What about Homer?"

Ames laughed. "He's exempt. He holds no public office. He's always a bridesmaid but never a bride. He's involved in campaigns all over the map, but he's never a candidate himself. I'd guess he's as bad off as everybody else, but he doesn't have to fill out a form saying so."

"Both broke," I mused.

"You have to have pretty deep pockets to be able to weather the kind of financial storm there's been in Seattle's real estate market the last couple of years. My indicators say it's starting to turn around."

"Are mine?"

"Are your what?"

"Are my pockets deep enough?"

Ames laughed again. "They are, Beau. Believe me, you'll do fine. Now, we should take a look at that penthouse. If you're going to buy it separately,

I can draw up an earnest-money agreement today."

I rummaged through my wallet and found the
business card of the real estate lady at Belltown
Terrace. "Call her," I said. "I liked the water view
best. Two bedrooms with a den."

Ames seemed startled as he took the card. He
had asked for a decision. I don't think he expected
one quite that fast. "Just like that?" he asked.

"I looked at it Friday. It has a grill. I'm a sucker
for barbecues."

Ames left a short time later, setting off happily
on his various missions. At least one Seattle real
estate agent was in for a pleasant surprise that
Sunday.

Alone, I mulled Ames' information. Broke.
Both Ginger and Mona had been dead broke, bat-
tling for survival, trying to stay afloat. I found it
hard to imagine Ginger living in that palatial estate, running like hell to keep up appearances. In
Chelan, Mona and Sig must have been caught on
the same kind of treadmill.

Ginger and Mona—both of them married above
their station, both young and attractive, and both
dead within days of one another, probably at the
hands of the same killer. Mona Larson and Ginger Watkins indeed had a lot in common.

Peters' phone call interrupted my reverie. We see
each other so little during the week that we have to
check in on weekends. Indulging in his favorite
vice, current events, he was determined to keep
me well informed, whether or not I wanted to be.

"I don't suppose you've read the paper."

"Good hunch."

"Your friend Max has hit an all-time-record low for bad taste, a Death Row telephone interview with Philip Lathrop from Walla Walla. Asked Lathrop what he thought about Wilson knocking off Sig and Mona Larson."

"I don't think I want to hear this," I said.

"Lathrop's comment was, 'It serves 'em right.' "

"That's why I don't read papers," I told Peters.

"Maybe you've got a point," Peters muttered.

Ida Newell dropped off my Sunday collection of crossword puzzles. I was working the second one when the phone rang. It was Hal Huggins. "They found him, Beau."

"Who?"

"Wilson."

"Where? When can I question him?"

"In Prosser. I'm on my way over there right now." Hal hardly sounded jubilant. "But St. Peter's the only one who'll be asking him any questions."

"He's dead? You're kidding! Who found him?"

"A troop of Boy Scouts out cleaning the bank along the Yakima River."

"How long's he been dead?" My mind did a quick geographic review. Prosser was in Benton county, the county next to Pasco where Mona Larson died.

"I don't know, but I'm going over to find out."

"What's the cause of death?"

"Initial report says drowning."

"Drowning?" I repeated.

"I'll find out when I get there."

I heard weariness and frustration in Hal's

voice. He had followed a trail of questions, only to be robbed of both his suspect and his answers. To a homicide detective, answers are life's blood.

"Tough break, Hal," I said.

"I know." He paused. "I'd better go." With that, he hung up.

I sat for a long time afterward holding the phone. When a recorded voice threatened me with bodily harm, I returned the receiver to its cradle.

Don Wilson was dead. That finished it, right? Supposedly.

Maybe it did for Hal Huggins. It sounded as if he was buying the whole program.

But I wasn't. Several things demanded consideration: Don Wilson's thawing chicken, his hungry cat, his unpacked protest gear, and an extraneous set of missing keys. All were perplexing loose ends that wouldn't go away, that refused to be tied up in neat little packages.

Loose ends bug me. If they didn't, I guess I'd be in another line of work.

CHAPTER 27

ANYONE WHO'S EVER BEEN ON VACATION KNOWS HOW hard it is to return to work that first day. In my case, the vacation had been the culmination of months of being miserable and disconnected. It felt like I was going back to work after six months rather than a mere two weeks.

Peters spent the day at the courthouse on the dead wife-beater case. Both Peters and I were rooting for the woman, Delphina Sage. Delphina's husband, Rocky, came home drunk one Friday night and beat the crap out of her, same as he did every payday. The only difference was that, the day before, Delphina had bought herself a .22 pistol.

If she had shot him while he was beating her up, it wouldn't have been so bad. We would have called it self-defense and let it go at that. Instead, Delphina waited until Rocky was sound asleep, then plugged him full of holes. From talking to the kids and the neighbors, Peters and I figured Rocky was a bully badly in need of plugging, but

Barbara Guffy, King County's chief prosecutor, has a thing about premeditation. She was after a murder conviction.

Peters and I had been working another case just prior to my leaving for Rosario. In two separate but—we believed—related incidents, some jackass had set fire to sleeping transients downtown. Detectives Lindstrom and Davis had one case, while Peters and I had the other. Our victim had died almost immediately, but the other transient still clung stubbornly to life in the burn unit at Harborview Hospital. Both victims remained unidentified.

I was reviewing what little we had to go on when Hank Wu stopped by my desk. "Any luck?" I asked.

He shook his head. "This stuff takes time, Beau. The Hmong don't come out of the woodwork and spill their guts just because Henry Wu snaps his fingers. What time did you say your interpreter leaves?"

"Today on the four-thirty Greyhound for Anacortes."

"I'd say chances aren't very good."

"Keep after it anyway."

"Sure, glad to." Hank sauntered away from my desk.

Ames had promised to call as soon as he heard anything on the real estate transactions. The penthouse earnest-money agreement called for a March closing date. "That way," Ames had told me with a sly grin, "we'll keep the money in the family."

He called just before lunch, sounding perplexed. "What's the matter, Ames? You sound upset."

"I don't understand. They jumped on the penthouse deal, but they refused to consider the syndicate offer."

"Why?"

"I don't know. Must have come up with another investor who's willing to buy in. That's all I can figure."

"What happened?"

"That's what's so strange. When I talked to the project manager this morning, he was hot on the idea. Said he had to talk to one of the principals. Five minutes later, the deal was off. Just like that. One minute they needed the money; the next minute they didn't. The way they grabbed at that penthouse deal, even with a delayed closing, they don't expect to lose Belltown between now and March."

At Ames' insistence I had studied the project's financial sheet. We were talking big money, several million dollars.

"How can someone come up with that kind of cash in five minutes' time?" I wondered aloud.

"I don't know," Ames told me, "but I intend to find out."

Ames was in no mood to go to lunch. Craving companionship, I tracked down Peters at the courthouse. The two of us walked to a salad bar at Fourth and Madison. He dismissed my questions about Delphina Sage with an impatient shake of his head. "I don't want to talk about it. You do any good this morning?" he asked.

"I went over everything we have on our char-broiled John Doe. This afternoon I thought I'd check to see if Manny and Al's guy up in the burn unit can talk."

"Don't hold your breath," Peters said. "He couldn't last week."

It sounded hopeless to me, and I said as much. "We'll never crack this one. There's nothing to go on. Besides, if bums kill bums, who gives a shit?"

Peters gave me a long, critical look. "We sure as hell won't crack it with that kind of attitude," he responded. "You were supposed to come back from vacation with your enthusiasm back, all pumped up and rarin' to go, remember?"

"Go to hell," I retorted. "What do you think about them finding Wilson?"

"We're talking burning transients, remember?" he reminded me.

"I'm not interested in burning transients. I want to talk about Don Wilson."

"What about him? According to the papers, Hal Huggins has him dead to rights. Left a note and everything. What's there to talk about?"

"A note!" I exclaimed. "Are you serious?"

"Damn it, Beau. When are you going to stop being stubborn and start reading the papers? Yes, a note."

For the first time I felt the smallest prick of annoyance toward Hal Huggins. My phone had worked well enough when he needed my help. So why hadn't he called me with the news of the note? "God damn that Huggins," I grumbled. "What did the paper say?"

"That they found Wilson's body on the banks of the Yakima River just outside Prosser. Said he died of exposure, but that somebody found a suicide note."

"Exposure? Initially they said drowning. Since when is exposure suicide?"

"I'm just telling you what it said in the paper."

"And where did they find the note?"

"The article didn't say."

I left Peters at the table and prowled the restaurant for a pay phone. Locating one in a hallway between the men's and ladies' restrooms, I placed a call to Friday Harbor. Hal Huggins was not in. The woman who answered had no idea when he was expected. I left word for him to call me and went back to Peters.

"Did they say how long he'd been dead?"

Peters shrugged and shook his head. "A couple of days, I guess. At least that's what they implied."

"What about the note?"

"Just that there was one."

I stared morosely into my cup. Peters was fast losing patience. "Look. This Wilson character isn't our case. When are you going to the hospital?"

"Right after lunch, I guess."

He watched me drain my cup. "Know what your problem is, Beau?"

"What?"

"You just don't give a shit about burned-up bums."

"We've been partners too long," I told him.

I drove up to First Hill, Pill Hill as it's called

because of all the hospitals. The burn victim in Harborview was in no condition to talk, at least not according to the dogfaced intensive-care nurse who barred my way. She said he had been hit by an infection and wasn't expected to make it.

I went down to Pioneer Square. I walked around talking to people, asking questions. It was tough. All of the drunks were too fuzzy to know who was sitting next to them right then, to say nothing of remembering someone who had been missing from the park bench almost three weeks. In their world, three weeks ago was ancient history.

By four o'clock I was parked outside the Greyhound terminal at Seventh and Stewart as Jenny and Ernie arrived by taxi. Ernie held two suitcases on his lap; Jenny struggled with a collection of shopping bags.

"Want some help?" I asked, coming up behind them.

They both turned. Jenny's face was radiant with that peculiar glow common to pregnant women. Ernie seemed relieved to find someone to help her with the luggage.

"She didn't spend it all," he said, grinning. "But she came real close." He wheeled along beside me as I carried bags and packages into the terminal and checked them onto the proper bus. "You never found Blia?" Ernie asked.

"No, and we've been looking."

"If you find her, I'd still be willing to talk to her, but I hate to miss a full day's work."

"What about a telephone conference call?" I

asked. "We could get you, Blia, and me all on the phone together."

Ernie shook his head doubtfully. "You gotta remember that for the Hmong, coming to this country is like stepping into a time machine. She was raised one step out of the Stone Age. A telephone conference call is asking too much."

"It was just an idea," I said dismally.

Promptly at four-thirty the bus left for Anacortes. I dropped my company car off at the department and rode a free bus as far as the Westin. I needed to talk. Ames was stuck with me whether he liked it or not.

As it turned out, Ames was glad to see me. "I've been hitting one brick wall after another on the Belltown thing," he complained. "I have some sources here in town, one in particular over at the *Daily Journal of Commerce*. He's mystified, too. Says nobody's acting like there's an outside investor. The real estate community is watching Belltown Terrace because of the sheriff's sale. He doesn't know who bailed them out."

"Well, somebody did," I said, settling onto Ames' bed. "Am I buying the penthouse?"

"If you still want it, considering you'd be buying it from them rather than the syndicate."

I thought about it, but I had been fantasizing about barbecued ribs for three days. My mind was made up. "I want it," I declared.

Ames nodded. "All right." He changed the subject. "Tomorrow I have to go back to The Dalles. They left word this afternoon. I catch an early plane to Portland."

"Want a ride to the airport? My car's back."

He shook his head. "I'll take the hustle bus."

We were ready to discuss our dinner when Peters called. "I figured I'd find you there. I just got out of court. What are you up to?"

"Ames and I are plotting dinner. Care to join us?"

He did. Afterward, Ames returned to the Westin and Peters dropped by my apartment to chat. Around ten, just as Peters was ready to head home, the phone rang. It was the department. Another transient had been set afire in an alley encampment between First and Western off Cedar. Officers were on the scene. We took Peter's Datsun.

The building at First and Cedar is an office building with a penthouse restaurant on the fifth floor. The narrow alley behind it separates the building from two pay-parking lots. Between them sits a no-man's-land of blackberry bramble eight feet high. A small clearing had been carved beneath the thorny, dense branches with pieces of cardboard for flooring and walls.

Al Lindstrom and Manny Davis were at the scene. We didn't need to ask what was under the blanket in the blackberry clump. Once you've smelled the sweetish odor of charred human flesh, you never forget it.

"Same MO as before," Al told us grimly. "Only it's a woman this time, one of the Regrade regulars. We've got a positive ID. Teresa Smith's her name. Looks like she was sleeping it off here in the brush when someone doused her with gasoline and lit a match." The very fact that someone knew her name gave us a big leg up over the other two cases.

"Who reported it?" I asked.

He gestured toward the building above us. "A guy up there in the bar looked down and saw the fire just as it started. The bartender called 911, but it was too late by the time they got here."

"Did he see anyone?"

"Saw a car drive off. Only headlights and taillights. No make or model."

"So we're not dealing with another transient," Peters commented. It was true. Downtown bums don't drive. They wander, foot-patrol style, throughout the downtown area, hanging out in loosely organized, ever-changing packs.

"How come she was by herself?"

One of the uniformed officers came up as I asked the question. "We found her boyfriend. The food bank up the street was open, and she passed out. The group left her to sleep it off while they went to get food."

A tall, weaving Indian with shoulder-length greasy hair broke free from a scraggly group at the end of the alley. He pushed his way toward us. "Where is she?" he mumbled.

Manny moved to head him off, but the drunk brushed him aside. "Where is she?" he repeated. He stopped in front of me and stood glaring balefully, swaying from side to side.

I brought out my ID and opened it in front of him. I motioned wordlessly toward the heap of blanket. He swung blearily to look where I pointed. When his eyes focused on the blanket, his knees crumpled under him. He sank to the ground, his face contorted with grief, shoulders heaving.

This was an empty hulk of humanity with nothing left to lose, yet I watched as he sustained still another loss. He stank. His hair and clothes were filthy. Blackened toes poked through his duct-taped shoes. But his anguish at the woman's death was real and affecting.

Grief is grief on any scale.

One of the patrolmen knelt beside him. "We've sent for Reverend Laura," he said.

In the old days, Reverend Laura would have gone searching for heathens in Africa or South America. Today, the tall, raw-boned woman is a newly ordained Lutheran minister with a pint-sized church in a former Pike Place tavern. She ministers to downtown's homeless. Wearing her hair in a severe bun and with no makeup adorning her ruddy cheeks, she is both plain and plain-spoken, but her every action brims with the milk of human kindness. She appeared within minutes and knelt beside the weeping man, taking his elbow and raising him to his feet.

"Come on, Roger," she said kindly, "let's go to the mission."

"Will you keep him there so we can reach him tomorrow?" I asked.

She nodded. An officer helped her load him into a car. We fanned out, asking questions of all bystanders, interviewing the patrons in Girvan's, including the man who had first reported the incident.

We found nothing, It took us until two A.M. to ascertain we had found nothing. Peters dropped me off at my place. "Why don't you stay here?" I offered. "You can have the bed. I'll sleep on the couch."

"No, thanks," he replied. "I'd better get home."

I'm sure I was sound asleep before he reached the floating bridge.

CHAPTER 28

I WOKE UP TUESDAY MORNING, TIRED BUT WITH A RE-newed sense of purpose. Roger Bear Claw's grief had catapulted burning transients out of the realm of the inconsequential. Years of discipline took over, bringing focus and motivation. Ginger, Mona, and Wilson were Hal's bailiwick. Teresa Smith and a dead John Doe were mine.

By seven-thirty I was at my desk. Peters stopped by on his way to the courthouse. He dropped a newspaper onto my desk. "Thought you'd want to read Max's column," he said.

It was there in lurid black and white, all about Ginger Watkins' murder. He told the whole story, including the blood-alcohol count, speculating what conversation she and Wilson might have shared over those last few drinks. Columnists speculate with impunity. They also rationalize. Cole's conclusion was that Wilson had taken his own life after destroying those responsible for the deaths of his wife and child. With typical tunnel vision, he ignored the fact that Mona Larson had never served on the parole board.

The moral of the story—and with Max there is always a moral—was couched in snide asides about inept law-enforcement officers. No one was exempt—from the Washington State Patrol and the San Juan County Sheriff's Department to the Pasco City Police. There was, however, one notable omission. J. P. Beaumont's name wasn't mentioned, not once. Evidently Ralph Ames' threat of libel had struck terror in Max's black little heart.

Peters was still there when I finished reading the article. I tossed the paper back to him. "Where the hell does he get his information? Huggins swears there's no leak in his department, but the stuff about the throttle linkage was known only by Huggins, Rogers, me, and the killer."

Peters shrugged. "It doesn't really matter, does it? Wilson's dead; the case is closed. Maybe now you can get your mind back on the job. I should be done with the Sage case by noon."

After Peters left, Al, Manny, and I did a quick huddle. "So who's got a grudge against bums?" Manny asked.

"Every taxpaying, law-abiding citizen," Al Lindstrom grumped. Al is a typical hardworking Scandinavian squarehead with a natural aversion to any able-bodied person who beats the system by not holding down a real job.

Al and Manny went to the Pike Place Mission for another talk with Roger Bear Claw, while I was dispatched to Harborview Hospital to check on the surviving John Doe. Before I had a chance to leave my desk, the phone rang. It was Hal Huggins. I tried to check the annoyance in my voice. "It's about time you got around to calling me."

"Lay off, Beau. I'm up to my neck. It's just as well Wilson's dead. The county couldn't afford two first-degree murder trials."

"You're sure Wilson did it? All three of them?"

"Absolutely. Didn't you hear about the note?"

"Vaguely. But exposure? People don't just go out in the woods and wait to die. Besides, it hasn't been cold."

"Who knows? Maybe he fell in some water. That'll do it. Look, Beau, I'm not calling the shots, the coroner is. . . . By the way," he added, "we found his car parked on a side street in Prosser. The note was there."

"How long had it been there?"

"I can't tell you that. We're trying to reconstruct Wilson's movements from the time he left Orcas. So far we're not having much luck, but there's no doubt the note is his. The prints check. Handwriting checks. What more do you want?"

"What about the chicken?"

"Oh, for God's sake, Beau, lay off that chicken. Maybe he didn't plan to kill them when he left home; but after he did, he couldn't very well go back without getting caught, not even to eat his chicken or feed his goddamned cat."

"So you're closing the case?" I asked.

"Not completely. As I said, we're still retracing his movements from the time he left Orcas until he showed up in the river."

"How long has he been dead?"

"Old man Scott says two to three days at the most."

"Not 'Calls It Like I Sees 'Em' Scott!"

"That's right. One and the same. He's still Benton County Coroner. He's up for reelection next week."

Only three counties in Washington—King, Pierce, and Whatcom—have medical examiners. All the rest rely on an antiquated county coroner system. Whoever runs for office is elected without any consideration of qualifications. Garfield Scott had earned both his nickname and a permanent place in the Bungler's Hall of Fame when he declared a man dead of a heart attack, only to turn him over and discover a knife still buried in the victim's chest.

"Can't you get another opinion? What if Wilson's been dead longer than that, like since before Mona died?"

"Dammit, Beau. I already told you, I'm not calling the shots. There's an election next week, remember? Scott would never hold still for a second opinion."

I changed the subject. "Who went to Maxwell Cole with Ginger's murder?" I asked.

There was a moment's pause. "I don't have any idea."

"Somebody did," I told him grimly. "It's front-page stuff in this morning's *P.I.*"

"Not anybody from my department, I can tell you that!" Huggins' hackles were up, and so were mine. He attempted to smooth things over. "Thanks for all your help, Beau."

"Think nothing of it," I said. Obviously he didn't.

On my way up to Harborview, I tried to shift
gears from one case to another. The same intensive-
care nurse stopped me. "He can't talk to you," she
snapped. "He's dying."

"Look," I said wearily. "Can he communicate
at all?"

"He can nod and shake his head. That's it."

"Even that may tell me something. Someone
else died last night, a woman. She never made it
as far as the hospital. Without his help, the toll
could go higher."

She relented a little. I could see it in the set of
her mouth.

"Please," I wheedled, taking advantage of her
hesitation. She glared at me, then marched briskly
down the hall, her rubber-soled shoes squeaking
on the highly polished tile floor. I stood there
waiting, uncertain if she was throwing me out or
taking it under advisement. She came back a few
minutes later carrying a sterilized uniform, boo-
ties, and a face mask. Wordlessly, she helped me
don compulsory ICU costume.

"You can see him for five minutes. No more."

One look convinced me that Teresa Smith was
a hell of a lot better off for dying on the spot.
What little was visible of the man's puffy face
was fused in a featureless mass of flesh that bore
little resemblance to a human being. Tubes went
in and out his arms and throat. His breathing was
labored.

"He's awake," the nurse said, although I don't
know how she knew that. "We call him Mr.
Smith."

I stood by the bed, astonished by my revulsion.

I'm a homicide cop. I'm supposed to be used to the worst life can dish out. Five minutes left no time for niceties. He was dying. I think he knew it.

"I'm a cop, Mr. Smith. A detective. They'll only let me talk for five minutes. Somebody else got burned last night, up on First Avenue. We think it's the same guy who burned you. Can you help us?"

There was no response. I couldn't tell if he heard me.

"Did you see anyone?"

He nodded, so slightly, that I wasn't sure he had moved.

"Someone you knew?"

This time there was no mistaking it. The mass of flesh moved slightly from side to side. The answer was no.

"One person?"

A minute nod. We were playing hardball Twenty Questions. Every question had to count. There wouldn't be any second chances, not with this Mr. Smith.

"Male?" Another nod. He groaned with the effort.

"Young?"

He nodded again, barely, but his breathing changed. The nurse took me by the arm. "Enough," she said firmly. "He's fallen asleep. You've worn him out."

She led me outside the intensive care unit, where I shed the sterile clothes. "Thank you," I said. She bustled away without acknowledgment. She was a tough old bat, but nobody with the least tendency to a soft heart could work there.

Back in the office I had a despondent Peters on my hands. "They convicted her," he said. "Not Murder One, but a minimum of twenty years for killing that worthless bastard. What the hell ever happened to justice?"

"Sometimes there's no such thing," I told him. "So get to work."

We did. We spent the afternoon with Manny and Al. The information that it was somebody young, probably a kid, constituted the first tiny break in the case. One kid, one young punk, who liked to burn people up. Who was he? Where was he from? Was he black, white, Asian?

Back to questions, always questions. The consensus was that, whoever he was, he wasn't a regular inhabitant of the downtown area. This wasn't your usual drunken brawl over a half-consumed bottle of Big Red. Fights over booze are generally harmless—a little gratuitous bloodshed among friends. This was deliberately malicious. And deadly.

We hit the streets, talking to known gang leaders and toughs. The patrolmen in what the department calls the David Sector of downtown Seattle know most of the street kids by name. They guided us to the various groups, pointing out kids who would talk and kids who liked to throw their weight around. All of them could have gotten gasoline; none of them had cars.

To quote one, a scrawny-looking kid named Spike who wore a black leather vest over a hairless bare chest, "Nobody knew nothin'," although he hinted darkly that there might be a club down at Franklin High with some allegedly vicious initiation rites.

Peters and I drove to Franklin High School in Rainier Valley. The principal, a tall black former Marine, sounded more like a drill sergeant than an educator. He admitted he had some tough kids in his school, but none who would go around setting fire to sleeping drunks, he'd stake his reputation on it. I was inclined to believe him.

Driving back to the department, Peters asked me what I thought. "He seems to know what's going on with those kids," I told him.

"Bullshit," Peters replied. "Nobody ever knows what's going on with a bunch of kids."

We agreed to disagree. It wasn't the first time, and it wouldn't be the last.

I found a note from Henry Wu on my desk. "See me."

Hank sat with his feet propped on his desk reading a copy of the *International News.* "What have you got?"

He put down the paper, a wide smile spreading under his impeccable mustache. "I think I've found her, Beau, in the Stadium Apartments out in Rainier Valley. You know where that is, out on Martin Luther King Way?"

"I think so."

"My source says she lives with her aunt and uncle and some cousins out there. Your interpreter's gone?"

"Yesterday," I said.

I must have sounded ungrateful. Hank bristled. "Look, I moved heaven and earth to get this far. Nobody rushes a grapevine."

"I know. Sorry. It's just that Ernie had to go home." Hank appeared somewhat mollified. "So what do you suggest?" I asked. "Is there anybody on the force who speaks Hmong?"

"Even if there was, I wouldn't advise your taking them along, not if you want her to talk."

"What should I do then, go by myself?"

"That guy who left on the bus—Ernie. . . . My source recognized the name, knew who he was. He's evidently widely respected in the Seattle Hmong community. It wasn't until I mentioned him that I started getting to first base. My suggestion is that you do whatever it takes to get him back down here."

If you call in an expert, you have to be prepared to take his advice. Henry Wu was the expert. "Thanks, Hank. I'll see what I can do."

I went back to my desk. Peters looked up as I sat down. "What gives?"

"Hank's got a line on the hotel maid from Orcas," I answered. I picked up the phone, ready to call Ernie.

Peters scowled. "Look, Beau, we're already on a case. Two and a half by actual count, if that guy at Harborview is still alive."

I felt like he'd stepped on my toes. "Don't tell me what to do," I snapped. I couldn't very well call Ernie right then, not with Peters peering over my shoulder. We spent the rest of the afternoon circling each other like a squabbling old married couple. By five, we still weren't ready to bury the hatchet.

"You having dinner with Ames?" Peters asked as we waited uneasily for the Public Safety Building's snail-like elevator. I hadn't told him Ames had returned to The Dalles. I didn't tell him then.

"Naw, he's busy," I replied noncommittally.

If Peters was fishing for an invitation to dinner, I didn't bite. We parted company in the lobby, and I walked home to the Royal Crest. I called Ernie right away.

"I think we've found Blia," I said, once he answered the phone. "Could you come down tomorrow if I had a float plane pick you up and take you back?"

"It won't work," he said. "I've got a motor home to overhaul. The Hansens are leaving for Arizona Saturday. I've got that job to do and another due by Friday."

"Nobody else can do it?" I insisted.

"I'm a one-man shop. Without me, nothing happens."

I couldn't very well argue the point. "Call me as soon as you see your way clear," I told him.

"Sure thing," he replied. "Glad to."

Disappointed, I hung up. Outside it was raining a steady fall drizzle. I put on a waterproof jacket and walked to the golden arches at Sixth and Westlake. I picked up a Big Mac and an order of fries to go. Peters would have pitched a fit if he'd glimpsed my evening menu.

Back at the house, I set the table with my good dishes and dined in solitary splendor. Bachelors are allowed their small eccentricities. After dinner I settled into my old-fashioned recliner and let my mind wander.

Maybe the guy who sent us to Franklin had been playing some game of his own, creating a wild-goose chase among the predominantly minority kids there. I was smart enough to recognize that the suggestion played on our own prejudices. Maybe our bum-killing fanatic was to be found at the other end of the spectrum, concealed among the well-heeled kids of Bellevue or the North End.

It was a thought that merited further consideration. Meantime, all we could do was keep looking for that rarest of all birds, the eyewitness.

The discipline of focusing on one issue at a time pushed Ginger and Sig and Mona and Wilson further and further into the background. I had to leave them alone until Ernie could return to Seattle.

For the time being, inconsequential as they might seem, three dead transients took precedence. Harborview Hospital had called the department to say that Mr. Smith was no more. My interview with him had been his very last opportunity to give us any help.

I fell asleep in the chair and didn't wake up until morning. That's something else bachelors can get away with. I'm not sure the good outweighs the bad.

CHAPTER 29

My back was broken when I woke up. In my youth I could sleep all night in a recliner and not have it bother me the next day. Maybe I'm getting old.

I was in the bathroom, my face slathered with shaving cream, when the phone rang. I hurried to answer it, Colgate Instant Shave smearing into the holes of the mouthpiece.

"Did you know?" an unfamiliar voice asked.

"Know what?"

"That Ginger was—" Tom Lander's voice cracked.

I waited while he got hold of himself. "I knew," I said grimly, silently cursing Homer and Darrell Watkins and Hal Huggins and J. P. Beaumont for not having broken the news to Tom earlier.

"Why didn't you tell me? Why did I have to read it in the paper?"

I didn't have an answer. I had known he wasn't told, but I had shut the knowledge out of my mind.

"Was it Wilson?" he continued doggedly.

"That's what Hal Huggins thinks," I countered.

"What do you think?" he demanded.

"I don't know." It was an honest answer.

"You could have told me."

"I expected Homer or Darrell would do that."

"They didn't."

I felt like I owed him something, but not enough to lapse into idle speculation about thawing chickens and hungry cats and extra keys. "Look, Tom, I'm following up on some leads. I'll be in touch if I find anything out, okay?"

"Why should I believe you?"

"No reason," I answered. "Because I asked."

"All right," he agreed reluctantly. "But was she really drunk, or was that just part of the story?"

"Her blood-alcohol count showed she had been drinking, enough to be drunk."

"Oh," he said, disappointment thick in his voice.

"Why, Tom? What does it matter?"

"It's personal," he replied and hung up.

I went to the bathroom and finished shaving, thinking about Maxwell Cole. I couldn't help wondering how he had gotten his information, particularly since Huggins was so sure it hadn't come through his department. I decided to pay a call on Max, for old time's sake. I called the *P.I.* He wasn't in and wasn't expected before ten.

I checked the phone book. Bingo. Maxwell Cole. It gave a Queen Anne phone number but no address. I dialed. He sounded groggy.

"Hello, Max. This is Beaumont. I want to talk to you."

"To me? How come?"

"Just a couple of questions. Can I come over?"

"I guess."

"Good. What's the address?"

He gave me a number on Bigelow North, an old-fashioned street strewn with fallen chestnuts and mounds of moldering leaves. The house was an eighteen-nineties gingerbread type set among aging trees and crowned with leaded glass gable windows. It surprised me. I had always figured Max for the swinging hot tub and cocktails type. This hardly fit that image.

I pulled up and parked. Before I could get out of the car, Max blustered out the front door and down the walk. He heaved himself into the Porsche.

"What are you doing here?" he demanded.

"You invited me, remember?"

"I was asleep. Let's go someplace for coffee." We drove to an upstairs coffee-and-croissant place on top of Queen Anne Hill. "So what do you want?" Max asked, once we settled at a table.

"I want to know where you got your information on Ginger Watkins."

Wariness crept over his flabby face. "Why do you want to know?"

"I do, that's all."

"My sources are confidential."

"You'd be forced to tell, under oath."

"There won't be a trial. Wilson's dead."

"Did Wilson tell you about Ginger? Were you in touch with him after that day on Orcas?"

Max shook his head. "Don't try to trick me, J. P. Why do you want to know? Huggins says the case is closed. He's satisfied Wilson did it."

"Who set up the meeting on Orcas? Was it Wilson?"

Max nodded.

"What did he say?"

"That something big was going to break, that it would be announced during the parole board retreat. He thought it should go in the special feature I was doing on him."

"Did he say what this 'something big' was?"

"He didn't. I thought it would be about the Victim/Witness Protection Program. That's what he was working on, but nobody's mentioned it since. He must have had his wires crossed."

"Did you ever publish it? The feature, I mean?"

Max looked stunned to think that I had missed a word of his deathless prose. "I used some of it in the column after Wilson died, but not much. I was still pissed at him for dragging me all the way to Orcas and then missing the interview."

"Was it Pomeroy?" I asked in a feint-and-thrust maneuver designed to throw him off guard. It didn't work.

"I'm not talking," Max returned stubbornly. "I already told you that." I wasn't able to get any more out of him. We finished coffee, and I took him home.

I turned up at the department around ten. Peters, glancing up from a stack of papers, glared at me. "What'd you do? Forget to set your alarm?"

I didn't answer. I sat down at my desk, hoping to reshuffle my priorities and get the two John Does and Teresa Smith back on top of the desk. Don Wilson, the wild card, refused to go away.

"I talked to Hal," I said to Peters as I passed his

desk. "Old Man Scott swears up and down Wilson was dead two to three days at most. If that's true, how come he floated to the surface? That usually takes five days to a week."

"Current," Peters offered helpfully. "The current could have washed him up on shore without him necessarily floating to the surface."

"I wish Baker could take a look at him." Dr. Howard Baker is King County's crackerjack medical examiner. Nothing gets by him. Dr. Baker is no coroner, but then King County isn't Benton County, either. "Why the hell couldn't Wilson have died inside King County? It would simplify my life."

"Wish in one hand, shit in the other, and see which hand gets full first." Peters' comment was philosophical. I love it when he lectures me in parables.

Just then Peters' phone rang. He listened briefly, then slammed down the receiver and jumped to his feet. "Come on," he said. "We've gotta go."

"Where?"

"Manny and Al are down in Pioneer Square. They may have a lead in the transient case."

That effectively put the cap on Ginger and Sig and Mona and Wilson. I followed Peters through the fifth-floor maze and out of the building. Pioneer Square is only a few blocks from the department, down the hill, off James.

As the name implies it's an old neighborhood made up of stately old buildings whose insides have been gutted and brought up to code. Gentrification has brought new tenants—law firms, trendy shoppes, and tiny espresso bars. The only glitch is that the new tenants haven't quite convinced the old ones, the bums, that they don't live there anymore. The merchants and the bums are constantly at war to see who controls the turf.

Peters and I walked down the hill. Manny and Al were in the Elliott Bay Bookstore, downstairs in the book-lined espresso bar. With them was a young woman in tennis shoes and a ponytail. She might have been any well-built teenager poured into a tank top and tightly fitting jeans, nipples protruding under the knit material. She looked like a teenager until you saw her close up. Her face was still attractive, but it showed signs of excessive wear.

Periodically she popped a bubble with a wad of gum, but she kept a nervous watch on a flashily dressed black man two tables away. He sat with both arms folded across his chest, silently observing the proceedings.

"So nothing happened," she was saying as Peters and I approached the table. "It washed off. He never lit the match, but I told Lawrence I'll bet it's the same guy. When I heard it on the news, I told him." She nodded toward the man I assumed to be Lawrence. "He said I could tell."

Al motioned us into two empty chairs while Manny spoke earnestly to the girl. "These are Detectives Peters and Beaumont," he explained. "They're working the case with us. Would you be willing to do a composite drawing, Sandra?"

She glanced questioningly toward Lawrence. He nodded. Evidently, anything that damaged the merchandise was bad for business. It didn't make sense to let someone set fire to the stable.

"Yes," she answered.

"This was three nights ago?"

I think she forgot she was talking to a cop. She gave Manny a bat of her long lashes as she answered. "Yes."

"And there were two of them?"

"Yes."

"Black or white?"

"White."

"Blond? Brunet?"

"One of each."

"How tall?

"I don't pay much attention. I mean, it's not important, you know? Maybe six feet or so."

"How old?"

"Twenty. Maybe younger."

"And they both paid?"

"I charge extra for two." Lawrence shifted uneasily in his chair, but I don't think Sandra noticed. At least he didn't tell her to shut up.

"Where did you go?"

"To a room at The Gaslight up on Aurora."

"So what happened?"

"Nothing. . . . Nothing kinky," she added. "Not even both together. But while the second one was getting it up, the first one pulled a bottle out of his coat pocket and poured something on me. It smelled terrible. It burned my eyes.

"The second one started yelling, 'What are you crazy?' and the first one said 'Just having a little fun.' I jumped up to call Lawrence, but one of them knocked me down, and they took off. The second guy didn't even get his shirt and shoes on. I followed them to the door, screaming like mad. They drove off before Lawrence could catch them."

"You're sure it was gasoline he poured on you?"

"Yeah. From one of those screw-top Coke bottles. Lawrence said if they'da lit a match I'da died."

Manny nodded. "It's true," he said. Sandra swallowed hard. I wondered how old she was. Probably no more than seventeen, although she looked half again that old.

"After that woman died, Lawrence said I could tell. He said this was one time we'd better cooperate."

Manny nodded again, encouragingly. "Lawrence is absolutely right," he agreed. "What kind of car was it?"

"White. One of those little foreign cars like maybe a Toyota or a Datsun. I don't know which."

"What year?"

She shrugged. "But it had some of those university parking stickers in the window. We watch for those. They're usually bad news."

Lawrence stood and motioned toward the door. Sandra caught the signal and rose obediently. "I gotta go."

"Can we call you for the composite?" Manny asked.

She nodded. "Lawrence knows how to get ahold of me."

Lawrence made a quick exit with the girl trailing behind him on an invisible leash.

"I'll just bet he does, the son of a bitch," Al Lindstrom muttered under his breath. "That makes me sick."

Manny glared at his partner. "Don't look a gift horse in the mouth, Al. We get paid for solving murders, not for busting hookers and pimps. She's the best thing that's happened to us all week."

CHAPTER 30

I FELT LIKE A GODDAMNED RUBBER BAND. TERESA AND friends bubbled to the surface while Ginger and friends receded. The four of us went to lunch—Manny, Al, Peters, and I. Manny was high as a kite, while Al was still pissed, speculating that Lawrence made more than all four of us put together. Well, three of us, anyway. I wasn't talking.

Other than comparing notes on what Sandra had said, there wasn't much to do until she completed the composite. We agreed that since Manny had done most of the talking with Sandra, he should make the next contact and set up the appointment. There was no sense in causing Lawrence to be any more squirrelly than he already was.

The idea that the car was a white Datsun or Toyota with a university sticker was some help, but not much. There are literally thousands of cars registered at the U Dub, as locals refer to the University of Washington. We figured somebody should contact the campus police and ask for a preliminary list.

Seattle P.D. and the campus police get along fairly well. As law-enforcement officers, campus cops suffer from a severely restricted sphere of influence. They do a lot of PR work within the confines of their narrow jurisdiction, keeping a lid on anything that might offend the tender sensibilities of well-heeled alumni. Peters and I were to brief them on the current situation. We figured they'd be overjoyed to be involved in a real crime that didn't involve property theft.

As soon as lunch was over, we split up the act. Manny and Al headed for the medical examiner's office to pick up the preliminary report on the Harborview John Doe. Dental charts were our only possible means of identification. There sure as hell wouldn't be any fingerprints. Peters and I were supposed to go to the university. About ten to one, we stopped by the department to pick up a car, but Margie Robles, our clerk, caught us before we got away.

"There you are!" she exclaimed. "I've been looking all over for you."

"Why? What's up?"

"Somebody named Ames. He's called three times so far. For you or Detective Peters."

"Why would he call me?" Peters wondered.

"Did he leave a number?" I asked.

"Not the last time. Said you should meet him at the airport at one forty-five. Both of you. Here's the flight number." She handed me a yellow slip of paper.

Once she was out of earshot, Peters turned on me.

"What's this about? More footwork for Hal Huggins?"

"I guess," I said.

He glowered at me. "We'd better not take a company car, then. We can just barely make it." He angrily strode toward the door with me right on his tail. I had an idea Ames wasn't calling about Ginger and friends. He had been in The Dalles, negotiating with New Dawn. If he had sprung the kids, it would be a kindness to give Peters some advance warning, but if he hadn't . . . I wasn't about to make that kind of mistake. I let Peters stay pissed.

The Datsun was parked in a cheapo monthly garage at the bottom of James. Peters ground it into gear and angrily fishtailed us out of the parking stall. "You've got more nerve than a bad tooth. We shouldn't work an unauthorized case during regular hours. You'll get us both in trouble."

I said nothing. It was pure luck that got us to Sea-Tac without a speeding citation. The parking garage was crammed to the gills. We searched through three levels before we finally spotted a little old lady vacating a spot. Peters beat two other cars to it. We were inside the terminal by one thirty-five. Naturally we had to hassle with the security guards over our weapons.

By the time we reached the gate, Northwest Orient Flight 106 from Portland was already parked in place at the jet bridge. Passengers were disembarking. I saw Ames first. He was packing one kid on his hip and dragging the other along by the hand. The girl Ames was carrying spotted Peters. "Daddy, Daddy," she squalled.

Peters whirled toward her, a look of stunned amazement on his face. As he stood glued to the floor, unable to move, the girl who was walking broke loose from Ames' grip and raced for Peters' knees. She hit him with a full flying tackle that almost toppled him. Meantime, the kid Ames was carrying set up such a howl, he had no choice but to set her on the floor and let her run too.

Peters sank to the floor, buried under a flurry of bawling kids. I moved to where Ames, looking inordinately proud, was attempting to smooth the wrinkles from his usually immaculate jacket. What appeared to be the better part of a Tootsie Roll was stuck to his silk tie.

I grabbed his hand and pumped it. "How the hell did you pull it off?"

"You've just funded their mother on a five-year mission to Nicaragua. No children allowed, of course."

"Of course," I said.

"Fully deductible," he added.

"Of course." With Ames in charge I should have known the solution would be fully deductible. Peters gradually emerged from the mêlée and came over to Ames and me, one child in each arm. They were cute little imps, five and six years old with baby teeth, long dark hair, thick lashes, and brown eyes.

Peters was more than a little choked up. "I don't know what to say," he blurted.

"How about introducing me?"

"This is Heather," he said, indicating the smaller one, "and this is Tracie. My friend, Detective Beaumont."

"Beau," I corrected.

The smaller of the two regarded me seriously. "Hello. Mommy says my name is Joy and she's Truth." She pointed at her sister. They had evidently lived under different names in Broken Springs, Oregon.

"I like Heather better," I said.

We stood there awkwardly, bottling up the hallway, not knowing what to say or do. It was a moment that could have become maudlin, given half a chance, but Ames took charge. He herded us down the hallway like a bunch of errant sheep, leaving us long enough to pick up luggage. When he rejoined us, he carried only his own suitcase and a briefcase.

"What about them?" I asked, indicating the girls.

"New Dawn's attorney told me I could have them this morning, as is, take it or leave it. I took it. I decided we could get them clothes once they got here."

One glance at Peters told me Ames had made the right choice. You can always buy new clothes. I doubted he would have gotten a second crack at the kids.

We crowded into the Datsun for the trip back to Seattle. Peters sat in the backseat with the girls. I drove while Ames attempted to clean the chocolate off his tie.

"I guess you're taking the rest of the afternoon off?" I asked.

Peters grinned. "Looks that way. I can't believe you did it!" he said to Ames.

I could believe it, all right. I counted on Ames to smooth it over so Peters would never know exactly how it happened. It would be better for him to believe that his ex-wife had experienced a sudden change of heart. There was no need to tell him certain amounts of money had changed hands.

I got out at the department, and Ames assumed the driver's seat. I tracked down Captain Larry Powell and told him that Peters was gone for the day, explaining that his kids had come home unexpectedly. Powell was glad to hear it, but he didn't press for details. I didn't volunteer any, either.

Once Peters dropped me at the department, I checked out a car and drove to the university. Driving there, I suddenly recalled an old undergraduate pastime that had been called Bum Bashing in my day. It involved dragging home a bum on one pretext or another and then beating the crap out of him once he was there. Of course, back in the old days, I couldn't remember anyone's ever dying of it. Obviously the current generation had elevated the sport from intramural to semipro. By actual count we had three victims dead. My hope was that Sandra's encounter had been with the same bunch and that we could somehow nail them.

As I expected, the officer of the day, Joseph Randolph, was more than happy to help me. He listened carefully as I explained the problem, then left me in a waiting room while he went to work on it. Forty minutes later, he called me back into his office. With a triumphant grin, he handed me a huge computer printout that must have weighed ten pounds.

"Here it is," he said. "Every single car that's registered on campus this quarter—make and license number."

I could tell he was proud of getting it for us so fast. I hated to burst his bubble. "Can you break it down by make and model?" I asked.

His face fell. "I don't know when we could schedule that much computer time."

I took the whole list back to the department. Manny, Al, and I divided it three ways and began weeding through it. By quitting time, we had found 73 Datsuns and 51 Toyotas. No colors. We called it a job and went home. That's one thing about this kind of work. When you're looking for a needle in the haystack, you don't have to do it all at once. Both the needle and the haystack will stay right there and wait until the next day.

I called Peters at home to find out how things were going. They had just come in from buying bedroom furniture. He said he'd decided to take the rest of the week off. It would take that long to get the girls registered for school and locate a baby-sitter. I told him not to worry, since sorting through the vehicle list would probably take the better part of a week.

Ames turned up, wearing a clean tie and jacket. The two of us went out for a celebratory dinner, co-conspirators congratulating each other behind Peters' back. With the kids in Peters' custody and the major real estate deal canceled, Ames planned to return to Arizona on Saturday. I was sorry to hear it. It cost me money, but I enjoyed having Ames around. I supposed, however, that he did have other clients.

"You making any progress on the Watkins case?" he asked as we left Rosselini's Four Ten Restaurant to walk home.

I shook my head. "Huggins is sure Wilson did it. Since it isn't my case, I don't have much to say about it."

Ames looked thoughtful. "I can't help but think that the murders and the project might be related."

"How's that?"

"I'm not sure. It's just a thought."

We walked together as far as Fourth and Lenora, then split up. I went up to my apartment, mulling Ames' words along with thawing chickens, hungry cats, and extra keys.

CHAPTER 31

ONCE MORE I HAD A FACE FULL OF SHAVING CREAM when the phone rang. It was Peters looking for a good pediatrician. In order to register the girls for school, they had to have a complete set of vaccinations. New Dawn believed in prayer, not science. As I tried to keep shaving cream out of the receiver, I considered growing a full beard.

I returned to the bathroom and had barely put razor to chin when the phone rang again. I jumped and left a good-sized nick. I'm sure I sounded exasperated when I answered. "Is this Detective Beaumont?" The voice was female, sultry, and dripping with the honeyed accents of the Deep South.

"Yes," I answered tentatively.

"My name's Colleen Borden with Armour Life Insurance." I steeled myself for the inevitable pitch. Various estate planners and financial advisors had crawled out of the woodwork ever since my windfall. "Ah'd like to make an appointment with you."

"I'm not interested in any life insurance. I'm going to live forever." It was the line that had given me the most luck in getting rid of pushy bastards.

"Ah'm not tryin' to sell you somethin,' Mr. Beaumont." She sounded clearly affronted. "Ah'm not a salesman. Ah'm a claims inspector."

That caught my attention. "A claims inspector?"

"Yes. Ah investigate death claims."

"Whose claim are you investigating?"

"That's why Ah want to see you. Ah'll be comin' to town tomorrow and wondered if maybe we could get together for dinner, say at the Westin, the Palm Court, at six."

"How will I know you?"

"The reservation will be in my name."

She hung up. I spent the next few minutes taking the phone apart and prying Colgate Instant Shave out of the holes with a toothpick. A death-claim inspector. I wondered which one. There were any number of deaths in need of inspecting.

I finished my shave on the third try. I was almost late by then. I hit the elevator with a tiny piece of tissue stemming the flow of blood on my chin.

Manny and Al were hard at work on the list when I got to my desk. I settled down with my portion of it, wishing Peters were there to lighten the load. Manny took off about eleven to oversee Sandra's composite drawing, while Al and I grappled with the list until our eyes burned.

Manny came back about two, practically

walking on air. He had two drawings. Each pictured a clean-cut, ordinary-looking kid. It gets me when a cold-blooded killer looks like the kid next door or maybe even *is* the kid next door.

But it wasn't the drawings that had Manny excited. Sandra had come up with one other tiny scrap of information. The white car had carried a bumper sticker. She couldn't remember the whole thing, just that some of the letters had been funny, maybe backward or upside down. The only one she remembered for sure was a K, and maybe a backward E.

A frat rat! From a house with *kappa* in it and maybe a *sigma*. Sandra, bless her little heart of gold, had saved our eyesight. Instead of having to go through the computer printout listing every car on campus, she had narrowed our investigation to the much smaller world of sororities and fraternities. A quick consultation with Ma Bell's Yellow Pages told us the university boasted only ten Greek houses with *kappa* in their names.

Manny, Al, and I drove to what we call Never Never Land in two separate cars. If Seattle is a liberal egg, then the University of Washington is the yolk, although the kids there now are far more conservative than the students of, say, the sixties or seventies. They still do drugs, and they still live in an aura of permissiveness where some students literally get away with murder, but it's a hell of a lot better than it used to be.

We didn't notify the campus police. It wasn't necessary. Greek Row isn't on campus proper.

Parking places are at a premium. We finally parked in front of two separate fire hydrants on

Seventeenth NE. Manny and Al took one side of the street, and I took the other, wishing the whole time that Peters were there to back me up instead of sitting in a doctor's office somewhere waiting to have his kids vaccinated for polio, tetanus, typhoid, and God knows what else.

I was the one who got lucky, if you can call it that. Kappa Sigma Epsilon at 4747 Seventeenth NE was a white, New England-style building. I remembered it as an old-line, socially prominent Eastern fraternity. Like fraternities in general, it had fallen on hard times. The paint was chipped and peeling, and a couple of broken windows were patched with plywood.

I knocked and waited. Finally a wide-eyed kid answered the door. I pulled out the two sketches. "I wondered if you could help me. Do you recognize either of these guys?"

He looked at the pictures, then back at me. "You a cop?" he asked.

I pulled out my ID. Five years ago, a kid at the university wouldn't have given me the time of day. That's what I expected now. I was wrong.

He nodded, pointing. "That's Howard Rayburn. The other's Vince Farley. Howie's upstairs. Want me to get him?"

Sometimes you make a decision that you spend the rest of your life regretting, playing it back over and over; wondering, if you had done something differently, would disaster have been averted. At that moment in the vestibule of Kappa Sigma Epsilon I made one of those bad decisions.

I didn't know what I was up against, and I didn't want to go in without a backup. "No, thanks," I said. "I'll be right back." I hurried to the grass median and waited until I saw Manny coming back down a sidewalk. I motioned for him to come. He in turn called Al.

"What have you got?" Manny demanded.

"Looks like they both live there. Only one is home."

"Want me to radio for more units?" Al asked. I nodded. He loped off toward their car. I motioned Manny to cover the back door, while I returned to the front porch. This time I didn't bother to knock. I met the same kid, coming down the stairs.

"I told Howie you were here," he said helpfully.

It was the worst thing he could have done, but I hadn't told him not to. "What room?" I said, taking the stairs three at a time.

"Turn left. Third door on the left."

I drew my .38 as I dashed down the hall. The third door on the left was ajar. I tapped on it, but there was no answer. I pushed the door open, but nothing happened. Cautiously I looked inside. No one was there. A dresser drawer sat open with half its contents spilled onto the floor. Someone had left the room in a hell of a hurry.

I flew back down the hall to the vestibule at the bottom of the stairs. The same kid was still standing there. When he saw my Smith and Wesson, his jaw dropped.

"Did he come this way?" I demanded.

Incapable of speech, he shook his head.

"Is there another way down from up there?"

He nodded dumbly.

"For chrissake talk to me! Where is it?"

"The fire escape comes out down by the kitchen."

I raced in the direction he pointed. I came to the backdoor and looked outside long enough to see Manny crouched behind a dumpster. I turned around and almost ran over the kid who had trailed behind me down the hall.

"If he didn't get out here, where else could he be? Is there a basement?"

This time he pointed to a darkened stairway leading down from the kitchen. I heard wailing sirens as backup units charged through traffic. Sprinting to the bottom of the stairs, I paused on a musty landing before dashing down a narrow hall. I checked rooms as I went—laundry room, boiler room, bicycle room, poolroom. All of them were empty.

If Howie hadn't made a run for it before Manny got to the dumpster, he was still hiding somewhere in the building. The question was Where.

I had started up the stairs to begin a systematic, room-to-room search when I remembered chapter rooms. Every fraternity had one—at least they used to—a secret room hidden somewhere in the house, where the whole fraternity gathered for formal meetings and initiations. I went back to the poolroom. One wall curved in a semicircle.

"Where's the chapter room?" I snapped. "There?"

The boy nodded.

"Where's the entrance?"

He opened the door to a seemingly small closet which became a black-walled stucco room, an Aeolian cave for initiation rites. He pointed toward a small door. I motioned him away from it and knocked. No answer. I tried the doorknob. It turned in my hand. I pushed the door open, but stayed outside.

"Howie?" I asked into the blackened room.

There was no answer, but I could sense another person's presence. Maybe I could smell his terror, hear his heart thumping. I knew he was there.

"Police, Howie. We know you're in there. Give yourself up."

Still there was no answer.

"Come on out, Howie. We know all about you and Vince. It's no use."

I heard a half-sob. "I didn't do it." His voice was a choked whisper. "I made him leave, but he said I was an accessory after the fact."

"Come on out, Howie. We can talk about it later."

I stood with one eye closed, hoping to adjust my vision to the deeper darkness of the other room. It didn't help.

There is no silence quite as stark as that between hunter and hunted. The two of us were alone in a frozen universe. The small click of a released safety catch shattered the silence.

"Throw it down," I commanded. "Come out with your hands up."

Instead, Howard Rayburn, age nineteen, put the gun to his head and blew his brains out.

CHAPTER 32

I WAS SICK AS I WALKED THROUGH THE PROCESS. Howie Rayburn was almost the same age as my own son, Scott. The media showed up outside, including the ubiquitous Maxwell Cole. I stumbled across him when I went outside with the medical examiner's team.

He waved to me, but I ignored him. It's a double standard. No one had been particularly interested when Teresa Smith burned to death. She wasn't as newsworthy as someone who might have lit the match. I returned to the building without acknowledging him.

Nobody could tell us where Vince Farley was. We sealed off both Rayburn's and Farley's rooms until Al came back with search warrants. By late afternoon we knew more about Vince Farley than we wanted. His father owned a string of racetracks all over the Southwest. Vince was flunking out of school. He kept a little scrapbook. We found clippings, not only of the three incidents in Seattle, but also one from Iowa City, Iowa.

Same MO. Vince Farley himself was nowhere to be found.

Howard Rayburn's mother, a widow, showed up. She appeared to be a nice lady—shocked, disbelieving, grieving, hurt. Al talked to her; I didn't. Couldn't.

The afternoon turned sunny, the blue clarity of the sky mocking what was going on below. We worked the rest of the afternoon. It was dark before we got back downtown and started writing reports; midnight before I came home and took a long shower, trying to wash away the day's filth. I fell into bed but couldn't sleep. I finally got up and administered a bottle of medicinal McNaughton's. It worked; I slept.

I stumbled to my desk at eight the next morning—sick, hung over, exhausted. Peters called to touch bases. "You guys got a line on Farley?" he asked.

"Not yet." I sighed wearily. "We've got a dragnet out, but it hasn't turned up anything. We heard rumors late last night that he might have crossed into Canada. His mother is divorced and lives in Toronto."

"That means extradition?"

"Fat chance, right?"

"Right," Peters echoed. "So what are you doing today?"

"We'll be back at the U, interviewing fraternity brothers. We didn't get to all of them last night."

And that's what we did. All day long. Back downtown late in the afternoon, we tried to put some international tracers on Vince Farley. Still no luck. We heard through the grapevine that his father's attorney was raising hell with the Chief about his son's name being plastered all over the media. It was the age-old story.

Poor little rich kid fucks up, and Daddy's attorneys ride to the rescue.

I got back to my apartment about five-thirty. I sat down in the chair long enough to take off my shoes. I made the mistake of leaning back, intending to rest my eyes a minute. The next thing I knew, it was six-thirty and the phone jangled me awake.

"Hello," I mumbled into the phone.

"Detective Beaumont, am Ah to understand you're standin' me up?" An angry Southern belle is anything but sultry.

"I'm sorry," I stammered. "I'll be right there."

"Ah've already been waitin' a whole half-hour."

"No, really, I'm only a couple of minutes away."

The Palm Court maître d' greeted me with a knowing smile. "You must be Mr. Beaumont. Right this way, please."

I had been far too preoccupied during the preceding thirty-six hours to give Ms. Colleen Borden from Armour Life Insurance Company any thought. Had I done so, I'm sure I wouldn't have pictured a platinum blonde in her late forties with an hourglass figure and a crimson smile. Her hair was pulled back ballerina-style and covered with a broad, brimmed fedora. A well-cut lavender dress, softly draped, showed her figure to good advantage. At the base of her throat lay a gleaming diamond pendant. Her eyes were a startling shade of violet, set in a timeless face.

The waiter held my chair. I slipped into it while

she gave me a shrewdly appraising once-over. "Well now," she drawled, "Ah don't believe anybody told me you were quite this cute, Detective Beaumont. Seein' you in the flesh maybe Ah'm not so mad at you for fallin' asleep."

It wasn't how I had expected our conversation to start. I mumbled an apology. She held up her hand. "No, now Ah don't want to hear another word about it. We'll just have ourselves a little drink and a little dinner. Then, if you still feel like apologizin', maybe we can work somethin' out." She gave me a sly grin. I would have had to be blind, deaf, and dumb not to have known what she meant.

I put a bland smile on my face and ordered a hair-of-the-dog McNaughton's. "What can I do for you?"

She took a long sip of Southern Comfort. "Mah daddy owns Armour Life Insurance Company," she drawled. "And his daddy owned it before that. We're not very big, but we're solid."

She paused and gave me a dazzling smile. "Years ago, Daddy called me into his office. He doesn't have any sons, you see, and he says, 'Cody.' That's what he calls me. 'Cody, Ah want you to come into the business so you'll know how to run it when the time comes, but Ah don't want you out sellin' none o' this stuff. That's too hard a life for a little lady. What Ah'd like you to do is make sure that when we pay a claim it's on the up and up.' And that's what Ah've been doin' ever since."

"What does this have to do with me?"

Instead of answering my question, she motioned to a waiter who hovered in the background.

"You decided what you want?" she asked. "Ah do believe Ah'll have the pheasant. Ah just love pheasant." Without looking, I nodded, and she ordered two of them. She turned back to me, the smile once more in place.

"Why do you suppose Homer and Darrell Watkins turned you down when you made them such a right tolerable offer?"

With that, any notion that Colleen Borden was a lightweight went right out the window.

"Ames says they found another investor."

"Ralph Ames is your attorney, the one who was handlin' your deal?"

"Yes."

"Do you have any idea where that man is?"

"Ames? Why, no. He said he'd head back to Phoenix tomorrow, but I don't know where he's been today."

"Ah've hung around here all day long, hopin' to run into him, left him messages. He hasn't returned a single call, not one."

"That's not like him," I said contritely, as though both Ames and I had been remiss. "Have you tried in the last few minutes?"

"Ah left word that he should join us." As if on cue, the maître d' hurried to our table. "Excuse me, Miss Borden. There's a gentleman outside who says his name is Mr. Ames. Should I show him in?"

"Oh, by all means. Do have him come in."

There was a flurry of activity around our table as a third place was set. Ames followed the maître d' uncertainly, as though not sure what to expect. I stood to introduce them. It was comical to see.

Ames fell into those violet eyes and never knew what hit him.

"Ah'm very pleased to make your acquaintance, Mr. Ames," Cody drawled. "Ah've been doin' my very best to find you all day long."

"I'm sorry to be so difficult," Ames apologized. "I've been out in Kirkland helping a friend of ours. I was actually . . ." Ames paused and cleared his throat. "Interviewing babysitters. He has to have one by Monday, you know."

Colleen nodded seriously, as though she understood perfectly.

"And then," Ames continued, Colleen's undivided attention making him babble, "once we got the girls registered for school, we had to take them shopping for clothes, shoes, lunch pails, bedding, everything."

I burst out laughing. The very idea of Ralph Ames, attorney extraordinaire, interviewing nannies and dragging tykes through Nordstrom and The Bon on a full-scale shopping marathon struck my funny bone, especially since he was so dead serious about it. Colleen took offense at my laughter. That moment sealed Ralph Ames' fate.

"Mr. Beaumont, Ah think it's perfectly wonderful that Mr. Ames has been helpin' his friend, and Ah don't see any reason for you to be laughin' at him."

Ames turned an interesting shade of red and took a long sip of the Southern Comfort that Colleen had ordered for him. By the time we were into the main course—three pheasants instead of two—Colleen Borden knew as much about Peters' custody fight as confidentiality would allow.

Then, just when I thought we were never going back to Armour Life Insurance Company, Colleen delicately laid down her fork, turned her violet-eyed charm full on Ames, and said softly, "Supposin' we get down to business."

Cody Borden was the consummate iron fist in a velvet glove. "To begin with, Ah've talked to Hal Huggins. He's a nice man, but Ah don't believe he's ever been involved in an insurance case of this magnitude." She blinked a long blink with her very long eyelashes. "You see," she drawled, "we're talkin' about three million dollars altogether."

"Insurance fraud!" Ames exclaimed. "A buy/sell agreement funded with life insurance. Why didn't I think of that?" Ames came on-line without missing a beat.

Colleen smiled at him. "That's right, sweetie. Five hundred thousand apiece, with a five hundred thousand accidental-death benefit."

Ames' accountant mentality took over. He whistled. "That would be plenty to get them out of the woods. When would the claim be paid?"

"Well, now," Colleen murmured, "that all depends, doesn't it? Two to three weeks if everythin's in order. Much longer than that if there's a problem.'

"Three weeks would be in time to ward off the sheriff's sale."

Colleen nodded. "These policies are all well beyond the contestable period. We'll be payin' the claims, regardless. Ah just want to be sure in my own mind that we're not payin' good money to a murderer."

She removed a sheaf of papers from a slender briefcase, handing them to Ames rather than me. Swiftly he skimmed through them. "It's essentially a buy/sell arrangement," he explained to me a few minutes later, "with all proceeds going to the surviving partners."

"And the surviving partners are?" I asked.

"Why, Darrell Watkins and his daddy, of course," Colleen answered sweetly.

"Have you talked to Hal Huggins about this?" I demanded.

"He's got it stuck in his craw that somebody named Wilson did it. But in talkin' to him, Ah kept comin' up with your name, Mr. Beaumont. And then, when Ah started looking into the Belltown Terrace situation, Ah saw your name again." She smiled. "Seemed like too much of a coincidence to me, wouldn't you say?"

Ames had been studying the papers throughout this exchange. He looked around as though waking from a long sleep. "If both surviving beneficiaries were implicated in the deaths of the other partners, what would happen?"

Colleen smiled again. "Why, sweetie, if someone proves that, the proceeds go to the insured's next of kin."

Dinner wasn't over. I believe we had dessert and coffee, but I bowed out of the conversation. I sat there thinking about Mona Larson's brother from Idaho and Sig Larson's three kids and Ginger Watkins' father, Tom Lander.

Maybe Hal Huggins was buying the Don Wilson story, but I wasn't. Cody's idea made perfect sense. Darrell and Homer could knock off the others, frame Wilson, and use the three million to bail themselves out of the hole. Greed for motive rather than revenge.

I made up my mind on the spot that, if Hal Huggins wouldn't do something about it officially, then I would unofficially.

I left the table with Ames and Colleen still huddled over a sheaf of papers. I had the distinct impression, however, that they wouldn't stick to business forever.

CHAPTER 33

HAL HUGGINS DIDN'T ANSWER EITHER AT HOME OR AT the office when I got back from the Westin. Why should he? After all, it was Friday night. As far as Hal was concerned, he had solved three murders that week. He was probably out celebrating.

I tried again the next morning, as soon as I woke up. Woke him, too. "What's going on?" he muttered, half asleep.

"Did you talk to Colleen Borden?"

"That dingey broad? Yes, I talked to her. God-damned insurance companies are all alike—do anything to avoid paying a claim. All they want to do is take your money; then, as soon as some-body dies—"

"Hal," I interrupted, "did you listen to her? I think she's onto something."

"Look here, Beau," Huggins bristled. "I'm tell-ing you once and for all. Wilson did it. We've got motive, opportunity, witnesses that place him near the scene, fingerprints on a confession. What the hell do you want?"

"I want to nail the guilty party."

"You know, Beau, I keep wondering why you're so involved. I heard you were up nosing around Wilson's house the other day. This isn't your case, remember?"

"Are you going to investigate Colleen Borden's allegations or not?"

"The case is closed as far as my office is concerned."

"My mind's made up, don't confuse me with the facts. Didn't you tell me that once? Does it have anything to do with the fact that Tuesday is election day and Darrell Watkins is a major political candidate? Did the sheriff tell you to stifle?"

"Go fuck yourself," Huggins replied, hanging up.

I got Ernie Rogers' home number from the Directory Assistance. "It's Saturday. What time are you coming over?" I asked, once I got him on the phone.

Ernie sounded surprised. "I didn't think you still needed me. I thought the case was closed. That's what the paper said."

"It may be closed there," I returned grimly. "It isn't here. How long will it take you to get to Seattle?"

"I'll check the ferry schedule and call you back."

"Screw the ferry schedule. Charter a float plane. I'll pay for it. Get here as soon as you can. Have him land at the Lake Union dock. I'll pick you up."

He called back a little while later to say that the soonest he could arrive would be one o'clock. It was almost ten. I had three hours to do what I needed to do.

I had kept one of Don Wilson's pictures. I needed to assemble a few others for a rogue's gallery. While I was at it, I decided to kill two birds with one stone.

Directory Assistance gave me Darrell Watkins' campaign headquarters. A quavery-voiced old lady answered the phone. "Do you have access to Mr. Watkins' calendar?" I asked.

"Certainly," she responded. "It's right here on the wall above my head. That way we all know what's going on at all times. Of course, he's canceled everything now that his wife . . ." Her voice trailed off.

"I know. I was wondering about some appearances during the last couple of weeks." I was playing liar's poker and doing my best to sound casual, unhurried. "I'm writing an article about Mr. Watkins. My records show he was in Vancouver and Longview on the eighteenth, and Chehalis, Centralia, and Olympia on the nineteenth. Is that correct?"

"I don't know where you got that," she snorted. "He was scheduled to be in Bellingham and Everett on the eighteenth and nineteenth."

There was a catch of excitement in my throat. Everett is a short hop from Anacortes and the ferry to Orcas.

"Is that all you wanted?" she demanded impatiently.

"Do you have any brochures with his picture?"

"Certainly. We could send you a whole packet. Are you interested in doorbelling?"

"No. All I need is one brochure. Can I pick it up?"

"Our campaign headquarters is at the corner of Denny and First North."

"Good," I said. "I'll be right over."

Getting a picture of Homer Watkins proved somewhat more difficult. Not impossible. I finally managed to dredge one out of a newspaper file. It was several years old and dated from Homer's tenure as president of the Washington Athletic Club. It was good enough for my purposes.

I stopped by the department and sifted through the collection of pictures we keep on hand to build montages for witnesses to use when they're trying to identify a suspect. You can't just hand them a picture and say, "Is this the one?" You have to give them a batch of pictures and say, "Do you see anyone you recognize?"

Ernie was true to his word. The float plane pulled up to the dock on Lake Union right at one. The pilot said he'd have lunch and then come back to the plane. Ernie had left his wheelchair at home. Assisted by a steel crutch, he hopped from the plane to the Porsche. Once inside, Ernie and I took off for Rainier Valley.

The Porsche created quite a stir among some kids playing a spirited game of soccer in the parking lot of the Stadium Apartments, a low-income housing complex on Martin Luther King Way. From the way he had put the Porsche back together, it was clear Ernie Rogers was a top-drawer mechanic, but his skill with language dumbfounded me. The kids broke up their game and admiringly surrounded the car, giving us a thumbs-up greeting. Within moments Ernie was speaking to them in a language I had never heard before. They responded by enthusiastically directing us to a building near the back of the complex.

People with two good legs never notice stairways. We were directed to a set of dingy stairs thick with the stale odor of boiled rice, rancid cooking oil, and old fish. Ernie turned around, sat down, handed me his crutch, then made his way up the steps on his butt without a word of complaint. We located the correct apartment number and knocked on a flimsy, hollow door.

It opened slowly, revealing an old woman, gray-haired and tiny, who peered cautiously up at us. Ernie spoke to her rapidly but softly in the same musical language he had used on the children outside. Her face brightened, and she favored him with a benign smile. A slight inclination of her head motioned us into the room.

It was empty except for one derelict chair and a floor covering of woven mats. I had the feeling that, moments before we entered, the room had teemed with people. Now it contained only two, the old woman and a venerable old man with white hair and a twisted driftwood walking stick. He sat regally on the only chair—a cane-backed wooden one that leaned slightly to one side. He nodded to Ernie, and spoke to the old woman who disappeared and returned with a folding chair for Ernie. The old man spoke again, addressing Ernie, who turned to me.

"He wants to know if Blia is in trouble."

"No," I answered. "We're looking for the man who stole her keys."

The old man studied me closely as Ernie translated. "The hotel didn't believe her when she said someone stole them."

"I do," I told him. When Ernie translated, the old man nodded sagely.

"He wants to know what you want with Blia."

I reached into my coat pocket and removed the packet of pictures. I handed them directly to the old man. "I want to show her these. One of those men may have been the one who stole her keys. Maybe she'll recognize him."

The old man examined the pictures minutely in the dim light of the curtained window, then he spoke quickly to the old woman who shuffled from the room. Moments later she returned, leading a shy young woman with waist-length jet-black hair. The younger woman seemed reluctant, but the old woman prodded her forward. When Blia saw Ernie, her face brightened. She moved forward more willingly.

The woman led Blia to the old man, who handed her the pictures. "Ask her if she saw any of those men at Rosario the day she lost her keys."

Ernie translated. The girl walked to the curtained window and studied the pictures. I held my breath as she leafed through them one by one. It was possible she had seen nothing, would recognize no one. Suddenly she stopped. She handed one of them back to Ernie, who passed it to me.

The face in the picture was that of Homer Watkins.

I'm sure my face betrayed the impact the picture had on me. I had expected it to be Darrell Watkins, wanted it to be him so badly I could taste it. There are very good reasons why neither doctors nor detectives should work on cases too close to home. It warps perspective.

I looked up. Everyone in the room was staring at me. "Ask her when she saw him," I said to Ernie.

He translated for her, then turned to me with Blia's long response. "She was cleaning her last room. Someone had checked in and then changed his mind. The desk wanted the room recleaned because they thought they could rent it again. When she came out of the room, he was standing by her cart. A few minutes later she realized her keys were missing."

"Can she remember exactly what time it was?"

"Late. After dark. Around seven o'clock." Blia hadn't moved from her place near the window. She watched me warily, gauging my reactions to each translation.

"Tell her thank you," I said. "And tell her there's a reward. Someone will be in touch with her next week to arrange it. He will be authorized to pay her five thousand dollars, but she may have to testify in court."

Ernie looked at me quickly before he translated. He spoke for a long time. Blia's face changed several times, mirroring surprise, joy, doubt, and, finally, after the old man spoke sternly, agreement.

"She'll testify," Ernie said. "If you need it."

The old woman showed us out of the apartment. "Five thousand dollars is a lot of money," Ernie said as he bumped his way down the stairs. "Where'd it come from?"

"Beats me," I replied. We were both quiet after that until we were in the car and halfway back downtown. "Whose picture?" Ernie asked.

"Not the guy I expected," I said.

"You can't tell me who, though?"

"No, I'd better not." He accepted my refusal good-naturedly. I felt obliged to explain. "If word leaks out before we're ready on this one—"

"Forget it," he said. "It's no big deal."

We stopped at the Doghouse for coffee before I took him back to the plane. Once the float plane was airborne above Lake Union, I went home.

There was no sense in calling Huggins. His mind was made up. And there was no sense in calling Peters. His hands were full. I called the Westin and was told Mr. Ames had changed his mind. He hadn't checked out, after all. I left a message saying that I would need him in Seattle during the week and that he shouldn't leave without checking with me first. I had a feeling Ames' virtue was no longer intact.

I settled into my recliner. I'm not one of the trendy types who sits in a half-lotus position to do his thinking. My legs would stick permanently. A recliner and a steaming cup of strong coffee are all I need to get the creative juices flowing.

The ball was definitely back in my court. What I had to do more than anything was think it through. There was far too much at stake to go off half-cocked.

Homer. Blia Vang had fingered Homer. He had been at Rosario that Friday afternoon, and no one had known it. So he had gotten the keys and then let Wilson into Ginger's room to get the calendar?

That didn't make sense, but that was the way it looked.

I tried to put myself back in that Friday afternoon, to remember all the events in the exact order in which they had occurred. It can be done. It's a process very much like a self-induced hypnotic trance. Or a time machine.

The parole board meeting got out at four. Ginger and Sig were supposed to meet at five, but Darrell called and held Ginger up, made her late. By the time she reached the rendezvous, Sig Larson was dead.

Homer Watkins and Don Wilson, an unholy alliance. Unless . . . Something Blia Vang had said jumped out at me.

Someone had rented a room at Rosario and then changed his mind. Who? And what about Darrell Watkins' campaign appearances in Everett and Bellingham?

The thought had no more than crossed my mind when I was out of my chair, emptying my cup in the sink and shrugging my way into the shoulder holster.

Either Homer and Darrell were in it together, or Darrell was next on the list.

CHAPTER 34

THE PORSCHE LOVES TO GET ON THE FREEWAY AND GO.
I headed north to Everett, driving directly to the
offices of the *Everett Herald*. It's a small-town paper.
The receptionist, a bored teenager, was happy to
have some company.

I flashed my badge at her, and she bustled
around, finding me what I needed—all papers
from the two-week period prior to October eighteenth. I located the information I wanted, eventually. Buried among wedding announcements,
Pop Warner football scores, and pre-holiday church
bazaars was an article detailing Darrell Watkins'
campaign swing through Bellingham and Everett.
He was to address the Bellingham Rotary and Jay-
cees on Friday afternoon and a League of Women
Voters convention at the Everett Holiday Inn Friday evening. Saturday morning he was scheduled
to be the keynote speaker at a Merchant's Fair
breakfast.

Thanking the receptionist for her help, I drove
to the Holiday Inn. I didn't mess around with the

desk clerk. I asked to speak directly to the manager. He was an eager Young Turk, fresh out of school with a degree in hotel management. His nametag pegged him as Mr. Young, which seemed entirely appropriate.

"What can I do for you?" he asked, after minutely examining my identification.

"I'd like to see your guest register for the night of October eighteenth."

"This is, of course, highly irregular."

"Mr. Young," I said firmly, "I'm attempting to prevent another homicide. There's not much time."

"Can't this wait until Monday when I could check with my superiors in Seattle?"

"No. Someone else could be dead by then." Youth can often be intimidated by a steady, middle-aged stare. It worked like a charm.

"Oh, all right. I don't see how it could hurt."

There were lots of registration slips. Many of the women had registered separately, even though they were staying in the same room—a variation on the female penchant for separate checks. I thumbed through them carefully. I was close to the bottom before I found the one I wanted, a slip that read Darrell Watkins. I jotted down the license number of the car, an '81 Audi.

Mr. Young had stood peering over my shoulder the whole time. "Did you find what you needed?" he asked.

"Yes. Can you make me a copy of this?" I showed him the slip.

"This is nuts. I shouldn't have shown it to you in the first place without a court order. Now you want me to make you a copy?"

"By the time I can get a court order," I said, "the killer may strike again. The score is four to nothing right now. The killer's winning."

He made me a copy. "One more question," I said as he handed me the paper. "Who on your catering staff handled the League of Women Voters convention?"

"That would have been Sue Carleton."

"Is she here?"

He sighed, exasperated. "She's upstairs."

Sue Carleton turned out to be a heavyset dame in her middle years. I had a feeling she had come up through the ranks—without a degree in hotel management but with a healthy regard for and an easy ability to work with other people. She had a pleasant manner and a sparkling sense of humor.

"What can I do for you, Detective Beaumont?" she asked.

"I wanted to talk to you about the League of Women Voters."

"They were awful." She smiled. "Too many chiefs and not enough Indians. I almost lost my mind."

"I wanted to ask you about one of the speakers, Darrell Watkins."

"That jerk. He was late. I had to pay my people overtime because they didn't finish on time."

"What happened?"

"He was supposed to speak at the beginning of the program. He didn't show up until nine when they were almost finished. They let him give his whole speech anyway. I was livid."

I stood. "That's all I needed to know. Did he offer any explanation?"

"Car trouble, I think. Does this help?"

"You'd better believe it. Thanks."

Galloping out of the Holiday Inn, I sped north to Anacortes, hoping I'd hit the ferry schedule right. No such luck. A ferry was just pulling away from the dock as I drove up to the ticket booth. There was nothing to do but cool my heels and wait for the next one.

It was possible Darrell could have been on Orcas with Homer at the time Ginger's room was broken into and still have made it back to Everett by nine. If, that is, he had better luck with the ferries than I did.

Once on Orcas, I drove straight to Rosario without notifying Huggins. I wanted to get in, verify the information, and get back out—without arousing attention.

It was Saturday evening. A laughing crowd was grouped around the massive fireplace in the Moran Room, and a clutch of people stood in front of the desk, waiting to register. The overtaxed desk clerk was far too busy to help me right then.

I went into the Vista Lounge. Barney was at his station. He glanced up and waved as I walked past. I had no more than taken a seat on a stool at the end of the bar when he brought me a McNaughton's and water.

"That's pretty good," I said as he set the drink in front of me.

He grinned. "I don't do much, but I'm good at what I do."

Someone signaled for a beer. Barney drew one

from the tap, delivered it, then came back to me. "So what's up? You get your car back all right?"

I nodded. "Ernie did a great job. I'm up here looking for some answers," I told him.

"What kind?"

"I need to see the guest register for the eighteenth. . . . Quietly," I added.

"Unofficially?" I nodded, and he grinned. "I might be able to help. Did you see the lady at the desk?"

"Just a glimpse. She was busy."

"We're engaged," he said proudly. "Tell me what you want. She'll get it for you."

Another customer summoned him. When he returned, he stood in front of me, vigorously polishing the bar. "What are you looking for?" he asked.

"At least one room was rented twice that day. Someone checked in, changed his mind, and checked back out. I need a copy of any registration slips on rooms that were rented twice that day."

He gave me a sly wink. "Looking for somebody sneaking around, eh?" He glanced at my glass. "You want another?"

"No. I'd better switch to coffee. It's a long drive."

"You're not staying over? We've got rooms."

I shook my head. I drank a couple of cups of coffee and ate a hamburger while I waited. It was almost an hour before Barney's fiancée delivered the goods. There were three rooms that had been rented twice on the eighteenth. Using a lighted hurricane lamp from one of the tables, I studied the copies Barney gave me. Five of the six names didn't ring any bells. Three of them had actually spent the night. The other two were probably respectably married people sneaking an illicit afternoon without their lawfully wedded husbands and wives.

The last name stopped me cold. Don Lacy. The address was in Burien. I wrote it down, 12823 S. 124th. The clincher was that the car was a 1981 Audi, the same make and model listed on Darrell Watkins' guest registration at the Holiday Inn. Naturally the license numbers didn't match. What a surprise! Don Lacy and Darrell Watkins had to be one and the same.

I left the lounge and walked to the last wing of the hotel where Ginger's original room had been. The room registered to Lacy was right next door to Ginger's. When Darrell had been talking to her, pleading with her not to divorce him, he had been directly on the other side of a narrow wallboard partition, not calling long-distance from somewhere on the mainland.

Hurrying back to my car, I barely had time to catch the last ferry to Anacortes. I sat by one of the huge windows, staring at glass that reflected the bright lights inside the boat rather than the midnight water outside.

My mind jumped to a dozen different conclusions. Wilson, Homer, and Darrell all had to be involved together. Somehow. All three of them had been at Orcas that afternoon. Funny how both Darrell and Homer had neglected to mention it.

The question remained, Were they in it together, or was one covering for the other?

I wanted to be the one to find the answers. I owed Ginger that much, but I wasn't working with a full contingent of soldiers. I didn't have all the resources of Seattle P.D. standing behind me, backing me up. I suppose I could have called Huggins and insisted he reopen the case, but I didn't. Pride, I guess. I wanted to nail the case down with a fistful of incontrovertible evidence before I called for reinforcements.

My mother used to say, "Pride goeth before a fall." It's true.

By the time I reached Anacortes, I had a game plan mapped out in my mind.

It was almost two in the morning when I hit Seattle. I drove straight through town and took the Sea-Tac exit to Burien. The address on S. 124th street wasn't hard to find. A silver Audi was parked in the driveway. I drove home.

Once in the house, I went searching for the phone book. I looked under Lacy, Darlene, 12823 S. 124th Street. That answered a lot of questions. I put the phone book away and went to bed.

Ames woke me Sunday morning. According to my count, that was two Sundays in a row. He wondered if I would care to join Cody and him for brunch at the Westin. Ames sounded smug. He couldn't quite conceal his lack of disappointment when I said no. Ames had never struck me as much of a ladies man. He was proud of what he regarded as a personal conquest.

I wasn't the kind of guy to tell him that he had

been duck soup for someone like Colleen Borden, and she was far too much of a lady to tell him herself. I left his delusions of adequacy intact.

"Too much to do, Ames, sorry. But I'll want to talk to you later today or tomorrow about some of the reward money."

"Okay," he said. "But if you don't reach me in my room, you might try Cody's."

"Right," I said.

I waited until ten o'clock before I called Janice Morraine at home. She's a criminalist in Seattle's Washington State Patrol Crime Lab. Over the months, she and I had become friends. I couldn't call the crime lab directly to ask for help. I didn't have an official case number.

"How are you at handwriting analysis?"

"So-so," she answered.

"How about trading breakfast for an off-the-record opinion."

She laughed. "Smooth talker," she said.

We went to an omelet house at the bottom of East Madison, right on Lake Washington. There, amid the early-afternoon Sunday brunch crowd, she smoked one cigarette after another and compared the two signatures from copies of the guest-registration forms. She studied them in silence for several long minutes, leaving me to sip my coffee and stare at the top of her head bent over the papers in total concentration. At last she looked up at me.

"You know I'm not the final word," she said. I nodded. "But in my opinion, they were signed by the same person."

"That's what I thought."

"Is this *the* Darrell Watkins?" she asked, pointing at his signature. I nodded again. "If this is something bad, you'd better not just take my word for it," she warned.

"I won't."

"And we haven't had this conversation?"

"How did you guess? Now, what do you want to eat?"

We each had huge omelets with crisp hash browns and thick, jam-covered toast. As far as I was concerned, it was a celebration. I was getting closer and closer to nailing those bastards. Nothing definite. Strictly circumstantial, but closer nonetheless.

Darrell Watkins, Homer Watkins, and the deceased Don Wilson. Gradually I was closing in on the truth.

Hurrying back to my apartment, I pawed through the receipt shoe box until I found my bill from Rosario. The long-distance phone calls were there—time, duration, phone numbers, and charges. Thank God for computer printouts.

I saw the problem immediately. How could Homer have been seen by Blia Vang at seven o'clock Friday night, less than an hour after he had phoned my room and left word for Ginger to call? Her answering call to Seattle was right there on my bill, dialed direct from my room. The time on the printout said seven-forty. The call from Orcas to Seattle had lasted six minutes.

Settling into my recliner, I studied the list of phone calls with minute care. Again on Saturday, there were calls to Seattle numbers, one to Homer in the early evening and one to Peters much later.

I didn't bother to work the crossword puzzles Ida Newell had dropped outside my door. I sat there and wondered why Blia Vang had lied to me, or if she hadn't, how had Homer Watkins managed to be in two places at once.

CHAPTER 35

MONDAY MORNING I WOKE UP EARLY AND WAITED UNtil six before I called Ray Johnson in Pasco. Evie answered the phone. "Just a minute, Beau. Ray's in the shower." Evie and I chatted amiably until Ray came on the phone.

"How the hell are you?" he boomed.

"I need your help, Ray."

"Sure thing. What's up?"

"Remember that morning when we were all there in your office and the governor's office called?"

"I remember. Just before the press conference. They wanted to make sure we had you safely under lock and key."

"Do you happen to remember the man's name? The governor's aide?"

Ray Johnson is an encyclopedia of names. Once he hears one, he doesn't forget it. When he left Seattle for Pasco, I felt as though I had lost my right arm. I had come to depend on him to remember names for both of us.

"Just a minute now," he said. "Hold on and it'll come to me. Something to do with a bird. Hawk . . . Hawkins. That's it, I'm almost sure. What do you need him for? I thought the case was all sewed up."

"Except for a couple of loose ends," I said.

By ten to eight I was suffering from a serious case of twenty-four-minute flu. I called the Department at eight. Peters wasn't in yet. Margie took the call.

"I'm not feeling well, Marge," I said, doing my best to sound feeble.

"I hope it's not stomach flu," Margie sympathized. "That's going around. My kids were both down with it last week and missed two whole days of school."

By five after eight, I was in the Porsche heading south on the freeway, feeling much better. It was a miracle. As I drove toward Olympia, my mother's words came back to me. "One thing about Jonas, he doesn't let good sense stand in the way of what he wants."

My mother's twenty-five-year-old words still held the ring of prophecy. What I was doing didn't make good sense. J. P. Beaumont, good sense to the contrary, was turning up the heat under Homer and Darrell Watkins, attempting to smoke them into the open. It was best not to use a direct attack.

I parked as close as I could to the governor's office on the governmental campus and walked in as big as life. I asked the doe-eyed young receptionist for Mr. Hawkins.

"Do you have an appointment?" she asked.

"No," I said, flashing my ID in her direction. "But I'm sure he'll see me just the same."

I was right. Within five minutes I was shown into Lee Hawkins' office. I handed him my City of Seattle business card which he examined with some care.

"Weren't you the one—"

"Who was mistakenly arrested in Pasco?" I supplied helpfully. "Yes, I am."

He nodded. "I thought so. The name looked familiar. What can I do for you?" He dropped my card onto his desk.

"I'm actually here about the Washington State Victim/Witness Protection Program."

"I see."

"What's going on with that?"

"Well, we've been involved in negotiations with the Senate and House Judiciary Committees. There's no question that the program will cost money, although the governor's office supports the idea wholeheartedly." He paused and looked at me. "Is this on or off the record?"

"Off."

"We've about ironed out all resistance. We're hoping it'll be presented as a joint bill early next session."

"No announcement will be made prior to that?"

"That would be premature, Mr. Beaumont."

"And no announcement was planned for the parole board retreat on Orcas?"

"Absolutely not."

Just in case my message hadn't gotten through,

I added one final hook. "That's funny. Don Wilson was sure there would be an announcement at Orcas."

Lee Hawkins smiled. "He must have been mistaken."

"Of course," I replied. "Thanks." I left and drove straight back to Seattle. If somebody called to check on my health, the invalid should be at home, in bed. And if somebody took the bait, the fisherman should be hanging onto the other end of the pole for dear life.

Predictably, the phone was ringing as I got off the elevator. It was Peters. "Where the hell have you been? You're supposed to be sick."

"I needed some medicine," I lied. "How're the girls?"

"They're in school. The baby-sitter Ames hired will pick Heather up after kindergarten. Tracie can walk home by herself. Mrs. Keen—that's the baby-sitter's name—will stay until I get home tonight. Do you have everything you need? Yogurt, or maybe some Pepto-Bismol?"

"Everything, thanks. I'm much better. What are you doing?"

"Manny and Al are trying to negotiate a peace treaty with the feds to extradite Farley from Canada."

"Good luck." I was glad I wouldn't be there to fight and lose the opening rounds of the paperwork war. I've seen more than one crook hole up across the border, hiding out in plain sight behind a mountain of red tape.

"Get well," Peters said. "See you tomorrow."

I fixed a pot of coffee, sat down, and put my

feet up. The next caller was Ames, totally focused on business. "What about the reward money?"

"Never mind. The witness may have lied to me. We'll have to see."

"Okay," Ames said agreeably. "Whatever you say."

"How's Cody?" I couldn't resist catching him off base. Ames was trying with some difficulty to concentrate on work. His obvious confusion was laughable.

He hesitated, half switching gears, attempting to maintain his dignity. "She's working today. I don't know doing what." He paused again, scrambling for what to say next. "I guess, as long as I'm here, I'll go ahead and mother-hen the penthouse deal. Are you going to do any customizing?"

I hadn't thought about it. "What do you suggest?"

Ames sighed. "I'll get a couple of decorators to take a look and see what they say."

"Just one thing, Ames."

"What's that?"

"Wherever I go, my recliner goes."

"Right," he said.

He hung up. I poured myself a cup of coffee. And waited. It was the calm before the storm. I was convinced the storm was coming. Who would call, Darrell or Homer? I figured it was a toss-up.

When the phone finally rang at four that afternoon, it was a delivery boy bringing flowers. I buzzed him into the building and opened the door without even bothering to check the peek-hole. The crime prevention unit would have drummed me off the force.

"Hello, Detective Beaumont," Darrell Watkins said easily. "I've got a gun. You're coming with me." He raised a snub-nosed .38 from behind the box of flowers.

He lifted my Smith and Wesson out of its holster and dropped it into a jacket pocket, all the while keeping me covered.

"I understand you were making inquiries about the Victim/Witness Protection Program."

"That's right."

"Was your interest personal or professional?"

"Both."

"Since that's a program I'm interested in, too, I thought maybe we should get together and talk. Where's your car?"

"In the garage."

"Let's go."

He directed me to the Watkins mansion on Capitol Hill. I walked ahead of him to the house and pushed the door open, half expecting to find Homer waiting inside, but the entryway was empty, the house itself quiet.

I stepped over the threshold, tensing as I realized we were alone, hoping I could catch him off guard, take him by surprise.

Instead, something hit me behind my right ear. I went down like a sack of potatoes.

The cold woke me. I opened my eyes, thinking I'd gone blind. I could see nothing. I struggled to move, and ran my nose into my knee. It startled me to find my knee jammed directly in front of my face. It shouldn't have been there. I tried moving my fingers and felt my feet. Slowly it started making sense. I was tied, trussed in a fetal position, with my hands and feet fastened together at my ankles.

I was also stark naked.

It's tough getting your bearings in pitch darkness. Under me were what seemed to be wooden slats. A humming motor clicked off, followed by ominous silence.

I was trapped in a refrigerator waiting to die.

Rocking painfully on the small of my back, I tried rolling as far as I could in one direction, hoping to find a door and figure out a way to open it. I rolled until I encountered a smooth, hard surface. Before I could ascertain whether it was door or wall, a door at the other end of the compartment jerked open. A single lightbulb next to the door snapped on, momentarily blinding me.

When I could see, Darrell Watkins was standing over me. "My, my. Aren't we clever. I didn't think you'd wake up before I got back. I had to take your car downtown and park it on Third Avenue. In the bus zone. By now it's being towed at owner's expense. It'll take days to find it."

"You're crazy."

"Maybe," he said agreeably. "But smart."

"Is this how Wilson died of exposure?"

He nodded. "I let him hang around long enough for the drug to get out of his system, then I sprayed him with cold water. Worked like a charm. I never had to tie him up. I'm afraid your rope burns will show."

I wanted to keep him talking. I gauged the distance between us, wondering if I could roll against his legs with enough strength to knock him down.

"You met him on the ferry?"

"He met me on the car deck so I could give him a copy of the governor's proclamation."

"But there was no proclamation."

Watkins shrugged. "Don Wilson didn't know that. He got in the car, I gave him one little prick with this, and he went night-night."

He held up a hypo, the needle glinting in the light from the bulb near the door. I made a tentative roll toward him. He laughed and stepped away. "None of that," he said.

"Wilson went off the ferry in your car?"

"That's right. Out cold on the floor of the backseat. I put him in the trunk later. He slept like a baby until Sunday when I finally got him back to Seattle. I had plenty of time to see Sig Larson."

"And kill him?"

He grinned. "That too." He sobered suddenly. "You puzzle me, Detective Beaumont. As far as I can tell, you're the only one who doesn't believe Wilson did it. How come?"

"Gut instinct. Wilson left a chicken thawing at home, and he didn't feed his cat. Looked like he planned to come back."

"He did. You think you're pretty smart, don't you! Guess that's why you're there and I'm here, right?" He laughed—the maniacal laughter of someone losing his grip. "Except for that, I was good, though, wasn't I? Framed Wilson every step of the way, that poor, stupid bastard. He wanted to make headlines."

"You're the one who called him to Orcas?"

He nodded, grinning. "You bet. I even arranged for that reporter to do a series on him. That was brilliant."

His words reeked of ugly truth. "You've been planning this for a long time."

"Months. This was my last chance before the sheriff's sale. After that it would have been too late."

"Mona too?"

"Mona too."

"How did you know she was at the Red Lion?"

"My father. I told him I wanted to explain why I couldn't go to Sig's funeral. I was waiting. When you drove up, I decided to use your car. That was masterful, don't you think?"

"You did it for the money?"

"Money isn't everything, but it helps. I'll need every penny to get back on even ground."

"You think you'll get away with it?"

"Absolutely!"

"How did you get Ginger drunk?"

He laughed. "You should have seen her face. She was real surprised to see me. I was waiting just outside the gate. I almost missed her because she was driving a different car. Your car. How come?"

I ignored his question and repeated my own. "How'd you get her drunk?"

"A hose, a soft plastic hose. That was for Tom's benefit. She promised him she'd never drink again. Little Miss Perfect. Shoved it down her throat and poured the booze through it. She was already unconscious. It worked, too. Did you see old Tom at the funeral?"

"What about the calendar. Did you take it?" If I was going to die, it would at least be *with* some answers.

"Sure. I had to put Wilson's fingerprints on something while he was passed out in the back of the car."

Far away, through the chill, I heard the chime of the doorbell. Darrell jumped as though shot. I tried to call for help. He covered the distance between us in one long step. A hand clamped over my mouth, and a needle pricked my arm.

The lights went out, literally and figuratively.

CHAPTER 36

WHEN I AWAKENED AGAIN, MY FINGERS AND TOES were numb. Trying not to succumb to panic, I moved them as much as possible, hoping to force circulation back into them. There was a gag in my mouth with sticky tape holding it in place.

The humming motor clicked off. In the subsequent silence, I could hear another person's breathing.

I strained to listen. The roaring beat of my own heart threatened to drown out the shallow sound. The person was sleeping a sleep very close to the big one. Panting with effort, I rocked toward the sound. Four painful rocks away, I encountered another naked body, bound and trussed as I was, with legs as hairy as my own. Another man. For some unaccountable reason, that made me feel better.

Positioning my back against his, I tried to jar him awake. He stirred a little, but immediately resumed his shallow breathing. Again I attempted to shake him. Exertion caused beads of sweat to pop out on my body. I was aware of further heat loss as cold, dry air met perspiration.

Painfully I scooted around until my feet were in his face. I kicked him, and his breathing changed. He was awake now, whoever he was. Some circulation had returned to my fingers and toes. I felt for the tape that covered his mouth. Grasping a corner of it between my thumbs and forefingers, I rolled away from him, taking the tape with me.

It took long, precious minutes to roll back again and reposition myself to remove the cloth material that had been stuffed into his mouth behind the tape. "Thank you," he choked once the gag was out. I recognized the voice.

Homer Watkins lay on the wooden slats beside me.

He had not yet mastered the fundamentals of movement in our condition. I rolled around until my face was against his fingers. His first numbed attempts at grasping the tape on my gag didn't work. It took numerous tries before he was at last able to hold the tape while I rolled away. Then I maneuvered my way back so he could remove the gag.

"Who are you?" he asked as soon as I could speak.

"Beaumont," I answered. "What time is it?"

"I don't know. It was morning when he put me in here. He kept me up all night, raving. He's crazy."

"We'll discuss that later. Let's get out of here first before we die of cold or suffocation. Can you untie me?"

We struggled in the dark, our fingers too numb

and clumsy to know what they were about. Time passed, I don't know how much. Finally I gave up in defeat. "Stay here," I ordered. "I'm going to find a bottle to break."

I remembered seeing a wine rack, but in the struggle to free us, I had become disoriented. I rocked back and forth across the confines of our prison, searching for the rack, my muscles screaming at the unaccustomed position. After what seemed like hours, I finally bumped up against the stack of corked bottles.

Deliberately breaking a bottle seems easy, but not if your hands and feet are tied together. The adult male body has long since lost the newborn limberness which allows a baby to suck its toes. Each movement was an agony, each failure unbearable. I wanted desperately to break the bottle in the farthest corner of our cage. There's an atavistic fear of bleeding to death in the dark. I didn't want to roll blindly and helplessly on broken glass.

At last I managed to return to Homer with a jagged shard from a bottle. "You do me," I said. "If anybody gets cut, it'll be me."

Fortunately, the insides of our wrists were tied together. The cuts and slices in my flesh, though painful and bloody, were also superficial. As Homer sawed at my restraints I asked him questions. The exercise served two purposes. It gave me some answers, and it took both our minds off the sticky blood that accompanied his work.

"Why did you go to Rosario that Friday?"

"Darlene said she thought that's where Darrell went. I was worried about him. He was upset."

"Why?"

"God knows he had no right to be jealous, but he couldn't believe she'd go ahead and divorce him."

"You took the maid's keys and broke into Ginger's room?"

"Someone had already been there. The room was a mess. I panicked."

"But I talked to you. Ginger called you back."

"When she didn't return my call at first, I was afraid he might have killed her too."

"Ginger called you in Seattle. I have the phone number on my bill."

"I have a phone in the car. I forwarded calls there."

A long silence ensued between us, with only the scraping of glass on the fibrous rope filling the emptiness left by the stilled motor. "Why didn't you turn him in?"

He waited a long time to answer me. "When they said it was Wilson, I believed it, wanted to believe it."

"It wasn't."

"I know," he said hollowly.

Eventually, after what seemed an eternity, the rope parted. My hands and feet were freed.

To my complete frustration, I wasn't instantly able to straighten up and walk to the light switch. My muscles were too cramped and stiff. I lurched across the wooden slats, crawling awkwardly on my knees, dreading the broken glass, groping blindly for the elusive switch I knew was there. Eventually I found it.

The sudden light from the single 40-watt light was dazzling. I found the thermostat and turned the refrigeration unit off, then I cut through Homer's bonds. Movement returned slowly. Even then, it didn't do us a hell of a lot of good: there was no latch inside the refrigerator door, only a smooth, seemingly impenetrable metal surface.

I turned from the door to Homer. "How long have you known for sure?"

"Since last night. I wouldn't let myself believe it. I never saw him in a jealous rage before."

"Jealous rage hell!" I said harshly, stripping away Homer's last vestige of justification. "He's after money, the insurance. He set it up to frame Wilson for the first three. You can bet he has some plan so it will look like J. P. Beaumont did away with you."

Homer swayed dangerously. I caught him and broke his fall. "He would, wouldn't he! He'd kill me too." Homer Watkins sank the rest of the way to the floor. You don't fake the kind of shock that spread across his face. Seeing it told me once and for all that Homer was innocent. Darrell Watkins had acted alone.

The naked old man, diminished, squatted brokenly on his haunches, a picture of abject defeat. I looked down, thinking to help him to his feet. In looking down, I saw our way out.

Our cell's wooden slats were actually the tops of pallets, wooden lathing on frames of sturdy two-by-fours. "Get up, Homer, quick," I urged, grasping him by the wrist and pulling him to his feet.

The pallets were about three and a half feet square. I picked one up, hefted it, stood it on edge. With both of us swinging in concert, we could use it as a battering ram. The latches on the outside of the door couldn't hold forever under that kind of treatment.

I explained the plan. "If the door opens and he's outside, chances are he'll have a weapon. Keep swinging, and hope we can hit him."

We took a first tentative swing at the door. The noise of the blow seemed deafening. We waited, breathless, expecting Darrell to charge through the door. Nothing happened. We swung again. Again nothing happened.

"All right," I said, "here goes. Swing together in rhythm. Back and forth. Eventually we'll build momentum."

I didn't tell Homer my other worry, that our air would run out and we'd suffocate before we ever broke through to the outside. At least we'd die warm.

Swing, blam. Swing, blam. Swing, blam. Obviously the house was empty, or the noise would have aroused a response. Swing, blam. Swing, blam. Swing, blam. The metal dented as the inside of the door crushed against an outer shell. Swing, blam. Swing, blam. Swing, blam. The door shuddered each time we hit it, giving way under every blow. Swing, blam. Swing, blam. Swing, blam. As the hinges crumbled, momentum carried us into the kitchen. We were out. We were free. We weren't going to die.

At least not then, and not in a refrigerator.

The kitchen was dark. It was night. Homer crossed the floor and switched on a light. A clock over the sink said nine o'clock. "What night?" I asked.

"Tuesday," he said. "Election night." The strength that had sustained him as we battered the door ebbed away. He leaned heavily against the stainless steel table in the center of the room. "What are you going to do?" he asked.

I gave the first answer that came to mind. It had no bearing on the question he was really asking. "I'm going to find some clothes."

There is something implacably sane about insanity. I found all our clothes, both Homer's and mine, in a dirty-clothes hamper in the laundry room. Where else? It was as though Darrell expected a maid to appear and wash them for him, maybe even dispose of the corpses in his refrigerator—a kind of macabre *noblesse oblige*. Darrell Watkins was no more accustomed to living without money than I was used to living with it.

Homer was still leaning against the table when I returned to the kitchen. He hadn't moved. "What are you going to do?" he asked again, his voice a plaintive monotone.

I countered with another question. "Where is he?"

"The victory party."

"Where?"

Homer took the clothes I handed him. "I won't tell," he said stubbornly. "I'll show you. Will you arrest him?"

"If I can."

"Don't," he said.

I was bent over, tying my shoe, convinced I had misunderstood him. "What did you say?"

"Don't arrest him. Put him out of his misery. He's a mad dog."

I knew what he was asking and why. I shook my head. "I'm an officer of the law, Homer. I can't do that."

My .38 had been in its holster at the bottom of the clothes hamper. I checked it now, making sure it was loaded, that it wasn't jammed. "Will he be armed?"

"No," Homer stopped speaking abruptly and stood examining his shoes as though unsure which shoe went on what foot. "I can't say," he resumed at last. "He's killed four people so far. What do I know?"

A phone hung on the kitchen wall. I had seen it the moment the light came on, but I waited to use it until we were both dressed. Homer's dignity had suffered enough.

While I waited, I washed the dried blood from my hands and wrists. When Homer finally finished tying his shoelaces, I picked up the phone and dialed the department. It was late, after nine, but I knew Peters would be there. We were partners. He would be working, trying to find me.

"Beau!" he exclaimed, relief evident in his voice. "Where the hell are you?"

Quickly I gave him the address. "Come as fast as you can. Bring a couple squad cars with you, but no sirens, understand?"

"Right," he replied without question.

Homer had disappeared from the kitchen while I talked on the phone. He returned now, wearing a heavy jacket over his suit. He still looked cold and pale. "Are you warming up?" I asked.

He nodded. "I'm coming with you." He was determined.

"You can't," I said. "It's too dangerous. It would be better if you stayed here."

"No. I know where he'll be. Maybe I can talk him into giving up."

It was remotely possible. "Where's the party?" I asked.

"Will you take me along?"

I relented. "Oh, all right. Now where are we going?"

"The Trade Center," Homer replied.

"Shit!" I remembered seeing live election-night coverage from the Muni-League party in previous years. It was usually held in the Seattle Trade Center. The candidates and their campaign workers would gather there, winners and losers alike, to watch the returns. There would be throngs of people, drunk and sober, television cameras, bands, lights, reporters. It would be chaos—the last place any cop in his right mind wants to go after a crazed killer.

Peters and four uniformed patrolmen arrived within minutes. The three of us—Peters, Homer, and I—rode in a squad car to the Trade Center at Elliott and Clay.

"Let me talk to him," Homer insisted as we made our way through traffic. "Maybe I can get him to surrender."

My initial reaction was to say no out of hand. We're not in this business to risk civilian lives. Peters, however, assumed the role of devil's advocate. "It's going to be a madhouse in there. If Homer can get him to come quietly, it could prevent wholesale bloodshed."

Spending well over twenty-four hours in cold

storage had put me in a mood to listen to sweet reason. "All right," I agreed. "So how do we handle it?"

Homer let out his breath as though he had been holding it. "I'll lead the way to our spot. We're usually on the first floor, near the escalator. Give me a minute or so to find him."

It was better than no plan at all.

We approached the Trade Center with lights flashing but no sirens. Not wanting to broadcast a warning, we maintained radio silence. Surprising him was our only chance. Alerting the world could create a riot.

Once there, Peters designated an officer to assume command outside the center. He deployed men to cover all building and parking-garage entrances. It was an empty gesture. We all knew that if panic ensued, no one would be able to tell Darrell Watkins from hundreds of other terrified partygoers crushing through the doors, racing to get outside.

Peters and I paused for a moment outside the door, giving Homer a head start in crossing the crowded room. "Are you sure you're okay?" Peters asked.

"Yeah. I'm all right."

"I'll go first," he said. "You follow."

"No deal, asshole," I told him. "You've got a couple little kids to raise. No fucking way you're sticking me with that job."

Before Peters had a chance to object, I pushed my way in front of him, following Homer Watkins into a wall-to-wall throng of people.

CHAPTER 37

AFTERWARD, THERE WERE CONFLICTING STORIES. A woman said she saw Homer Watkins walk up to Darrell, pull a gun out of his jacket, and try to shoot him. Others said there was a struggle, the gun went off, and Homer fell mortally wounded.

I heard the report of a pistol and a woman's scream. Time froze. The sea of people turned as one man, moving toward the disturbance and away from it at the same time, surging forward and back, closing ranks. I fought my way through, moving in slow motion, flinging people aside, only to have others blunder into my path.

"Out of the way. Police!" Peters roared behind me, but the crowd became denser, more compact. Absolutely silent, and compact. To this day, I don't know if that silence existed anywhere but in my mind. It ceased when I reached the escalators.

People coming down screamed and swirled back up the moving stairs, attempting to escape the carnage below. They encountered a wall of people above them who stood unable to move, transfixed by fear.

I saw Darrell Watkins as he broke and ran. Gun in hand, he dashed up the escalator three and four steps at a time, plunging over people, pushing them aside.

Delayed pandemonium erupted through the crowd as I touched the rail of the down escalator. Maybe the noise was there the whole time and I only just then heard it. Clearing the way with my drawn .38, I charged up the downward treadmill, desperate to reach the top. My only hope was to drive him farther up into the building. Away from the crowds. Away from doors that would lead him outside.

Peters must have been only one or two steps behind me at the outset, but the crowd caught him in a crushing wave of panic and carried him back toward the door with them. I paused and turned briefly at the top of the stairs, hoping he was with me. He wasn't.

It would be Darrell Watkins and J. P. Beaumont. Alone.

The Trade Center is made up of a soaring atrium, with a ground floor and two layers of shops arranged around circling balconies under a huge skylight. Watkins charged up the second escalator. On the second level the crowd had thinned. I raced across the landing to the up escalator and followed, watching in dismay as he disappeared around a corner and down a hall before I reached the next level.

He was halfway down the long corridor when I

turned the corner in hot pursuit. "Stop or I'll shoot," I shouted.

I paused to fire, but he was out of range. My slug ponged harmlessly off the wall behind him. I ducked my chin into my chest and sprinted down the corridor after him as he vanished into a stairwell. Gasping for breath, I flung open the fire door. I stood on a concrete landing, listening to the echo of retreating footsteps. For one heart-stopping moment, I thought they were going down. Then a gust of fresh air rushed down the stairwell into my face, followed by the warning shriek of an alarm on an opened emergency exit.

He had gone to the roof.

I crept up the stairs. It could be a trap. He might have opened and shut the outside door to trick me. Maybe he was lying in wait around the blind corner of the stairs, ready to blast me into oblivion. I held my breath as I rounded the turn. He wasn't there. The stairs leading to the emergency exit were empty.

Below I heard the wail of sirens as ambulances and emergency vehicles raced to the scene. They would set up a command post and summon the Emergency Response Team, trying to position them to negotiate a surrender or, as a last resort, to fire off a clean shot. Peters would direct officers through the building, evacuating the crowd, securing first one area and then another.

But all that was happening in another world, far below us. Out on the roof, Darrell Watkins was waiting. For me.

I pushed open the heavy door. Over the wail of

the alarm, I heard a bullet whine past the door's metal frame above my head. That was his second shot. I counted, wondering subconsciously what kind of a gun Homer had smuggled into his jacket. How many bullets? Did Darrell have four more shots, or seven? And did he have another gun of his own?

Standing in what amounted to a metal bunker at the top of the stairwell, I was better off trying to draw his fire and exhaust his ammunition while I could use the heavy door as armor between us. Each bullet he expended was one less available to slaughter innocent bystanders. Or me.

I yanked the alarm wire off the wall, silencing its bloodcurdling screech. In the sudden quiet that followed, a surprising calm settled over me. He was trapped. His only way out was past me. If I could drive him to a frenzy, force him to attack me in the open, maybe I could end it.

The irony struck me with the force of a physical blow. Darrell Watkins and J. P. Beaumont, men who had possessed the same woman, were locked in mortal combat.

I remembered Homer's hopeless pronouncement in the kitchen. "Put him out of his misery." I was tempted! God, was I tempted! But shooting was too easy, too good for him. I wanted him to live to know his loss, to pay a price, to suffer humiliation and defeat, to live out his days with Philip Lathrop as his lifelong companion. They deserved each other.

I would take him alive. I steeled myself to use every weapon at my disposal.

Somehow Ginger Watkins would forgive me. I opened the door a crack so he could hear me.

"She was a hell of a lay," I called into the night.

"What?"

"Ginger. She was one hell of a lay," I taunted. "Too bad you didn't know how good she was."

Another bullet whined off the metal door. That was three.

"You lying son of a bitch!"

"What's the matter. Can't take a dose of your own medicine? She was hot stuff, Darrell," I continued, soft enough so he had to strain to hear me. "She was so hungry. You never gave her what she wanted. She needed a man to take her, to make her know she was a woman."

I waited, silence brittle between us, hoping another bullet would crash into the wall near my head. Nothing happened. He was across the roof from me, crouched out of range behind a small fenced terrace outlined in a sudden splash of moonlight. Needing to draw his fire, I opened the door and spun around toward the back of the rooftop box that formed the top of the stairwell.

It worked. Too well. A slug ripped into my upper left arm, spinning me against the wall. Searing pain came quickly, making it hard to talk, to concentrate. How many bullets was that now, four or five?

"You couldn't handle that, could you?" I rasped through gritted teeth. "You had to have young ones like Darlene, girls you could impress with money if not performance. Ginger had been empty so long I couldn't fill her up."

"Liar," he said.

"Just because you couldn't get it up for her didn't mean nobody could."

"No," he croaked, his voice a hoarse, broken whisper. "It's not true."

"It is, too. Ask me. Ask Sig. Didn't he tell you? He could have."

"Maybe with him, not you." His voice rose dangerously. A tongue of flame spewed from his pistol in the darkness. The shot whistled harmlessly away into the night sky. Five or six? Let there be only six bullets, I prayed, not nine.

"I can prove it. How about the stretch marks from Katy? Remember those, or had it been so long since you looked at her that you forgot?"

I waited to see if he would reply. There was nothing. No response. "She'd have been stupid to divorce you," I continued. "She should have just screwed around behind your back. That would have been fair."

Several separate shots peppered the wall of the stairwell, followed by silence. For a long time we remained motionless, frozen in place, him across the fenced balcony and me behind the stairwell, a sticky stream of blood oozing through my jacket sleeve. I couldn't tell for sure if he had emptied the bullet chamber. Or if he had another gun.

It was time to play Russian roulette.

I stepped into the open. If he had only one shot left, he could squander it on me. Whether or not he got me, Darrell Watkins was finished.

"I always knew she was fucking around. She had to be."

"Is that why you killed her, Darrell, or was it the money?"

He raised up, his form outlined on the other side of the terrace. "Both," he said simply. "She was going to divorce me." He spoke with the wonder of a philosopher contemplating life's fundamental mysteries. He seemed quiet, subdued.

"Drop the gun, Darrell."

"I won the election. Did you know that?"

"Put your hands on your head. You're under arrest."

My words were a catalyst, spurring him to action. With an enraged roar, he vaulted over the fence, charging at me like a wounded bull. He landed on the terrace.

Except it wasn't a terrace at all.

It was the skylight.

The glass shattered. With an agonizing screech, he plunged out of sight, crashing into the mêlée of television cameras and milling people three stories below.

I walked over to the jagged hole and looked down. Far below, Darrell's crumpled body lay in a broken heap, seeping blood on the red brick floor. Around him television cameras hummed, fighting for focus and position, recording live footage for the people staying up late to watch election-night returns. Viewers would have their full recommended daily dose of blood and guts before they fell asleep. In living color.

The door behind me flew open. Peters burst onto the rooftop, his .38 glinting in the moonlight. "Are you all right?" he demanded.

"I am now."

CHAPTER 38

WE WENT TO PETERS' HOUSE IN KIRKLAND THE FOL-
lowing Sunday for dinner. My left arm was in a
sling. Cody Borden insisted she knew just what I
needed. She would cook Southern for us—
Southern Fried Chicken, black-eyed peas, and
cornbread. She bustled around Peters' kitchen
with Peters serving as cook's helper. She wore
stiletto heels. One of Peters' oversized aprons was
cinched tightly around her tiny waist. She looked
better than any middle-aged woman has a right
to look.

Peters was catering to the invalid. I had been
off work the rest of the week, recuperating. In
the interim, Peters, Cody, and Ames had joined
forces to spoil me rotten.

Ames, content for once to let Cody out of his
sight, sat on a couch with Heather and Tracie cud-
dled on either side of him. He was teaching them
the Pledge of Allegiance. They had never learned
it while they lived with New Dawn in Broken

Springs, Oregon. At Greenwood School in Kirkland, they were required to memorize it.

I listened on the sidelines. Uncle Ralph, as they called Ames, showed infinite patience. It was funny that the man who inspired stark terror in the heart of Maxwell Cole was meek as a lamb with those two little ankle-biters. They had him wrapped around their fingers.

It was a quiet family setting, as American as apple pie. I sat in an easy chair across from them, my arm safe from squirming little bodies, sipping a McNaughton's. Physically, I remained in the room, but my thoughts roamed far afield.

Had Homer Watkins lived, things would have been different. Since there were no surviving partners, however, Armour Life would pay the insurance proceeds to each person's next of kin.

Tom Lander had put his 76 Station on the market. He planned to buy a motor home and hit the road. Sig's children had been notified and were in the process of filing a claim. No one had yet been able to locate Mona's brother, but Cody said she was working on it. Cody said it would be only a matter of days before death benefits owing them were paid.

As far as we could tell, Homer had no surviving kin, and his attorney said that his will left everything he owned to Children's Orthopedic Hospital.

I understood Blia Vang had used her reward money to make a down payment on a small house with room for a large garden. Ames was handling those details, including getting Blia hired on in the Westin laundry. Blia's whole family—aunt, uncle, and cousins—would be moving out of the low-income housing development and into a place of their own.

I didn't go to Homer and Darrell's double funeral. I sent flowers to Homer, not Darrell. The funeral was widely attended. And televised.

Thinking about Ginger still hurt, but Anne Corley's pain was a little more remote. I had Ginger to thank for that. She had helped me say goodbye to Anne, to move beyond that chapter in my life. Without her, I don't know how long it would have taken to get back on track.

I returned to Peters' living room in time to hear the girls repeating in singsong unison: "One nation, under God, invisible, with liverty injustice for all."

"And justice for all," Ames corrected gently.

I took a long sip of McNaughton's. Thinking about Ginger and Mona and Sig and Homer, I wondered if the girls hadn't gotten it right the first time.

Here's a sneak preview of
J.A. Jance's new novel

QUEEN OF THE NIGHT

Available now
wherever books are sold

PROLOGUE

THEY SAY IT HAPPENED LONG AGO THAT A YOUNG TOHONO O'odham woman fell in love with a Yaqui warrior, a Hiakim, and went to live with him and his people, far to the South. Every evening, her mother, Old White-Haired Woman, would go outside by herself and listen. After a while her daughter's spirit would speak to her from her new home far away. One day, Old White-Haired Woman heard nothing, so she went to find her husband.

"Our daughter is ill," Old White-Haired Woman told him. "I must go to her."

"But the Hiakim live far from here," he said, "and you are a bent old woman. How will you get there?"

"I will ask I'itoi, the Spirit of Goodness, to help me."

Elder Brother heard the woman's plea. He sent Coyote, Ban, to guide Old White-Haired Woman's steps on her long journey, and he sent the Ali Chu Chum O'odham, the Little People—the animals and birds, to help her along the way. When she was thirsty, Ban led her to water. When she was hungry, The Birds, U'u Whig, brought her seeds and beans to eat.

After weeks of traveling, Old White-Haired woman finally reached the land of the Hiakim. There she learned that her daughter was sick and dying.

"Please take my son home to our people," Old White-Haired Woman's daughter begged. "If you don't, his father's people will turn him into a warrior."

You must understand, nawoj, my friend, that from the time the Tohono O'odham emerged from the center of the earth, they have always been a peace loving people. So one night, when the Hiakim were busy feasting, Old White-Haired Woman loaded the baby into her burden basket and set off for the North. When the Yaqui learned she was gone, they sent a band of warriors after her to bring the baby back.

Old White-Haired Woman walked and walked. She was almost back to the land of the Desert People when the Yaqui warriors spotted her. I'itoi saw she was not going to complete her journey, so he called a flock of shashani, *black birds, who flew into the eyes of the Yaqui and blinded them. While the warriors were busy fighting* Shashani, *I'itoi took Old White-Haired Woman into a wash and hid her.*

By then the old grandmother was very tired and lame from all her walking and carrying.

"You stay here," Elder Brother told her. "I will carry the baby back to your people, but while you sit here resting, you will be changed. Because of your bravery, your feet will become roots. Your tired old body will turn into branches. Each year, for one night only, you will become the most beautiful plant on the earth, a flower the Milgahn, *the Whites, call the Night-Blooming Cereus. The Queen of the Night."*

And it happened just that way. Old White-Haired Woman turned into a plant the Indians call ho'okwah'o *which means witch's tongs, but on that one night in early summer when a beautiful scent fills the desert air, the Tohono O'odham, know that they are breathing in kok'oi 'uw, Ghost Scent, and they remember a brave old woman who saved her grandson and brought him home.*

Each year after that, on the night the flowers bloomed, the Tohono O'odham would gather around while Brought Back Child told the story of his grandmother, Old White-Haired Woman, and that, nawoj, *my friend, is the same story I have just told you.*

April, 1959

Long after everyone else had left the beach and returned to the hotel, and long after the bonfire died down to coals, Ursula Brinker sat there in the sand and marveled over what had happened. What she had allowed to happen.

When June Lennox had invited Sully to come along to San Diego for spring break, she had known the moment she said yes, that she was saying yes to more than just a fun trip from Tempe, Arizona to California. The insistent tug had been there all along, for as long as Sully could remember. From the time she was in kindergarten, she had been interested in girls not boys, and that hadn't changed. Not later in grade school when the other girls started drooling over boys, and not later in high school, either.

But she had kept the secret. For one thing, she knew how much her parents would disapprove if Sully ever admitted to them or to anyone else what she long suspected—that she was a lesbian. She didn't go around advertising it or wearing mannish clothing. People said she was "cute," and she was—cute and smart and talented. She suspected that if anyone learned that the girl who had been valedictorian of her class and who had been voted most likely to succeed was actually queer as a three dollar bill, it would all be snatched away from her, like a mirage melting into the desert.

She had kept the secret until now. Until today. With June. And she was afraid, if she left the beach and went back to the hotel room with everyone else and spoke about it, if she gave that newfound happiness a name, it might disappear forever as well.

The beach was deserted. When she heard the sand muffled footsteps behind her, she thought it might be June. But it wasn't.

"Hello," she said. "When did you get here?"

He didn't answer that question. "What you did was wrong," he said. "Did you think you could keep it a secret? Did you think I wouldn't find out?"

"It just happened," she said. "We didn't mean to hurt you."

"But you did," he said. "More than you know."

He fell on her then. Had anyone been walking past on the beach, they wouldn't have paid much attention. Just another young couple carried away with necking; people who hadn't gotten themselves a room, and probably should have.

But in the early hours of that morning, what

was happening there by the dwindling fire wasn't an act of love. It was something else altogether. When the rough embrace finally ended, the man stood up and walked away. He walked into the water and sluiced away the blood.

As for Sully Brinker? She did not walk away. The brainy cheerleader, the girl who had it all—money, brains, and looks, the girl once voted most likely to succeed would not succeed at anything because she was lying dead in the sand—dead at age twenty-one—and her parents' lives would never be the same.

1978

As the quarrel escalated, Danny covered his head with his pillow and tried not to listen, but the pillow didn't help. He could still hear the voices raging back and forth, his father's voice and his mother's. Turning on the TV set might have helped, but if his father came into the bedroom and found the set on when it wasn't supposed to be, Danny knew what would happen. First the belt would come off and, after that, the beating.

Danny knew how much that hurt, so he lay there and willed himself not to listen. He tried to fill his head with the words to one of the songs he had learned at school: Put your right foot in; put your left foot out. Put your right foot in and shake it all about. You do the Hokey Pokey and you turn yourself around. That's what it's all about.

He was about to go on to the second verse when he heard something that sounded like a firecracker—or four firecrackers in a row, even though it wasn't the Fourth of July.

Blam. Blam. Blam. Blam.

After that there was nothing. No other sound. Not his mother's voice and not his father's, either. An eerie silence settled over the house. First it filled Danny's ears and then his heart.

Finally the bedroom door creaked open. Danny knew his father was standing in the doorway, staring down at him, so he kept both eyes shut—shut but not too tightly shut. That would give it away. He didn't move. He barely breathed. At last after the door finally clicked closed, he opened his eyes and let out his breath.

He listened to the silence, welcoming it. The room wasn't completely dark. Streetlights in the parking lot made the room a hazy gray, and there was a sliver of light under the doorway. Soon that went away. Knowing that his father had probably left to go to a bar and drink some more, Danny was able to relax. As the tension left his body, he fell into a deep sleep, slumbering so peacefully that he never heard the sirens of the arriving cop cars or of the useless ambulance that arrived too late. The gunshot victim was dead long before the ambulance got there.

Much later, at least it seemed much later to him, someone—a stranger in a uniform—gently shook him awake. The cop wrapped the tangled sheet around him and lifted him from the bed.

"Come on, little guy," he said huskily. "Let's get you out of here."

June, 2010

It was late, well after eleven, as Jonathan sat in the study of his soon-to-be-former home and stared at his so-called "wall of honor." The plaques and citations he saw there—his "Manager of the Year" award along with all the others that acknowledged his exemplary service were relics from another time and place—from another life. They were the currency and language of some other existence where the rules as he had once known them no longer applied.

What had happened on Wall Street had trickled down to Main Street. As a result his banking career was gone. His job was gone. His house would be gone soon, and so would his family. He wasn't supposed to know about the boyfriend Esther had waiting in the wings, but he did. He also knew what she was waiting for—the money from the 401 K. She wanted that, too, and she wanted it now.

Esther came in then—barged in really—without knocking. The fact that he might want a little privacy was as foreign a concept as the paltry career trophies still hanging on his walls. She stood there staring at him, hands on her hips.

"You changed the password on the account," she said accusingly.

"The account I changed the password on isn't a joint account," he told her mildly "It's mine."

"We're still married," she pointed out. "What's yours is mine."

And, of course, that was the way it had always

been. He worked. She stayed home and saw to it
that they lived beyond their means which had
been considerable when he'd still had a good job.
The problem was he no longer had that job, but
she was still living the same way. As far as she
was concerned, nothing had changed. For him
everything had changed. Esther had gone right
on spending money like it was water, but now
the well had finally run dry. There was no job
and no way to get a job. Banks didn't like having
bankers with overdue bills and credit scores in
the basement.

"I signed the form when you asked me to so we
could both get the money," she said. "I want my
fair share."

He knew there was nothing about this that was
fair. It was the same stunt his mother had pulled
on his father. Well, maybe not the boyfriend part,
but he had vowed it wouldn't happen to him—
would never happen to him. Yet here it was.

"It may be in an individual account but that
money is a joint asset," Esther declared. "You
don't get to have it all."

She was screaming at him now. He could hear
her and so could anyone else in the neighborhood. He was glad they lived at the end of the
cul-de- sac—with previously foreclosed houses
on either side. It was a neighborhood where living beyond your means went with the territory.

"By the time my lawyer finishes wiping the
floor with you, you'll be lucky to be living in a
homeless shelter," she added. "As for seeing the
kids? Forget about it. That's not going to happen.
I'll see to it."

With that, she spun around as if to leave. Then, changing her mind, she grabbed the closest thing she could reach, which turned out to be his bronze Manager of the Year plaque, and heaved it at him. The sharp corner on the wood caught him full in the forehead—well, part of his very tall comb-over forehead—and it hurt like hell. It bled like hell.

As blood ran down his cheek and leaked into his eye, all the things he had stifled through the years came to a head. He had reached the end— the point where he had nothing left to lose.

Opening the top drawer of his desk, he removed the gun, a gun he had purchased with every intention of turning it on himself. Then, rising to his feet, he hurried out of the room intent on using it on someone else.

His body sizzled in a fit of unreasoning hatred. If that had been all there was to it, any defense attorney worthy of the name could have gotten him off on a plea of temporary insanity, because in that moment he was insane—legally insane. He knew nothing about the difference between right and wrong. All he knew was that he had taken all he could take. More than he could take.

The problem is that was only the start of Jonathan's problems. Everything that came after that was entirely premeditated.

CHAPTER 1

PIMA COUNTY HOMICIDE DETECTIVE BRIAN FELLOWS loved Saturdays. Kath usually worked Saturday shifts at her Border Patrol desk job which meant Brian had the whole day to spend with his girls, six year old twins, Annie and Amy. They usually started with breakfast, either sharing a plate-sized sweet roll at Gus Balon's or eye-watering plates of chorizo and eggs at Wags.

After that, they went home to clean house. Brian's mother had been a much-divorced scatterbrain even before she became an invalid. Brian had learned from an early age that if he wanted a clean house, he'd be the one doing it. It hadn't killed him, either. He'd turned into a self-sufficient kind of guy and, according to Kath, an excellent catch for a husband.

Brian wanted the same thing for his daughters—for them to be self-sufficient. It didn't take long on Saturdays to whip their central area bungalow into shape. In the process, while settling the occasional squabble, being a bit of a tough task-master, and hearing about what was going on with the girls, Brian made sure he was a real presence in his daughter's lives—a real father.

That was something that had been missing in Brian's childhood—at least as far as his biological father was concerned. He wouldn't have had any idea about what fathers were supposed to be or do if it hadn't been for Brandon Walker, Brian's mother's first husband and the father of Tommy and Quentin, Brian's half brothers.

Brandon, then a Pima County homicide detective, had come to the house each weekend and dutifully collected his own sons to take them on non-custodial outings. One of Brian's first memories was of being left alone on the front step while Quentin and Tommy went racing off to jump in their father's car to go somewhere fun—to a movie or the Pima County Fair or maybe even the Tucson Rodeo—while Brian, bored and lonely, had to fend for himself.

Then one day a miracle had happened. After Quentin and Tommy were already in the car, Brandon had gotten out of the car, come back up the walk, and asked Brian if he would like to go along, too. Brian was beyond excited. Quentin and Tommy had been appalled and had done everything in their power to make Brian miserable, but they did that anyway—even before Brandon had taken pity on him.

From then on, that's how it was. Whenever Brandon had taken his own boys somewhere, he had taken Brian as well. The man had become a sort of super-hero in Brian's eyes. He had grown up wanting to be just like him and it was due to that, in no small measure, that Brian Fellows was the man he was today—a doting father and an experienced cop. And it was why, on Saturday afternoons after the house was clean, that he never failed to take his girls somewhere to do something fun—to the Randolph Park Zoo or the Arizona Sonora Desert Museum. Today, as hot as it was, they had already settled on going to a movie at Park Mall.

Brian was on call tonight. If someone decided to kill someone else tonight, he'd have to go in to work, but that was fine. He would have had his special day with his girls, well, all but one of his girls, and that was what made life worth living.

Brandon Walker knew he was running away. He had the excuse of running to something, but he understood that he was really running from something, something he didn't want to face. He would face it eventually because he had to, but not yet. He wasn't ready.

Not that going to see G. T. Farrell was light duty by any means. Stopping by to see someone who was on his way to hospice care wasn't Brandon's idea of fun. Sue, Geet's wife had called with the bad news. Geet's lung cancer had been held at bay for far longer than anyone had thought possible, but now it was back. And winning.

"He's got a set of files that he had me bring out of storage," Sue had said in her phone call. "He made me promise that I'd see to it that you got them—you and nobody else."

Brandon didn't have to ask which file because

he already knew. Every homicide cop has a case like that, the one that haunts him and won't let him go, the one where the bad guy got away with murder. For Geet Farrell it had been the 1959 murder of Ursula Brinker. Geet had been a newbie ASU campus cop at the time her death had stunned the entire university community. The case had stayed with him, haunting Geet the whole time he'd worked as a homicide detective for the Pinal County Sheriff's department and through his years of retirement as well. Now that Geet knew it was curtains for him, he wanted to hand Ursula's unsolved case off to someone else and make his problem Brandon's problem.

Fair enough, Brandon thought. *If I'm dealing with Geet Farrell's difficulties, I won't have to face up to my own.*

Geet was a good five years older than Brandon. They had met for the first time as homicide cops decades earlier. In 1975, Brandon Walker had been working Homicide for the Pima County sheriff's department, and G. T. Farrell had been his Homicide counterpart in neighboring Pinal. Between them they had helped bring down a serial killer named Andrew Philip Carlisle. Partially due to their efforts Carlisle had been sentenced to life in prison. He had lived out his remaining years in the state prison in Florence, Arizona, where he had finally died.

It turned out Brandon had also received a life-long sentence as a result of that case, only his had been much different. One of Carlisle's intended victims, the fiercely independent Diana Ladd, had gone against type and consented to become

Brandon Walker's wife. They had been married now for thirty plus years.

It was hard for Brandon to imagine what his life would have been like if Andrew Carlisle had succeeded in murdering Diana. How would he have survived for all those years if he hadn't been married to that amazing woman? How would he have existed without Diana and all the complications she had brought into his life, including her son, Davy, and their adopted Tohono O'odham daughter, Lani?

Much later, long after both detectives had been turned out to pasture by their respective law enforcement agencies, Geet by retiring and Brandon by losing a bid for reelection, Geet had been instrumental in the creation of an independent cold case investigative entity called, TLC, The Last Chance started by Hedda Brinker, the mother of Geet's first homicide victim In an act of seeming charity, Geet had asked that his old buddy, former Pima County sheriff, Brandon Walker, be invited to sign on.

That ego-saving invitation, delivered in person by a smooth-talking attorney named Ralph Ames, had come at a time when, as Brandon liked to put it, he had been lower than a snake's vest pocket. He had accepted without a moment of hesitation. In the intervening years, Working with TLC had saved his sanity if not his life.

All of which meant, Brandon owed everything to Geet Farrell, and that was why, on this amazingly hot late June afternoon, he was driving to Casa Grande for what he knew would be a deathbed visit.

The twin debts Brandon Walker owed G.T. Farrell were more than he could ever repay, but he hoped that taking charge of Ursula Brinker's file and tilting at Geet's insoluble windmill of a case would help even the score. Just a little.